ESCAPE TO EROTICA

These sexy encounters will inspire you to pack your bags, let go, and get kinky. Whether the destination is exotic or ordinary, it's the electricity that ignites between wild and ready wayfarers that makes the experience magic. So get ready for the wildest journeys imaginable in the land of pleasure.

OTHER BOOKS IN THE SERIES:

LETTERS TO
PENTHOUSE
XXVI
DESTINATION
S-E-X

THE EDITORS OF
PENTHOUSE® MAGAZINE

WARNER BOOKS

NEW YORK   BOSTON

Copyright © 2006 by General Media Communications, Inc.
All rights reserved. No part of this book may be reproduced in any form or by any electronic or mechanical means, including information storage and retrieval systems, without permission in writing from the publisher, except by a reviewer who may quote brief passages in a review.

Cover design by Tony Russo

Warner Books
1271 Avenue of the Americas
New York, NY 10020

Printed in the United States of America

First Printing: August 2006

10 9 8 7 6 5 4 3 2 1

INTRODUCTION

Vacation—a time to let go, have some fun, and perhaps even try something new. The adventurous people featured in this racy collection do all that and much more. From chance meetings to the rediscovered joy of a familiar lover, these letters detail the erotic expeditions of the most daring couples featured in the pages of *Penthouse*.

Your itinerary begins with an outrageous tryst in Aruba and continues on to a passionate threesome in Mexico. You'll also experience the erotic exploits of a couple in Bombay, wife-swapping in the tropics, and other sensual delights in exotic locales.

Not to be outdone by foreign affairs, you'll also be taken on a red-hot road trip across America, including a lusty lap dance in Las Vegas, a mysterious interlude in New York City, and an airport layover that lives up to its name.

There's nothing like a change of scenery to get you looking at life a little differently. So sit back and relax, and enjoy the journey—you never know where you'll wind up!

Barbara Pizio

WHAT MADE OUR STAY IN ARUBA SO PERFECT WAS WATCHING MY WIFE THRILL ANOTHER MAN

My wife and I took a trip to Aruba last January and stayed in a little bungalow on the beach. Lyla fell in love with our private quarters, which were nestled among the trees, giving an impression of seclusion. Taking advantage of the privacy, Lyla became very frisky, prancing around naked every day. One night she even did a striptease for me outside, as I watched from the window.

Lyla and I were in paradise and so turned on that we seldom went more than four hours without making love. So, I was quite surprised when Lyla returned from a solo trip to the beach to tell me that she had made a new "friend." She explained that her friend, a tall sexy blond named Derek, had made a pass at her, exciting her to the point where she had considered fucking his brains out.

We talked about this riveting possibility, and the more it became apparent that our fantasy of her doing another guy while I watched was going to come true, the hotter we became. Soon I was slipping my erect cock into my wife's wet hole, pumping slowly in and out of her as she described how she wanted to take Derek's cock in her ass and how she would milk it till he came, squeezing her butt cheeks to heighten his sensations. By the time she started telling me how she would take his cock into her mouth, we were thrashing about wildly on the bed. Neither of us could remember the last time we came with such intensity.

While regaining our composure, Lyla devised a plan. She said that she would tell Derek that I had to leave Aruba to attend to some urgent business and wouldn't return until the following day. She knew that he would seize this opportunity to make another play for her.

The next night, as she prepared to leave our bungalow, my wife told me to leave the curtains open and to find a spot outside the window from which I could watch—that was, if I wanted to watch.

Waiting for her to return with her soon-to-be lover, my whole body trembled in anticipation of what the night might bring. Lyla had dressed in a tight-clinging blue minidress, sans undergarments. Her nipples were straining against the fabric so hard that I could almost count the little bumps on her areolas. I tried to coax her to have a quickie with me before she left, but she said that she wanted to be fresh and ready for only the second cock ever to fill her cunt.

While she was gone I arranged a place for myself to watch outside the window. I even checked the sound capabilities, ensuring that I would be able to hear their moans of pleasure. Then I settled back, heart racing, palms sweating, and waited until I heard them coming down the trail.

They entered the bungalow clinging to one another tightly, and the second the door shut they shared wet, passionate kisses. My cock was already throbbing at full attention, and when Lyla unbuttoned his shirt and kissed his smooth chest, stopping only to suck his tiny nipples, I was sure that I was going to shoot my load on the windowpane without even having touched my cock!

Derek began running his hands all over Lyla's body,

saying how beautiful she was. But she was impatient and quickly undressed and then stood before him in all her naked glory. As if this were the final go-ahead he was waiting for, he grabbed her and brought her closer to him, snuggling his head into her breasts. I thought about how delicious she must smell to Derek with his nose buried in her cleavage, and then he suckled each firm tit, one at a time.

I watched, mouth hanging open, as Derek circled each nipple with his tongue, starting with her left tit. Cupping her breast with his hand, he flicked his tongue tip quickly over the hardened nipple—a technique Lyla had often used on the rim of my cock when blowing me. I wet my fingers with saliva then and brought my hand to my shaft.

Although Lyla was obviously loving it all, she wanted more. Dropping to her knees, she pulled down Derek's pants and freed his erect organ. As she quickly guided it into her mouth, my cock throbbed again, eager to be in her mouth as well.

My wife gave this man an expert blow job, taking his whole length in her mouth, massaging his balls, gliding her hand up and down in rhythm with her mouth, and it wasn't long before Derek cried out in pleasure, filling her throat with his semen. A bit of pre-come seeped from my cockhead as I watched my sexy wife swallow another man's come and then clean the tip of his cock with her tongue. Wanting to get off as well, I began stroking my cock with greater urgency.

Far from being satisfied, Derek had my wife lie back on the bed where he worked his finger diligently over her clit and pussy lips. He rubbed her labia in a circular motion, causing her to tense up and close her eyes, her face contorting with pleasure. He dragged his tongue down to her clitoris and slid two fingers into her pussy. Lyla let out a loud moan as he finger-fucked her and flicked his tongue across her clit. It seemed as if she were going to come at any moment, as her legs were trembling and her hands were holding Derek's head tight to her sex. But before she could come, Derek stopped eating her.

I moved right up to the window, so close I was in danger of being seen, but I had to get a close-up view of my wife taking another man's cock inside her snug pussy. "Fuck me," I heard her say as he slid his cock up and down her opening, teasing her.

I continued to play with my cock as Derek slowly slid all the way inside Lyla's cunt. I could almost feel the velvety wetness of her vaginal walls embracing my cock as I watched Derek pump in and out, in and out, his shaft glistening with her juices. Soon they were thrashing wildly on the bed, fucking so fast I could hardly see Derek's cock as it pounded into her cunt. I worked my cock faster as well, but it was only moments before Lyla cried out, "Oh, yes, yes, I'm coming." And Derek came, too, with one last, quick thrust into her convulsing pussy. It wasn't easy, but I let go of my cock, wanting to be inside my wife when I came.

The two of them lay together, stroking each other for a while, until Derek went to the bathroom. Lyla came to the window and teased me by scooping Derek's come from her cunt and licking it from her fingertips. I had already ducked out of sight when Derek returned, but remained in earshot to hear Lyla telling him that he had to go now, but that maybe they'd have a chance to fuck again before the week was over.

When he was gone, Lyla came to the window and instructed me to stay where I was. She came out and found me seated in a hard-backed chair in the darkness outside the window, naked, with my hard dick standing straight up. Without a word Lyla straddled me, sinking her freshly fucked pussy down on my aching member. Neither of us lasted long, both of us coming so hard we almost fell out of the chair!

It was a truly wonderful night that made our vacation in Aruba especially memorable.

—*J.E.S., Delaware*

LUSTY PICTURES CAPTURE MEMORIES
OF THEIR WILD AND SEXY VACATION

Recently, I was on vacation with my girlfriend, Betty, and our good friends Mark and Audrey. We were all excited about soaking up some rays, working on our tans, and totally relaxing. Both girls had brought skimpy bikinis. Betty's was black and a little smaller than Audrey's red one, but both looked incredibly sexy and emphasized their generous curves.

The real fun started when I went to the store to get some groceries. When I returned, I found Mark taking a nap on the king-size bed, with Betty and Audrey dozing naked on either side of him. What a sight! I knew that it was too precious not to record for posterity, so I grabbed my camera and snapped a few shots. I'd be sure to tease Mark later about letting such a delectable opportunity go to waste!

Mark was still asleep when the girls awoke. The two began making out and fondling each other's breasts. I couldn't believe that he hadn't woken up, but my cock was certainly awake from watching all their touching. I told both girls to wake Mark up by stroking him through his shorts. They did as I commanded and I photographed their every move. We all watched as his cock grew in his pants, but he still hadn't woken up. Finally, his eyes started to flicker and he looked around in amazement. I could see his mind turning over the possibilities, trying to figure out how he'd come to be in such a situation. I nodded at him, letting him know that it was more than okay to go with his instincts and touch the girls.

It didn't take Mark long to get the hint because they started touching and kissing him, their hands gliding along his body and reaching out for his cock. I watched through the camera lens as my Betty got things started by wrapping her hand around Mark's meaty cock and stroking it slowly. She always keeps her hands soft with lotion, and I knew from my hand job this morning that they were the perfect smoothness for her task. While she pumped his cock slowly and tenderly, Audrey leaned down and began licking and pinching Mark's nipples. He clearly enjoyed it, because the minute she started, he closed his eyes and whimpered. I moved aside and snapped a photo that captured their action in all its fullness. My cock was rock-hard, but instead of joining in, I was content to watch as the girls worked in tandem to give Mark what had to be the most memorable sexual encounter of his life.

As they got more comfortable, I noticed the girls touching themselves as well as Mark. Betty used her free hand to begin tweaking her own hardened nipples, while Audrey rubbed her pussy along the mattress, then spread her legs to give me a view of her glistening sex. I snapped away, my eyes riveted on all three of them getting completely turned on. Mark looked like he was in absolute heaven as the girls went to town. When they paused to give each other a long, seductive kiss, I thought he might pop right then. He didn't, even though Betty had increased the pace of her pumping. The girls continued kissing, moving closer so that their breasts rubbed against each other. All the while, they kept touching Mark while moaning into each other's mouth.

I put down the camera and moved forward so I could grab both girls' asses at the same time. They turned toward me, peppering me with tiny kisses. I joined Mark on the bed, getting a new angle on their bobbing breasts and sensuous bodies.

I figured that Betty would come over and sit on my cock, but instead, Audrey climbed on top of me. Her pussy was radiating heat as she wiggled around my cock, teasing me by not sticking it inside her right away. The two girls mimicked each other's actions, holding our cocks in their hands and rubbing the bulging heads against their slits. I reached for the camera and snapped a photo of their glistening pussies teasing our dicks, and then I put it down as I sank into the ecstasy of Audrey's cunt.

From this angle, everything about her was enhanced; her breasts looked bigger and her face prettier. I grabbed her and pulled her on top of me. She giggled as she tumbled forward, and I kissed her, watching with pride as Betty did the same with Mark. Even though we'd never done this before, it seemed perfectly natural to swap partners for the night. Listening to the mewling sounds Betty made as Mark pressed his cock up against her spurred me on. As I got more worked up, I flipped us over so I could really pound into Audrey. She opened her eyes, and they were glassy with lust as I held her arms down at her sides and rammed into her as hard as I could. Acting on pure animal instinct, I pulled back and then arched forward, and she clearly appreciated this roughness, because she wrapped her legs tightly around me and let out a tantalizing moan every time my cock plunged back into her.

Betty, who was still on top of Mark, reached over to touch my shoulder, and when I looked back at her, we kissed. This kiss connected the four of us and made me feel even closer to my girlfriend, even while my cock was buried inside her best friend's pussy. I pulled back and watched her slide up and down along Mark's cock, her pussy lips engorged and beautiful. It was a rare treat to see her from this angle, and as she eyed me up and down, I knew she appreciated this special view of my ass. Mark seemed like he was in a dream as he took in the surroundings. I reached for the camera again, holding it slightly above me to capture all of us in our group-sex glory.

I didn't have time to dawdle any longer, because my cock was urging me to continue slamming into Audrey. I looked into her eyes, and she smiled up at me, licking her lips as I felt her deliberately squeezing my cock with her pussy muscles. I heard Mark slap Betty's ass and glanced back to see him pulling apart her asscheeks, fondling her behind in a way I knew would spark her orgasm.

I reached beneath me and toyed with Audrey's clit, feeling the bud harden even more against my fingers as she got even wetter. I fondled her button, trying out different sorts of touches, all of which seemed to drive her crazy with lust. She started to twist her hips and shake her head, beating her fists against the mattress while I maintained my rhythm. Betty was grunting by now, too, the way she always does before she's about to come. I pressed my thumb against Audrey's clit, mashing it against her pubic bone while I pushed my cock as far inside her as I could. I was thrilled when I felt her bathe my cock with her juices, and from the look on her face, her orgasm was clearly a powerful one. I could hear Betty's cries getting louder and the sound of their bodies slapping together, and I came, shooting deep into Audrey.

We both turned to watch Betty and Mark's finale. She stretched her hands above her head like a rodeo queen while he bucked and humped beneath her. Their echoing cries of pleasure filled the room as they both reached their peaks. I made sure to capture the three of them in postcoital bliss and took many more naughty pictures that we keep locked away in our bedside drawer. Whenever life seems dull, I look over those photos and remember what a wild girl I've got, and what special friends Mark and Audrey are to share that kind of fun with us.

—*T.E., Oakland, California* O┈▪

EXTRA! EXTRA! READ ALL ABOUT IT! REPORTER GETS NAUGHTY IN NAGANO

I watched as Masato closed the drapes, the expanse of mountaintops being concealed from my view. Before my eyes could adjust to the change in light, Masato had taken me into his arms and pressed his lips to mine. In between kisses and groping, we removed each other's clothes. I slid my hand up and down the now-familiar terrain of his naked body, his nearly hairless flesh soft and smooth to the touch. As his hands moved down to my chest and he cupped my breasts in his palms, an unslakable need fluttered inside my belly.

Moving with the alacrity I knew his pulsating cock craved, I dropped to my knees and took his shaft in my mouth. I felt him shiver and saw his legs twitch as I began running my tongue up and down his length. He moaned as my tongue tip slid over his mushroom-shaped head and then ran down the other side of his shaft.

Masato's legs began to shake, and he pushed his groin into my face, loving the licking but wanting all of his cock down my throat at the same time. I knew the effect my slow, deliberate licks had on him, and as I witnessed his burgeoning desire, I grew horny as well.

I stuffed him inside my mouth, allowing my breasts to occasionally brush his smooth legs as I sucked his shaft in and out. Soon he was pushing himself into me with ramrod intensity, his hips nearly knocking me off balance as his cock slid farther down my throat. I grabbed his ass-cheeks to control his movement, and seconds later he spewed his sweet come into my mouth.

I recalled that evening fondly, as well as the few others I spent with Masato, as I checked out of Nagano First Hotel. Consumed by my thoughts, I walked out into the chilly February air and paused to take a last look at the web of narrow streets. I was enamored by the quaint little neighborhood with its wide array of small shops and restaurants.

When my car arrived, I hopped in and peered at Zenkoji Temple, shrouded in lush gardens, perched high on a hill above the city. High-peaked mountains greeted the clear skyline, and serene valleys lay below the snow-covered alps. The car quickly swept away from the hotel, and as images began to move past my window, I was catapulted back to the first time I met Masato.

I was one of four reporters from the newspaper I worked for to be sent to Nagano, Japan, to cover the Winter Olympic Games. Assigned to report on the figure skating and short track speed skating events being held in the Mashima district in southeast Nagano City, I spent a lot of time scurrying around the White Ring—located on the site of the ancient battlefield of Kawanakajima—trying to get quotes and shoot great pictures to be sent home via my laptop computer.

The atmosphere during the games was intoxicating, with tourists roving the city streets donning Olympic paraphernalia. When I wasn't in the press box, taking in the events and writing, I was making my way through throngs of tourists and fans in an attempt to do a little local sightseeing and take some photos for my personal album. One morning, while focusing in on the entrance to the arena, a man stepped in front of my camera. I weakly said, "Excuse me," probably too softly for him to hear, because he did not move out of my way. I tried a second time and he quickly turned to face me.

"Oh, I am so sorry," he said, rather formally. He smiled politely and moved away, his eyes lingering over me fondly. I looked briefly into his deep black eyes and figured that he was a native.

When I had clicked the picture, he moved toward me and extended his hand in invitation. "Masato. Welcome to Nagano."

"Thank you. I take it you are a resident here."

"Yes, I live nearby. But currently I am working here, selling keepsake programs. And you? Are you just here to see the Olympics?"

"I am a reporter."

"Ah, I see," he said, pointing to the camera and smiling once again.

"Well, have a nice day," I said, beginning to walk away.

"Wait!" He stopped me. "I—maybe we can have breakfast."

The restaurant he chose was just a few blocks away from White Arena and, despite the early-morning hour, already bustling with tourists. The estimated wait was a half hour, so Masato suggested that we go back to his place, which was a short walk from there, and he would prepare breakfast. Nothing like a home-cooked meal, I thought, as my stomach grumbled. In minutes we were in his small and cozy kitchen.

During breakfast, Masato and I barely ate because we

were talking so much. He looked so intently in my eyes as he spoke, I thought I would melt right along with the butter on my toast. Soon we had delved into stories about our past romances, and as I imagined him in the arms of a lover, my desire for him became a need so palpable, I could almost taste it.

The conversation ebbed, but Masato and I continued to sit motionless, staring into one another's eyes, listening to each other's breath. And then, finally, Masato leaned over the table and kissed me hard on the lips. I was taken aback, though somewhat conscious of his shirt dangling in his cup of coffee, so I pulled away.

Masato seemed gravely disappointed as I began to stand, and then surprised when I came around the table and plopped myself down on his lap and wrapped my legs around the back of the chair. This time I kissed him, pressing my lips softly to his, and then slowly sneaking my tongue in his mouth. I could taste the coffee he had just consumed—light and sweet, just like his kisses.

During our kiss, I allowed my hands to play in his hair and then explore the curve of his back, our tongues performing a beautiful dance. Masato's gorgeous cock had hardened and was jabbing into my crotch as he slid his hands down my back to cup my bottom.

Soon Masato was kissing my cheeks, my neck, sucking my fingers into his mouth, opening my blouse. I shivered when he unsnapped my bra and glided his fingers delicately over each swollen nipple of my breasts. He slid down to my belly button with just the lightest touch of one fingertip, and then worked his hands down my pants.

Masato explored the folds of my pussy, my juices allowing his fingers to glide smoothly over my labia and clitoris. His touch was sensational and suddenly I was light-headed. I unbuttoned my jeans to give his hand some room to work, and then unbuttoned his. His cock-head was peeking out of his boxers. I shook hands with it, gripping it tightly before I began to stroke it.

Masato and I worked to a steady rhythm, kissing and moaning as the chair began to squeak. My pussy became hot as his hand motion built to a frenzy, and soon I was shaking through a delicious orgasm that I felt from the tip of my toes to the tip of my tongue.

When my quivering subsided, I felt a little cramped and got up from Masato's lap. He stood as well, and instead of taking me into the bedroom, he began to remove his clothes and drop them on the linoleum-covered floor.

Naked, he was quite muscular, and I couldn't help but reach out and touch his chest and arms. He stared at me longingly and removed my clothes. He clutched his cock and held it out like some fragile offering. Taking my cue, I moved in closer to him until my naked breasts were squishing against his chest.

Once again our lips met. As he kissed me, his hands lazily danced over my flesh, making my every hair stand on end. Once his fingers had found my sopping wet pussy again, he lined his cock up with my slick hole and steered it right in.

At first we moved slowly, taking and giving, touching and kissing, our bodies forging a greater intimacy with every buck and thrust. The slowness of it made it more hot, but soon both Masato and I grew hungry for it faster, harder. I could hear Masato's breath grow ragged just before he moved me backward, pressing my rear end into the sink.

He took one quick lunge inside me, my weight supported by the sink, and then began pumping his cock with ferocious tenacity. It felt as if he were hitting my kidneys as he moved with the skill of a samurai swordsman, coaxing my wet pussy to spasm again and again. I grabbed his ass as I felt his body stiffen, and pushed him in farther and farther as he shivered through his sweet release.

In the airplane on the trip home, I glanced out the window at the dramatic peaks that loomed over the sprawling valleys. I picked up the Shinmai paper I had folded in my bag and smiled, thinking that thanks to Masato I'd never forget Nagano.

—*K.P., Brooklyn, New York*

TRIP TO BRUSSELS SPROUTS
WILD DESIRES IN FUN-LOVING PAIR

I stared at Melinda as she lay sprawled across the chaise, her bare legs swaying over the side as she sat, the hotel room-service menu in her lap, writing out postcards to her friends and family at home.

"What do you think? Dear Mom, Dan and I have been having a splendid time here in Brussels, fucking like crazy."

"You might want to be a little bit more to the point, Mel." I smiled at her warmly as I stood to pull on my boxers. A new desire was already welling within me as I eyed my wife's naked body, still gleaming with sweat from the exalted experience we had shared just moments before. Breasts bouncing above me, she had ridden me with feline speed to an orgasm of exorbitant proportions. Mel has always been a track star in bed, but this time she beat her own record, and I was still reeling from it ten minutes later.

Melinda threw her postcards on the floor when she noticed me buttoning up my shirt. "What are you doing, hon?"

"Well, I figured that since we've come all this way, we might like to see what the capital of Europe has to offer." She knew that I was full of it. I couldn't care less about bourgeois palaces or baroque guild halls when given Melinda as an alternative option. I'd much rather wrap my lips around one of her gorgeous orbs than be stuffing my face with *pommes frites* with béarnaise sauce bought from some street vendor. And I know a helluva lot more about human physiology than I do about architecture anyway.

Melinda, her hair mussed from our sex romp, pressed her naked body to mine, rising up on her tiptoes to deliver a cock-throbbing kiss to my already dried-out lips, and she knew I was putty in her hands. After weeks of perusing travel guide upon travel guide, I thought for sure that Melinda and I wouldn't find time to breathe during our vacation to Brussels. She had an itinerary written out with the names of restaurants, shops, and museums she wanted to visit, as well as approximated wake-up times and bedtimes. I joked with her about whether or not she had figured in time for us to use the restrooms, but in truth I was more concerned about whether or not I was going to get laid.

But, suddenly, there we were, the city sprawled out before us right outside our hotel room window, Avenue Louise and its famous shopping district waiting to make friends with our Visa Gold, and my wife was naked, pleading for me to take my clothes off again.

Needless to say, I was undressed in seconds, and we were wrinkling my slacks with the soles of our feet as we kissed, our bodies pressed together, our hands exploring and petting.

My stiff cock was nestled between her thighs, being tickled by her thin spread of pubic hair, when she began kissing me from my neck down to my chest. I cupped her firm buttocks in the palms of my hands and pulled her closer to me, my cock pressing into her legs, the fresh dew of her pussy juices gliding onto my shaft. We kissed for a few more moments, her breasts squished into my hard chest, her cunt slathering me with its honey, until I was infused with desire.

I tore myself away from Melinda long enough to guide her by the hand to the bed, and then I laid her down on the lumped-up bedclothes. I lay on top of my gorgeous wife, our lips seemingly sutured together, as I slipped my cock inside her waiting cunt.

We began a slow and deliberate bump-and-grind, moving in the knowing rhythm that comes with several years of intimacy, our every buck and thrust collaborating to perform a dance of inexplicable pleasure. My wife's tight cunt grasped my cock with her every thrust, and she hugged it for a brief moment before releasing it with a swift downward movement of her hips.

The hot wetness was too delicious to withstand, and in moments my body was quivering in orgasm as all my blood rushed to my head and left me sated and exhausted.

We carried our afterplay into the tub where we lathered each other's body with bubbles and fondled each other to yet another orgasm underwater. Then we dressed in fresh clothes and hurried out the door.

Our trip to Brussels had been inspired by the art nouveau class my wife had taken the previous spring. We had spent our first day in Brussels visiting the Horta Museum and checking out the private house and workshop of Victor Horta, the famous nouveau architect. Today, Melinda wanted to visit the Grand-Place square.

We walked along the cobbled streets arm in arm, my wife popping *pommes frites* with curry into her mouth, and occasionally taking out her itinerary (written on various Post-it notes) to check off things we'd seen and make mental notes of the ones we hadn't. By the early evening I'd had enough architectural splendor to last me a lifetime, and I felt as old as the fifteenth-century Town Hall that had tourists clicking away at their cameras to capture the Gothic essence of its soaring skyline.

After taking some of our own pictures of the various small statues around the Town Hall, Melinda and I had dinner in one of the many luxurious restaurants in the square. We hung around long enough to catch some of the nightly music and light show and then, pretty much pooped, trekked back to our hotel.

Once we had settled into our bed, though, Melinda was back on the itinerary kick, telling me that she wanted to get some pictures of the "darling" Mannekin-Pis statue before the end of our trip.

"I have a lot more to offer than that chubby little boy," I said as I climbed on top of my wife and began kissing her neck.

"Oh, I am sure you do," she laughed, still clinging to her various itinerary notes as I slid my tongue up her neck and squished it into her ear.

I had already unbuttoned my wife's nightshirt and was stroking one of her full breasts as my tongue outlined the labyrinth of her outer-ear canal. With that, I plunged down to her hips and pulled off her pajama pants. The scent of her freesia body lotion wafted up to my nostrils, and I quickly buried my face in my wife's blonde muff of pubic curls.

I kissed her crotch several times before going for the gusto, and I peeked up to see that my wife's eyes were closed, and all of her sticky notes had been discarded with the exception of one that had stuck to the sleeve of her half-removed pajama top. It amused me slightly, but I could not be distracted for very long from the delicious juicy fruit that awaited me.

Drawing my attention back to between Melinda's legs, I began licking up and down the folds of her labia and then sliding my way down to her clitoris. I took the swollen little nub into my mouth and sucked and kissed it, which made my wife moan and writhe with burgeoning pleasure. As I pulled and tugged on her clit, her juices came pouring out, and I dragged my tongue to her hole to lap them up before jamming two digits inside her. Melinda pushed my head down as if to ram it between her legs, and I sucked at her lips, my fingers working in and out of her cunt.

Soon I could feel her body tremble beneath my oral ministrations, and I knew that she had come. My cock was already rock-hard and leaking pre-come, but I didn't want just plain sex tonight. I sat up and maneuvered my wife so that she was lying on her stomach. She knew just where I wanted to sightsee, and in seconds was up on her hands and knees offering her ass to me.

Dipping my cock in and out of her wet cunt, I slathered my shaft with her juices. Then I slid my cock inside her ass with one swift push. Her asshole tightened up around my shaft and held me still for a brief moment. Then she began thrusting back at me, allowing my cock farther visitation rights inside her rear canal.

Bucking and thrusting, we were both moaning, our bodies sweat-drenched as a cool August Brussels breeze swept through our hotel room. My come rushed through my shaft, and I pulled out to paint Melinda's asscheeks with my cream before settling down beside her.

I was tired from a long day of sightseeing, but I stayed awake even after Melinda had drifted off to sleep, staring at the loveliest sight Brussels had to offer—my beautiful wife.   —*D.K., Dayton, Ohio* ⊶∎

NUDE BEACH PROVIDES THE PERFECT LOCALE FOR COUPLE'S DARING UNDERWATER TRYST

My husband, Clay, and I are pretty adventurous, but we'd never tried anything as daring as what we did last summer while visiting a nude beach.

Looking for a vacation getaway, we recently bought a condo in Florida. One day we were driving out of the Bal Harbour shops in a ritzy part of town, when I read in our guidebook that there was a nude beach not too far away. It was very hot out, and my clothes were sticking to me, so the idea of getting naked and jumping into the ocean sounded divine. Neither Clay nor I had ever been to a nude beach before, but as soon as I read the description of the nudist playground to my husband, he looked over at me with the most devilish expression. I immediately noticed a bulge beginning to tent his shorts. That only added to the heat I was already feeling, and pretty soon we were keeping our eyes peeled for the exit to Haulover Park Beach.

Pulling into the parking lot, we could barely contain our excitement. Before we left the car, Clay leaned over and thrust his tongue into my mouth, kissing me deeply. My husband groped my breasts through my clinging tank top and I crossed my legs tightly, squeezing my aroused pussy between my thighs. I reached for my husband's lap and felt his hard member yearning to bust through his pants.

Knowing that we would soon be stripping off our clothes in front of a beach full of strangers got me so hot that I could barely keep from riding my husband's rigid cock right there in the parking lot! But I was also eager to get out of the steamy car and feel the ocean water lapping at my body, so I tore myself away from Clay's kiss and jumped out of the car. My husband soon followed, and together we headed toward the shore.

As soon as we emerged from the shady underpass, naked bodies filled our vision in all directions. We stood, awestruck, for a few moments as we took in the amazing sight of all of that bare flesh. There were bodies of all shapes and sizes, cocks with piercings through the head and some that even attached to the scrotum! I also saw a woman with a gold labia ring that was gleaming beautifully in the sunlight. I was stunned and stood staring in my place until Clay pulled me by the arm toward the ocean.

We spread out our towels near the water, right next to another couple about our age. To be frank, the man had the largest penis I'd ever seen. When his companion caught my gaze, she giggled and said, "You can see why I like to show him off."

I nearly choked on my own laughter, and suddenly Clay and I both felt self-conscious, realizing that we were the only people on the beach wearing clothes. So as not to seem like voyeuristic gawkers, we gave each other a nod and then peeled off all our clothes. Clay's cock was still at half-mast, but my nipples stiffened to peak hardness as soon as they encountered the warm ocean breeze. Wow, did that feel good!

There was something so freeing about standing there

completely naked, where everyone could see us. I keep my pussy shaved, so I felt even more exposed, knowing that there was nothing between my delicate folds and the world around me. I lay down on the towel and took a deep breath, enjoying the warm rays of the sun blanketing my skin until I felt a shade come over me. I opened my eyes to see Clay looming above me, wearing nothing but a smile.

"Let's go in the ocean," he said, reaching his hand out for mine and helping me up. We started running toward the waves as my hair blew in the wind and kept running, straight into the water until we were shoulder-deep in the sea. I closed my eyes and dunked my head back, enjoying the feel of the refreshing water engulfing my entire body.

When I came up, I slicked back my long dark hair and opened my eyes. I didn't see Clay, but seconds later I felt his hands encircling my waist underwater and his wet lips kissing my neck. He moved even closer to me and pressed his muscled chest against my back while his hard cock throbbed against my ass. Our skin was moist and pliant, and our bodies floated in the water as I turned around to meet his kiss face-to-face.

As our tongues swam in each other's mouth, I captured Clay's torso with my legs, my heels clasped around his tapered waist. His erection was flush against my pussy as the waves of the water made it brush back and forth against my labia, further arousing my clit. The sensation made my hot little button swell, and it felt so different in the water, like it was pulsing in slow motion with the ebb and flow of the tide. I quickly became insatiably horny and attacked my husband with furious kisses. I wrapped my arms around his neck, urging him to thrust his dick into my needy cunt.

"You want to do it right here, babe?" Clay said. "Are you sure?"

"Yes," I murmured against his ear as I nipped it roughly with my teeth. "I need it now, I'm so turned on and I can't wait."

I held on to Clay tightly as he moved us out a little farther, so we wouldn't be too close to any other people. Luckily he's a strong swimmer, so he was able to maneuver us in that awkward position. It was worth it, though, once he met my gaze and slowly worked his dick in between my folds. He hovered his cockhead at the entrance to my hole, letting my slippery pussy juice coat the very tip to make it easy for him to slide inside.

My inner walls quivered, aching to be stuffed full of his cock as my body floated in the water. Finally I moved myself closer to Clay, urging him inside me, relishing the slow stretching of my pussy around his massive girth. Ah, it felt so good to be spread open like that as he shoved deeper inside my hungry canal.

Once my pussy had swallowed his entire length, I made him stay still as my vagina pulsated around his shaft. Together we took a deep breath and went underwater, connected at the core. When we came up for air, I was ready to bounce on his cock, which I did as he swirled us around in the waves, each rise making him move deeper in as I dug my heels into his back. We felt weightless in the water, and as the pleasure rose inside me I let go of Clay and lay back to float as he grabbed hold of my hips and continued to pump into my pussy.

I looked up at the sky, feeling the warm sun caress my

nipples as they poked out from the water's surface. Then I closed my eyes and grabbed my breasts, pinching my nipples, making them even harder as the ecstasy of orgasm spread from my seething center throughout my body. Waves of pleasure coursed through me as my husband's stiff cock gracefully thrust in and out of my hot pussy.

Clay's fingers dug into my hips and I knew he was close, too. I sat back up and hugged him tightly, feeling every inch of his steely cock twitching inside me. "It's so wet," he whispered, then groaned deeply as he filled me with a warm load of come. We held each other like that for a while, hoping the waves were giving us some cover from the other swimmers in the distance, but in the back of my mind, I hoped at least someone had seen the fun we had.

We parted, and the water felt cool on the front of my body, then we both swam back to shore, emerging from the water holding hands, like we were the only two people on earth.

Somehow the sea of naked people on the sand no longer seemed so novel, but more beautiful and natural. We made it back to our towels and, spent and relaxed, lay down to soak in the sun, watching the salt water bead up on our bare skin.

It was an incredible day and a real awakening for Clay and me. We stayed on the beach until the sun went down, huddled together and wrapped in our beach towel for warmth. Reluctantly, we put on our clothes and walked back to the parking lot.

Once in the car, we made out for a few minutes until Clay's dick began to swell again. I reached down and freed it from his shorts and then swooped down to suck the whole length into my throat. I delighted in the salty taste of the sea on his skin and slurped and swirled my tongue all over the head. Clay moaned each time I swallowed him deeply, and it wasn't long before he filled my mouth with another delicious load of cream. After drinking it down, I wiped the corners of my mouth and told him I was ready to go home.

It wasn't too long a drive back to the condo, which was good, considering we went back to the nude beach every day during that trip, and we continue to visit it every time we're in Florida. We've even made some friends who we're looking into vacationing with elsewhere—though only at destinations that have a spectacular nude beach, of course.

—*E.P., New York, New York*

VACATION INSPIRES LUSTY COUPLE TO FIND
CREATIVE PLACES TO SPANK HER

A favorite sexual activity for my husband, George, and I is spanking. We do it any chance we get, and have from the moment we met each other. But our upcoming vacation to Cape Cod to visit his family left us in a quandary—where could we go for some privacy in order to fulfill our spanking quota? We'd learned from past experience that we're loud when he spanks me, so I took it upon myself to scope out any possible private nooks when we arrived. Lo and behold, I found a secluded cabin only five minutes away, and as soon as we could manage it, we made our getaway.

We held hands on the way over, and just knowing that I was finally going to get ravaged by my sexy husband was enough to make me dripping wet. Once inside the cabin, I looked up at him and immediately dropped to my knees, needing to have his cock in my mouth at that very moment. He undid his pants to reveal his impressively hard cock, and I quickly took him all the way down my throat, my pussy aching all the more as I tasted every inch of his manhood. But before I could really get into it, he stopped, sat down in a chair, and motioned for me to lie across his lap. The time for my spanking had arrived.

I got a chill throughout my body as he lowered my shorts and panties to reveal my bare bottom. I love nothing more than when he takes his strong hand to my butt, delivering hard smacks that redden my asscheeks and get me turned on beyond belief. He started off with a slight warm-up, a tease really, because he knows I can take much more. I longed to say something to urge him on, but knew he would work his way up to what I could take. So I lay there, one hand pressed to the floor for balance as he brought his hand across each of my cheeks, spanking me over and over again. With each blow, I absorbed the glorious stinging feeling and reveled in the warmth that raced through my body.

I squirmed on his lap, feeling his increasingly hard erection pressing against my stomach, thrilling me with the temptation of what was to come. But for now, I let his hand rain smack after smack down on me. He had developed quite the technique over the years, and with the slightest cupping of his hand could make his whacks feel that much more forceful. I loved the way he peered down at me so intently, like my every reaction and every mark he caused to form on my asscheeks mattered to him.

He took his spanking seriously and wanted to be the best spanker he could be. I could tell because during our many sessions, every once in a while he would try something new. He would move me slightly or use more force or try out a new toy, just to see how I would react. Usually, his impulses were correct, and he'd have me howling with that delicious blend of pleasurable pain that I adore. This time was no exception, as he ordered me to stand against the wall and put my hands up flat. When he hit me next, I felt the impact deep inside my pussy. I gasped in ecstasy, and dared to turn around. "What was that?"

My ass felt like it had just been pounded with something incredibly hard, yet I knew that there was nothing special in this room. "This," he said, showing me his fingers balled up, and when he did it again, I peeked over my shoulder. Rather than stinging, this technique of his created a thud that seemed to settle deep into my body, creating new layers of arousal.

There always comes a point in my spankings when I am so overwhelmed with lust that I'm not sure if I want him to keep spanking me or to fuck me. Well, in all honesty, I want it all. But I know that he will always make the best decision for me—he's done it every time so far, which is why I continue to trust him.

"Are you ready, Marcy?" he asked, his voice playful but with a deep current of desire lurking just below the surface.

"Yes, please, I'm ready for your cock, baby," I said, shivering as he turned me around so I was straddling him on the chair, his member pressing urgently up against me. I lifted myself slightly, feeling the stretch in my thighs, and stared into his eyes as I slowly lowered myself down onto his length. He held me steady as his cock entered me, stretching me and filling me all at once. I settled my weight on to his thighs and held on to him, then truly let myself go, focusing my entire being on the way his cock felt inside my pussy. It was glorious, and after all the erotic heat generated by his spanking, my body was tingling. Every move we made felt amazing, like he was fucking my whole body, and I kept shuddering against him. When he grabbed me by the hips, his fingers digging into my tender backside, I lost it, collapsing against him as my orgasm raced through me. As soon as my pussy started to spasm, George also unleashed his own load, quivering beneath me as his come spurted into my cunt.

We walked back to the beach house, and I felt goose bumps form on my arms every time George lightly brushed against my asscheeks. I was already looking forward to my next spanking.

The next day, we were both horny all over again, and we headed to a secluded beach about a mile down the road. Once the sun had properly roasted us, we swam out to a raft we'd seen from the shore. It was the perfect resting spot, and we took a little nap. When I woke up, squinting my eyes against the sun, George had positioned himself behind me. I could feel his cock against my backside, making itself known, and wiggled against him, darts of desire invading my pussy as I felt his nearness. I moved again so that I was sliding along his cock, and then I made a truly bold move by peeling down my bikini bottoms so that nothing separated us.

I reached behind me and fondled his cock underneath his swim trunks, smiling as I felt it jerk in my hand. My pussy was now completely slick with my juices, anticipating his cock plunging into me. But when I turned over and tried to take off his shorts completely, he stopped me, turning me back around with his muscular arms. I opened my mouth to speak, but when I felt his hands fondling my asscheeks, I remained silent, letting him arouse me as he increased the pressure until he was squeezing my cheeks with a good amount of pressure. Automatically, I rolled over onto my stomach, and he moved with me. He brushed his fingertips across my slit, but that was just a momentary tease, because in moments, he was striking my ass with his hand, giving me those firm smacks that I craved so dearly.

I pressed my body against the surface of the raft, grinding my clit against it as he increased the pace and intensity of his whacks. He leaned toward me and blew on the back of my neck. Each time his hand hit my ass, I felt a wave of heat, quickly followed by a pleasant chill, pass through my body. Every movement he made caused us to rock the raft slightly, so we teetered on the water. The sun beat down on my back as he continued to turn my ass a rosy red. "Marcy, you have the most gorgeous butt I've ever seen, and it's all mine."

"That's right, baby, you can do anything you want to it," I told him, thrilled that what he wanted to do was spank every inch of my firm, curved rear end. I prided myself on keeping my body in shape, but made sure to keep enough flesh on my ass to make the spankings enjoyable for both of us. He sped up his smacks, hitting me over and over again in the same spot, one on my right cheek and one on my left, until I thought I might simply melt into the water. My whole body felt liquefied with pleasure.

When he let loose with a torrent of his hardest smacks yet, I knew he was gearing up to fuck me. His cock had to be aching by now. When he was done, he rubbed his hand over my warm buttocks, tenderly patting them. George knows me so well that he didn't even bother asking if I was ready for his cock, he just spread my legs wide and shoved the entire length of his dick inside me. I'd been ready since the first smack, so the feeling of his cock filling me up was perfect. I opened my legs as wide apart as I could and kept my pussy tightened around him.

What could be more wonderful, I thought, than getting spanked and then fucked into oblivion under the sun's rays? Absolutely nothing. In no time at all, I was coming, bucking back against him and shaking the raft with my orgasm. "Yes, yes, yes!" was all he could say as he pulled out and shot his load onto my backside, the warm liquid hitting my sore asscheeks. This was a great place for him to come on me, because all we had to do was hop in the water to wash off!

Nobody was the wiser about our extracurricular activities, and we managed to keep our hands off each other except when we had some privacy. When we got back home, all we had to do was mention Cape Cod to get us in the mood for some good, old-fashioned spanking.

—*M.L., Portland, Maine*

LONDON DAY-TRIPPERS ENJOY SEX
AMONG HUGE STONE MONUMENTS

London has always been one of my favorite cities. Until recently all my visits there were for business reasons, and although I was usually in and out of the city in three days, I still managed to take in the city's major tourist sites. What I had never had time to do was explore the attractions on the outskirts of London. The countryside. Magical castles, medieval country manors, Stonehenge, the birthplace of the Bard—that was the part of England I wanted to see.

"So let's do it now," suggested Abigail, my business partner of five years and my wife of two, as our plane taxied to a stop at Heathrow Airport. "You're here on vacation, not business, remember? No time like the present, hon."

We had decided to spend a week, perhaps ten days, in Europe, enjoying time in France, Italy, England, and Scandinavia. Abby had convinced me that we could lock up the store (we have an upscale gift shop specializing in fine china, linen, glassware, and the like) for a short while with minimal damage to the bottom line while we enjoyed a brief and overdue vacation.

I had to agree with my wife that there was no time like the present to explore the English countryside, so the next morning, after breakfast at a restaurant near our hotel, we visited the British Travel Centre near Piccadilly Circus and got a handful of maps. With a sense of adventure, we started out of the city in our rental car, heading west toward Windsor Castle.

And what a magnificent structure it is! Over nine hundred years old, with much rebuilding over time, it reflects the history of English architecture. Inside are priceless tapestries and furnishings, as well as works of art by Leonardo and Rembrandt. Continuing northwest, we took in Blenheim Palace, and then, farther up on A34, we found Stratford-upon-Avon. No Shakespeare buff, of which I'm one, should fail to visit this fascinating place.

As it was getting late and we were hungry, we decided to call it quits for the day and return home. The day's outing, equally fun and educational, had invigorated me and Abby as well. We were hotter for each other than we had been in some time.

"Maybe it's all the fresh air we got today," my wife offered with a twinkle in her eye. "Or the exercise."

I really had no idea, nor was I about to think more about it as that night, back in our hotel room, I hammered my hard-on into Abby's hot, wet pussy. She held on tight as I used my cock like a fleshy cudgel in her sex, spitting out her lust in some very un-Abby-like language.

"I'd love to fuck in one of those castles," she blurted out at one point. "That would be wild." Sitting back on my haunches, I draped my wife's legs over my shoulders and then resumed fucking her, my cock going deep into the heavenly cove of her cunt. The thought of doing her in a castle, or medieval country manor, or soaring cathedral was wickedly appealing, and while I doubted we could actually pull it off, the fantasy fueled my passion and Abby's.

We finished up doggy-style, my wife's favorite, she and I coming within seconds of each other and then collapsing on the bed to cuddle before dropping off to sleep. Tomorrow we'd be up early for another day trip, this time venturing southwest of London to view the mysterious monuments at Stonehenge. We both anticipated another day of fun and adventure.

The day dawned cool and cloudy, but our spirits could not be dampened. We set off in our rental car and before too long found ourselves at Winchester in Hampshire, where stands the beautiful Norman cathedral. William the Conqueror was crowned in Winchester, and more English kings and princes are buried there than anywhere else but Westminster Abbey. Jane Austen is buried in Winchester Cathedral.

From Winchester, we drove through the West Sussex countryside and found Arundel Castle, yet another eye-popping structure of a time long, long ago. And then it was on to Stonehenge, which lies on the edge of the Salisbury Plain in the county of Wiltshire. As we wandered the grounds, Abby and I, like thousands before us, gazed in awe at the huge stone monuments of Stonehenge. The mystery of who erected them and why has fascinated the world for centuries.

I was deep in thought when Abby nudged me. "Wouldn't it be great if we could have sex behind one of those stones? We'd be making a little history of our own." I chuckled, but in truth I found the idea wickedly appealing. And it stayed with me on the drive back to London and our hotel, thanks in large part to Abby painting vivid images of how we would suck and fuck among the centuries-old monuments. Like an artist she created her fantasy, giving it shape and form, adding a detail here, an observation there, with the result that by the time we entered the hotel room we were both so into it we had no choice but to strip and jump into bed.

"Just imagine we're at Stonehenge," my wife said as she dropped to her knees in front of me, "and you're leaning against one of those—what do they call them—oh, yeah, trilithons." I was still digesting the word for the structures comprised of two uprights under a horizontal lintel when I felt Abby's wonderful mouth engulf my already fully erect cock. Closing my eyes, it was easy enough to imagine that we were back at Stonehenge, perhaps on a summer solstice morning, with the sun rising in exact and perfect alignment with the Heel Stone. Truly a lovely fantasy.

Abby continued licking and sucking on my pulsating member, pausing once in a while to add little touches to our shared fantasy of doing it at Stonehenge, reminding me of what we had seen and learned, helping me to keep the image sharp in my mind. Now she took me deep, little gurgling sounds emanating from her throat as she swallowed the shaft, her nostrils tickled by my pubic hairs. All the while she was fondling my balls, cupping the sac, squeezing gently. Occasionally she'd let a finger wander back to my asshole for a teasing tickle.

Finally, my wife stopped sucking me and said, "Now we're going to fuck. Over by the Altar Stone." With my mind's eye I saw again the single slab of gray-green sandstone about sixteen feet long that lies on the surface of the ground at Stonehenge. Abby swiveled around so that she was on her hands and knees. "Doggy-style, babe. That's how they did it back then, I'll bet."

I gave silent thanks for my vivid imagination as I got

into position behind my sexy wife and in one easy, fluid movement buried myself to the hilt in the cozy confines of her butter-soft pussy. "Oh, babe, that's what I like," my wife crooned happily. "I'm getting screwed at Stonehenge! Can you see it, babe? Is it in your head?"

I mumbled something unintelligible. I was really caught up in this now. I was at Stonehenge, that magical place of "hanging stones," giving it hard and fast to my grunting, moaning wife, who was as lost in this delightful dream world as I was.

"More, babe. Give me more," Abby pleaded.

And I responded, pictures of Stonehenge flashing across the screen of my mind, as I was sure was the case with Abby. The trilithons, Slaughter Stone, the bluestone horseshoe, and all the rest were so clear in my head, imagination transported me and my wife back to Stonehenge.

Abby and I came within seconds of each other, crying out with joy as our orgasms rocked us to and fro. Breathing hard, we collapsed right there on the plushly carpeted floor of our hotel room.

"That was cool," my wife said when she could speak. She thought for a moment. "We're going to Bath tomorrow, right? We'll be able to see the excavated remains of the Roman baths." I could see my wife's devilish mind working overtime. And when she gave me that mischievous smile of hers, accompanied by a wink, I knew where we'd be fucking tomorrow night.

—*M.G.L., Buffalo, New York*

KINKY CRUISING COUPLE WARMS TO SEX AT SEA

When my wife, Zoe, suggested we go on a cruise together, I let her make all the arrangements, because she's
the travel expert in our house. She told me what dates to
take off work, which I did, and then she handled all the
rest—reservations, transportation, and packing. So it
wasn't until we arrived at the dock that I really wondered
just what it was we'd be up to for the next week. Somehow, our fellow passengers didn't look all that much like
"normal folk." They were wearing chains and latex and
seemed to be getting quite intimate with each other on the
ship's deck. When I questioned Zoe about it, all she said
was, "It's a surprise, sweetie, just trust me," and she
beamed that same smile I've been agreeing to for ten
years.

We settled into our cabin and she let me lie down
while she made quick work of unpacking our clothes. I
watched her cute, slim figure as she scurried around, then
closed my eyes and started to drift off to sleep. Before I
knew it, Zoe was shaking me awake and standing in front
of me, looking decidedly kinky. She'd put on a tight
black PVC top I'd never seen before. It hugged her ample
curves. Completing the outfit was a bright red skirt that
barely covered her ass. I felt like a slob lying around in a
T-shirt and shorts.

Then Zoe revealed what she'd been holding behind
her back, and out of my view, a riding crop. My cock

jumped in my shorts; we'd talked about her dominating me, but that conversation was as far as we'd ever gotten. Now here she was, looking the part of the perfect domme. She tapped me on the arm with the crop. "Get up. You can't be a lazy bum, or at least you shouldn't look like one. I know we're on vacation, but you should try to show a little style." She grabbed my arm and pulled me up. My cock had become completely hard.

I put on a pair of lightweight black pants and a tight black T-shirt that I found among my luggage. All the while, I felt her hovering over me, the crop poised, awaiting any transgression. When I turned back to face her, my pants couldn't hide my bulging erection. Judging from the smile on her face, I didn't think this was a problem. "Now, I will give you a choice—we can go upstairs and join the others or stay here. I have plans for you either way. Which will it be?" She stepped toward me, the crop held off to the side until she was standing in front of me, so close that my cock was almost touching her. She moved her hips just enough to brush against my hardness, sending a shudder through my body.

"Let's go upstairs," I said, suddenly turned on by the idea of other people watching us.

"Good answer. That way everyone can see that I'm in charge," she said. I reached for the door, but she pulled me back. "Wait, there's just one more thing," and with that, she fastened a studded collar around my neck and then attached a metal chain that jingled as she adjusted it. Feeling the cold material brush against my skin and hearing it jangle made my face flush and my cock even harder.

We headed upstairs to join the many other couples

who were in similar configurations. I relaxed a little; clearly this cruise was slightly out of the ordinary, and I needn't have worried what anyone else might think. But I didn't have much time to ponder things because my wife quickly led me into a room that looked like a dungeon. It was empty, save for all the black leather furniture adorning it. I saw a big X-shaped cross up against the wall, a padded bench, and various hooks hanging around the room. A huge mirror hung on one wall and she brought me over to it so that we both faced it. Seeing myself on her leash caused my cock to jump once again, this time visibly.

"Does it turn you on to know that I can do whatever I want with you? I'm here to give you what you've always wanted, the ultimate in domination," Zoe said. As she spoke, my face got redder and redder, because every word she said was true and completely arousing. My little Zoe had transformed into a sophisticated domme, and I loved it. She tugged on the chain, and I felt the snugness of the collar around my neck. I was almost shaking with arousal, wondering what she'd do to me next. She is smaller than I am, but my desire to submit to her was so strong that I let her turn me around and shove me up against the wall. I put my hands above my head instinctively, and she praised me. I beamed like I'd just won the Nobel Prize.

Next she stripped me of all of my clothes. I glanced at the door; she'd closed it, but anyone could see what we were up to through the window. Even though we weren't the only ones engaging in such kinky behavior, the idea that strangers might see me at my wife's mercy felt both embarrassing and arousing. She raked her nails down my back, not hard enough to break the skin, but enough to make my backside tingle. Then her hand traveled down to my ass, and she let loose with two smacks to each ass-cheek in quick succession. She'd never spanked me before, but I'd dreamed about it plenty of times, and the sensation was amazing. Once she'd reached around and felt just how hard all of this play was making my cock, she kept going, raining smack after smack down on my eager ass as I glowed under her attention.

At one point, I let a hand slip down to stroke my cock. She immediately stopped what she was doing, took the offending hand, and deliberately placed it back to its proper spot above my head. She turned my head so that my cheek was pressed against the wall and stared directly into my eyes. "If we're going to do this, you'll follow my directions. Do you understand?" She pinched my cheek and I swallowed hard.

"Yes, ma'am."

I returned back to my original position, my cock now even harder. She took out the crop and proceeded to initiate my ass and upper thighs. She started off with light taps that weren't painful, and I was mesmerized by her rhythmic strokes. Zoe increased the intensity of her whipping, and I tensed my asscheeks as she landed another sharp blow on my butt. As much as I was bracing myself for her hits, I found that I was thrilled by the intensity. Each time the crop hit my ass, I felt the momentum travel to my cock, and when she was finally done whipping me, I was as aroused as I can ever remember being.

She finally put down the crop, then stood behind me and rubbed herself against me. I heard her playing with her pussy, and the slurping noise from her wetness drove me insane. Then she wrapped her wet fingers around my cock and said, "Now, if you're ready, you may have the honor of fucking me."

I turned around, and she tilted upward to kiss me deeply. Then she took up my previous position, leaning against the wall with her hands over her head. I sank low enough so that my cock was aligned with her opening and slid my hardness right inside. I lifted her hips as she thrust her ass backward, and we moved in a perfect rhythm. The cool air and motion soothed my reddened ass, and I pressed against her aroused clit while still holding her tight. Clearly, doling out my punishment had made her just as horny as I was.

Somehow, she managed to retain her air of coolness, even while my cock slammed into her again and again. I knew that at any moment, she might turn around and order me back into my subservient position. Out of the corner of my eye, I thought I saw someone walk by and turned my head around, half worried and half excited that someone might have seen us. But then my full attention was drawn back to my wife's ass as her tight pussy sucked my cock into her. I slowed down, savoring this moment of being so tightly encased by her clenching walls, looking down to watch my dick enter her.

"Yes, fuck me just like that!" she yelled, finally losing her composure as she approached her climax. I smiled as she reverted back to her old self, and then I slammed into her cunt, pinning her to the wall. I pumped my cock into her in short, quick strokes. In seconds, I squirted a hot load into her. She cried out when my liquid filled her cunt, and I held on to her as she went limp in my arms.

Later that evening, she made sure I learned my lesson

for the unspoken sin of coming before her, even though we both knew there was no way I could have stopped. But who was I to complain as she led me around by my beloved leash for the rest of the cruise?

Zoe continues to plan our vacations, and I trust her to come up with a good time that will always keep me on my toes.   —*D.G., Boulder, Colorado* O╾▪

MAGICAL MYSTERY TOUR IN NEW YORK CITY FOR WILDLY ADVENTUROUS LOS ANGELES COUPLE

My wife, Marla, and I normally go on two vacations a year, taking turns choosing the destination and making all the plans. It's all the more exciting because we try to keep the destination a secret from each other. Naturally, the one in charge gives some assistance concerning passports, visas, and appropriate clothing—but that's about it.

Now it was Marla's turn to choose the destination, and on the way to the airport, I was all delicious anticipation as I wondered where we were going. I managed not to gain clues at the terminal, but then we boarded the plane. Unfortunately, it was hard to drown out the sound of the pilot's voice when he said, "Temperatures in New York are hovering in the forty-degree range . . ." so the jig was up. New York Very interesting.

Both Marla and I are Midwestern at heart, but have adapted to the West Coast lifestyle like fish to water. The East? Well, we'd spent some time at JFK and La Guardia airports during stopovers, but that was about it. I hoped the Big Apple would be ready for me and my adventurous wife, who began to slide her hand down the waistband of my pants as the stewardess passed by with her drink cart. I could tell already this was going to be a great trip.

Six hours later we collected our luggage and found a taxi to take us into Manhattan. We checked into a rather nice hotel in midtown, but instead of handing us one room key, the desk clerk gave us two. On different floors! I had no idea what was going on until my wife told me in the elevator that we would be staying in separate rooms, spending our days apart, but the nights . . . well, if I did the right thing maybe she'd succumb to a chaste good-night kiss.

A good-night kiss! I was speechless as she got off the elevator on her floor and let the door close between us. Once I settled into my room, I pondered what my next move should be. I called the front desk and asked for my wife's extension, but was told there was no one with that name staying at the hotel. So she had used a fake name! Fine, I figured, two could play at this game. But the truth was that I was too intrigued to be annoyed. She obviously had something interesting up her sleeve.

As I dressed for dinner, I noticed a brochure on the desk describing a local restaurant that specialized in Thai cuisine, a favorite of mine and my wife's. I looked forward to a nice meal, figuring that I should just do my own thing and let Marla give me clues.

An hour later I sat at a table for one, enjoying some Mee Krob noodles. The waiter discreetly brought me a folded note that said, "Noticed you from across the room. Thought you might want some company. If so, meet me at the café around the corner. Simone."

I finished up my meal as leisurely as possible, actually quite anxious to get on with the night. Once outside, I started down the street. As I turned the corner, I noticed a tiny café with blue lights in the window. Stepping inside, I realized that this was some kind of a hot spot for young, pierced, artistic types with enough collective tattoos to cover a billboard.

Wearing my chinos, a button-down shirt, and penny loafers, I felt decidedly out of place. Just as I turned to leave, someone grabbed my arm to stop me. When I turned around, I was face to face with a woman with pixie-short hair, the eyes of a cat, and lips painted red and glossy. "Don't go," she whispered above the din. "I'm Simone."

She led me to a tiny table in the back, motioning for the waitress to bring us two Cosmopolitans. As she told me a little bit about her career as a graphic artist, I felt someone staring at me. I chalked it up to some middle-age phobia, but glanced through the thick crowd just to be sure.

That's when I saw her. If it weren't for her unmistakable almond-shaped eyes, I never would have recognized her in the black velvet cape and long blonde hair. My wife, the sexy yet conservative brunette, had somehow managed to transform herself into this erotic magnet, and in slow motion I got up from the table and walked toward her. Simone was quickly forgotten in all the excitement.

Marla simply smiled and said something in French, a language in which she's fluent while I'm clearly faltering. It didn't matter to me one franc as she led me through a tiny door behind the bar, the scent of an unfamiliar perfume floating off her skin.

She took me inside a small, square room with no windows. It took a moment for my eyes to adjust to the dim, sultry light provided by a few candles placed in the corners. She enveloped me in her arms and began to kiss me, her lips tasting somehow spicier, more exotic than normal. She pressed her body against mine with a fervor I nearly didn't recognize, and within seconds I was rock-hard.

She quickly undressed me, keeping herself swathed in black velvet as I stood curiously naked in the center of the room. My cock stood out straight with a spot of pre-come glistening on the head. I was so horny I thought I might explode. Marla stepped back to lean against a wall, opening her cape slightly to stroke her breasts and then her pussy. She had even dyed her pussy blonde! I moved toward her, but just then the door opened again and a slim figure slipped in. It was Simone!

My wife took her in her arms and began to kiss her, opening up the cape to let her inside. Some movement went on beneath the luxurious fabric and soon I could see that Simone had dropped her own pants down around her ankles. Marla was taller than Simone, and she seemed to wrap one leg up around her waist. It was just dark enough for me to be teased by their interplay without really being able to make out any details—but that was all about to change.

The two women seemed to be moving with one another in an erotic dance, and as my wife's head dropped back in ecstasy, I knew she was about to come. As she started to moan with increased urgency, the cape slipped off her shoulders and she stood there nude in the arms of Simone.

Simone was wearing an oversized blazer over some kind of dark underwear with a dildo attached. I could see its shaft as she pulled out of my wife's hot cunt, shiny and thick and pale in the dim light. I changed my vantage point so I could see her delicate pussy lips stretch around the bulbous cockhead of the toy as Simone pulled it nearly all the way out before shoving it back in.

"Fuck her hard," I said, wanting my wife's pleasure as much as I wanted my own. "Do it! Fuck her hard!" Simone pushed Marla up against the wall and, with surprising strength, managed to hold my wife's legs apart and in the air as she drove into her at a furious pace. My wife's face took on an expression of sensual anguish as she clearly lost control.

Simone gently lowered my wife's feet to the ground and pulled out of her. The dildo was obscene as it hung between her legs. Marla looked satiated but still ready for more, getting down on the floor doggy-style. I pushed the cape up around her hips and gripped her bare skin as I speared into her dripping pussy with one firm stroke. I fucked her hard, using all the building mystery of the day to fuel my passion, and she eagerly bucked back into me.

Simone knelt before us and watched with a small smile on her face, waving her still-wet "cock" near Marla's face until my wife started to suck it. I slowed down my thrusts a bit as she found her rhythm, and soon we were in a very erotic threesome. I could tell that the pressure of my wife's mouth on the dildo was pressing it against Simone's clit as she closed her eyes in blissful satisfaction, rocking her hips in time with Marla's attentions.

My wife, who is multiorgasmic to begin with, was coming in wave after wave, her moans muffled by the dildo in her mouth, but I could feel by the clenching and pulsing of her pussy that this was the best fucking she'd ever received. My cock was grateful for the pressure, especially as her muscles contracted around my cockhead near the entrance of her marvelous pussy. She felt so tight and smooth that it took every ounce of discipline not to erupt.

When I did come, it was so loud and so long that I wonder to this day if the entire café crowd heard us. No one seemed to notice as the three of us quietly left the secret room a while later, Simone fading into the night as my wife and I held hands for a midnight walk down Fifth Avenue. —A.D., Los Angeles, California ⚬━■

RAVISHING SEA NYMPH AND BOLD SCUBA DIVER
PUT ON SPLASHY SHOW

Thousands of tiny bubbles fluttered from my scuba gear and swirled up toward the surface of the water forty feet above me. All around me fish of many colors filled my field of vision with what looked like a kaleidoscope splintered into a million pieces. The water was as warm as broth and window-clear.

Far above, a large shadow passed between me and the sun. My first thought was a shark or manta ray. The waters in the Sea of Cortez are famous for both. I eased over on my back and looked straight up.

She was swimming slowly and languidly on the surface, nude, her skin golden brown, her full breasts swaying with the gentle rhythm of her breaststroke, her long, slender legs undulating with the grace and flexibility of the fish that swam all around me.

I was mesmerized; I couldn't take my eyes off her. I froze because she was looking straight down into the depths, but she wore no face mask and her feet were free of the ungainly flippers that snorkelers wear. Her nipples were dark and rosy pink against the brown of her breasts, her black hair long and spread out behind her, her bush a tiny ebony triangle.

I'd been diving in this cove for over a week and she was the first person I'd seen. This was my cove, I'd started to believe, just for me and the astonishingly beautiful sea creatures that filled it with pulsing life. Who was this interloper? I kept my distance behind and below her as she swam slowly toward the sea cave.

Inside the cave was a lagoon, the water so transparent it was invisible, with swaying schools of small fish, silver and blue and scarlet, like glittering gems flung across the limpid emptiness. Light shone from cracks in the rock high above, creating shafts of gold across the dim light.

She swam in and climbed out onto a huge slab of rock as black and smooth as a cheek from aeons of the wash of high tide. I felt like a transgressor here, watching this lovely young woman innocent of clothing. I watched, my face barely above the water, in the shadows only a few feet away.

She stretched out on the polished black rock, spread-eagled, legs wide open, arms over her head. Her long hair snaked out on the rock, black on black. The pink of her pussy glistened against the black of her bush. Her breasts were large and firm. I could hear her breathing, rhythmic and sweet.

Slowly she began to stroke her still-wet breasts, gently pushing them together, squeezing and releasing them as though she were trying to bring milk from her nipples. They were swollen now, like rosy little buds, full and erect.

Her smile seemed to look inward as she pleasured her slick, firm globes, kneading her nipples between her long brown fingers. Soft gasps of her pleasure echoed in the cavern like a strange sensual kind of water music.

My cock was bulging in my bathing suit and I reached down just to get it into a more comfortable position, but my hand stayed there, stroking myself just as she was stroking herself. I eased my cock out into the water, milking it, stroking, unconsciously mimicking her rhythm. Hundreds of tiny fish, silver and scarlet, swam past me, some of them brushing against my chest, flicking like butterflies across my nipples. They swam between my legs, gliding past my hard cock, touching, caressing my balls.

I watched as she slid two of her slender brown fingers into her vagina and her thumb fluttered against her clit. In a faster and faster fucking pulse, her fingers plunged in and out of her pussy. Up and down she gently thumbed her swollen clit as she got closer and closer to her orgasm. Her throbbing cadence increased bit by bit, and mine did, too, as I fisted my rock-hard cock.

Her back arched as she came, her scream of passion slicing the moist air like a mad seagull, echoing back and forth in the cavern. I came with her, my hot juice spurting out into the water, a fountain of milky fire drifting slowly past the silver darts of the tiny fish.

She was breathing long and slow, spread-eagled still, her legs open, her pussy swollen, shiny wet, and flushed dark pink. With each breath her large firm breasts rose and fell, swaying gently. I wanted to suck her rosy nipples, lick them while they were still full and swollen with passion.

But I couldn't. I was an intruder here, a voyeur invading this beautiful young woman's privacy. I slipped my mouthpiece in and sank into the crystalline depths. Slowly I swam out of the sea cave, expecting never to see her again. At least she hadn't seen me spying on her secret passion—or so I thought.

I went to bed early that night in my hotel room and

tried to read one of the books I'd brought with me about
sea life. I was considering changing professions from the
world of computers, which had begun to bore me, to marine biology. I couldn't concentrate, though, nor could I
sleep. She haunted me.

About two in the morning I gave up and went down to
the beach. The throbbing surf masked the music from the
disco. Clouds were gathering in the distance.

There she was, walking toward me on the sand, naked,
with her long black hair swaying free in the breeze. She
was barely visible in the starlight. We didn't speak until
we stood so close I could feel the warmth of her body.
She tossed her head fetchingly as she said she'd enjoyed
me watching her and was glad I'd liked what I saw.

I nodded and gasped because I felt her hand stroking
my cock. It had risen at the sight of her, but now it was
alive, straining against my skimpy bathing suit. I felt
overdressed. Her smiling lips met mine as her other hand
stroked across my nipples, which suddenly grew hot and
erect. Then both her hands cupped her breasts and offered
them to me, to my hot gaze and my eager mouth. I kissed
her swollen nipples. She moaned with passion as I sucked
first one and then the other into my mouth, tonguing them
gently.

Her body shuddered as she thrust her hips against
mine. My cock was spear-hard as I pushed it against the
softness of her belly. My tongue and lips felt the throb of
her heart in her nipples like the stormy beat of a drum.
Warm waves swirled around our legs as I pulled my
bathing suit down over my straining cock. Our arms
around each other, we tumbled down onto the soft sand
as the water lapped around us. The wind picked up a lit-

tle and big, dark clouds moved across the sky. Far in the distance was a glow of lightning.

Her legs opened to me and my cock entered her pussy. The rhythm of the sea slowly rolled us back and forth. As I eased into her inch by inch she moaned, gripping my thighs and pulling me in deep. She was gripping my cock so hard I thought I'd come right away. I wanted this to last forever as I gentled the power of my thrusting to match the soft back and forth of the warm waves.

Suddenly a blaze of lightning arced across the sky and she laughed as thunder boomed over the ocean. Under her then over her, I thrust into her hot slick pussy, her long slender legs wrapped around me, her nails raking across my chest, flicking fire as they ran over my nipples. The water wrapped around us, the rain sluiced down our naked bodies as we fucked. She moaned as I drove my cock into her delicate pussy. She leaned against me and her sharp white teeth found my nipple.

I felt my juices begin to overflow as her pussy tightened and her gasps came faster and faster. We exploded together, twin volcanoes in a whirlpool of sea and rain. The tide was ebbing and the waves left us spent on the sand, the rain washing us clean.

I came again that night as she sucked my cock. She seemed shy as she took me in her mouth, but that impression was quickly washed away. Deep she took me in a sea-slow rhythm, tonguing my shaft, and when my passion roared through me she gripped my ass tightly, sucking me dry and holding me lovingly in her mouth as the waves tumbled us about.

At dawn she said she had to leave me. I asked how I

could find her again, but she gently evaded my questions. We said good-bye with a long, gentle kiss, deep and tender. Then she turned out of my arms and walked out into the surf. —*K.A., Cedar Rapids, Iowa*

A MARRIAGE PROPOSAL IS MADE
AND ACCEPTED IN CARACAS, VENEZUELA

"Donde puede cambiar dolares?" I heard Deanne's dulcet tones as she read from her book of Spanish words and phrases. She had been brushing up on her Spanish for a month in anticipation of our trip to Caracas, while I was hunting down the perfect engagement ring.

From the moment Deanne suggested we take a trip to Venezuela, I knew that that was where I would propose. And I wanted to slip that princess-cut diamond on her finger in just the right place, at just the right time.

A flamboyant, metropolitan atmosphere seemed to swallow us up upon our arrival in Caracas. Brimming over a narrow valley and divided from the coastline by the imposing Mount Avila, the city feels chic and exotic.

After we had settled into our hotel room, I told Deanne I was eager to get out and see the sights. In truth, I was in a hurry to find the perfect place to propose to her. She, however, was content to make herself at home.

"Oh, it's so hot! Aren't you hot?" she said as she began taking off her clothes. That's my Deanne, always looking for an excuse to get naked. That was something I found out about her early on in our relationship. It was probably our third date or so, and I had yet to make any moves on her. I really liked her from the start and wanted things to go smoothly. I figured if she knew I wasn't dating her just to get in her pants, she'd be a lot happier. So I decided to abstain from any sexual advances until the time was right.

Apparently Deanne and I had different ideas about when the time was right. Because there she was in her apartment on our third date whining, "Oh, no, I must have spilled something on my favorite shirt during dinner. I better take this off immediately. I can't stand to look at it. It breaks my heart."

I just assumed she'd go into the bedroom to change, but Deanne saw no need for another shirt (and when she took off her shirt I realized she hadn't found a need for a bra either). Faster than you can say "good riddance," my vow of abstinence was out the door and my hands were squeezing Deanne's full breasts.

Now, two years later, Deanne was still abandoning her clothes every chance she got, and I watched as if seeing her for the first time as she slipped out of her shorts and pulled off her crop top. Her large breasts spilled out of her bra as soon as she undid the clasp.

I couldn't ignore the protrusion between my legs, so I took off all my clothes and brought Deanne to bed where we fell into each other's arms. You would have thought we were first-time lovers the way we pawed each other like two wild animals.

I trailed gentle kisses down her neck until I reached her breasts, where my mouth moved to one of her hard little nubs. I sucked it in my mouth and pulled on it lightly, stretching it away from her skin and then releasing my hold. Then I teased her other breast in the same manner before making my way down the smooth expanse of her stomach.

I stuck my tongue inside her belly button and then

dragged it down to her pussy, where I traced her lips with my tongue tip. She wriggled beneath me as I began to flick her clitoris and she raised her pelvis to grind against my mouth as I explored her hot sex. With my tongue stroking up and down her labia, and then rubbing her little clit, she soon erupted in orgasm, grabbing my head and pushing my face harder into her cunt.

Once we finally left the hotel room, Deanne and I made our way over to Plaza Bolívar, one of the many squares in the city and home of the equestrian statue of Simón Bolívar. It occurred to me that the plush gardens of the square would make for a romantic proposal site, but it was an extremely hot day and with sweat dripping down my sweet Deanne's face and my stomach rumbling, I quickly changed my mind.

There was not another chance to propose on our first day there, because after visiting Plaza Bolívar we went to dinner and then returned to our hotel room for a good night's sleep.

The following day was Sunday, and both Deanne and I thought it was the perfect time to go see the Roman Catholic cathedral. After mass, while standing outside the majestic chapel, holding Deanne's hand, I continuously fingered the ring box that was tucked securely in my jean-shorts pocket while debating if now was the time. Deanne turned around and smiled that sweet, cherubic smile of hers.

"Deanne," I began, slightly stuttering. "Would you . . ."

Deanne stopped me in mid-proposal by hitting my shoulder and screaming at the top of her lungs. Startled, I asked her what was wrong. "You just had some kind of big bug on you, that's all." She had collected herself but the moment was lost. "What was it you were going to ask me? Would I what?"

"Mind if we took a trip to the men's room," I answered with a faint smile.

And so our trip went, with Deanne and I going from sight to sight, with never an opportune time to propose presenting itself. By our last night, as we packed our bags, I had given up. I was starting to think that maybe it was all a sign of some kind.

Sure, I had enjoyed our trip, but what I had anticipated more than anything was seeing the look on Deanne's face as I slipped that band of gold on her finger, and hearing her say the word "yes."

We decided to pack in the early evening to get it out of the way so we could enjoy a nice dinner on our last night in the city. We left the Caracas Hilton International at about seven and took our rental car over to La Estancia restaurant.

I ordered rabbit basted in orange sauce and Deanne ordered parillas, which is a criollo-style grill. It seemed my feeling of disappointment was contagious because Deanne was quiet during dinner as well. When we returned to our room, however, her usual playful mood had returned.

"Oh, it's so hot in here. I'm just going to have to sleep naked," she announced.

I had to laugh as Deanne took off all her clothes and jumped into the bed. "You're going to be very uncomfortable tonight if you sleep in those," she said, pointing to my briefs. The air conditioner hummed on high as I slipped into bed. I didn't have to pretend I was hot. Deanne always got me hot.

She didn't waste any time, either. Before I knew what hit me, she had jumped on my lap and started to nibble on my ear, which never fails to get my dick in an uproar in mere seconds. With just a few licks of her tongue, Deanne had me rock-hard and dripping with pre-come.

My honey was ready to go as well, and in one fluid motion she slipped my cock inside her cunt and began riding me. It was delicious being inside her, feeling her velvety walls as she bopped up and down on my shaft.

I grabbed her asscheeks and helped her move up and down on my cock, ranging my speed from slow to fast. Several times I thought I was going to lose it, but I held out, wanting to savor the feel of Deanne's breasts brushing over my chest as they bounced up and down, and to luxuriate in the taste of her salty neck as I kissed it.

When Deanne started moaning and twitching, though, I couldn't hold out any longer and joined her in the kind of sweet climax that only true lovers can know.

Just as I was about to turn out the lights so we could go to sleep, Deanne slipped something on my wrist. I looked down to find a gorgeous Rolex watch. "*Esto es para usted*," she said in Spanish. I had to rack my brain to recall that what she said meant: This is for you.

"What is this for?" I asked, genuinely surprised.

"Read the inscription."

I turned over the watch and read: Will you marry me, James?   —*J.O., Cincinnati, Ohio*

GIRLFRIEND IS A WINNER WITH RACY LAP DANCE FROM SEXY VEGAS STRIPPER

Sure, I had been to strip clubs with my boyfriend before, and I'd enjoyed staring at all the sexy half-naked women, especially when they were giving lap dances to customers. But I had always been too shy to actually get a lap dance myself. That, however, changed when Sean and I spent a crazy weekend in Las Vegas.

Gambling not really being our thing, we took a cab from our hotel to a gentlemen's club a little ways off the Strip that a friend of Sean's had highly recommended. After paying the cover charge, we found two seats at one of the stage tables where a stunning woman was dancing. There were about ten of us sitting around the table, but I was the only woman and I could feel all the men's eyes on me as I sat down. Their looks of longing, coupled with the fact that the sexy dancer seemed to be paying extra attention to me, all served to turn me on more than I'd thought possible.

The stripper was at least six feet tall in her clear lucite high heels, with long, sleek legs that seemed to go on forever. All she was wearing was a satiny black G-string that barely covered the pink of her pussy. The perfectly round globes of her ass were on complete display as she moved sensually across the tabletop. Her dark hair was long enough to cover her breasts, but when she lay down on her back, propped herself up on her elbows, and tossed back her head, her silky mane swished behind her, revealing a pair of gorgeous, firm mounds capped with rosy red nipples.

I couldn't take my eyes off her, and if it weren't for my boyfriend's hand gently squeezing my thigh, I'd have forgotten he was there entirely. She got onto her hands and knees and crawled around the table, pausing along the way to let each patron slide a dollar into her G-string. When she got to me she moved in real close and locked her big blue eyes with mine. She smiled and teasingly offered up her hip, pulling the thin string away from her flesh. She was the sexiest woman I'd ever seen, and when I reached forward to tuck my dollar into her string, I fumbled a bit and it fell to the table.

"Naughty, naughty," she said as she wagged her finger at me. Then she looked over at Sean and whispered, "You must not take her to strip clubs often enough." And then she smiled and reached behind her for two dollar bills. She coiled them around two of her slender red-tipped fingers and reached forward, sliding them into my ample cleavage. When her fingers lightly grazed my breasts, a thrill surged through me and a gush of juice escaped my pussy, making me instantly wet.

"That's the double-dip," she said, leaning forward to whisper hotly into my ear. Her breath caressed my sensitive skin and I couldn't believe how aroused she was making me. She giggled and started to push back from me to the center of the table, but not before saying, "There, now you've made your first two bucks at a strip club."

Sean kissed my cheek as I sat awestruck, my gaze fixed on her as she finished her set on the tabletop. She rolled over the glass, her legs flying overhead in a straddle, showcasing her tiny triangle-covered pussy. She would arch her back, her high breasts reaching up like cherry-topped vanilla sundaes. She really looked good enough to eat.

As the song was ending, with my eyes still focused on the dancer, I tilted my head toward Sean and said, "I want her to give me a lap dance." Faster than I'd ever seen him move, Sean got up and approached the dancer as she descended from the stage, and soon she was walking back to me with him, all six glorious feet of her.

"How about a dance against the wall," she said. "That way I have more leverage." I liked the sound of that, and she grabbed my hand, leading me to the back of the club, my overjoyed boyfriend trailing behind us. She introduced herself as Carly and said that she was excited to earn her two dollars back by dancing for me.

I could hardly contain my own excitement as she sat me down in a plush armchair and leaned in close. Her sweet perfume filled my nostrils as her soft body covered mine. "You're going to enjoy this," she said. "Women are my specialty." And as the song started she kissed my neck, her silky hair pooling in my cleavage, tickling my skin.

My pussy was on fire, aching to be touched, and she must have sensed how much because she stood up and pressed her knee between my thighs. I spread my legs wider as she worked her knee into my crotch. My clit was hard and throbbing against her knee and my pussy was swollen with desire. She stood back and turned around, pressing her body up against mine and then gyrating slowly and sensually to the music, her warm skin covering every inch of my body.

I took a quick peek at my boyfriend and saw that his jaw was nearly on the floor and his hand was resting on his own stiffening bulge. I blew him a kiss and then brought my attention back to Carly, placing my hands on her hips. I was amazed at how soft her skin was, and I helped guide her smooth ass between my spread thighs. She looked over her shoulder at me, her eyes half-closed. She seemed to be enjoying this as much as I was.

She continued to grind her cushiony ass against me, practically riding it against my hot little button. The dampness of my panties made them stick to my slick pussy lips as each thrust of her ass brought me a little closer to my climax. Still wriggling madly, she arched her back and leaned her head against my shoulder. I reached my arms around her, stroking her flat stomach and urging her to grind even harder into me.

The sensual pleasure of another woman's body against mine was bringing me to the edge of ecstasy. I cried out against her soft shoulder, wishing I could scream. She grabbed my hands and brought them to her breasts. She sighed deeply as I clutched her tits and squeezed my thighs against her. She continued her sexy dance, thrusting against me until she felt me shudder beneath her. The sensation of her beautiful body pressing up against mine sparked a fabulous orgasm that left me shaking in the chair. Carly gradually slid off the chair and turned around to face me. Then she squatted down low and moved her face toward my crotch, breathing in deeply at the very hem of my skirt to smell my oozing honey. "Mmm, I wish I could taste you," she said.

As the song ended she leaned in close and kissed me on the neck, thanking me for inspiring her best dance of the night. I sat there speechless, her perfume still lingering in the air. "How do I match that?" Sean asked Carly as he handed her a generous tip.

"I suggest you take your girlfriend home and fuck her right now," she said. And lucky for me that's exactly what Sean did, only after I performed a special lap dance for him first, using all the techniques I learned from Carly, of course.   —*M.L., St. Paul, Minnesota* ⚷

WHEN THEIR PLANE IS DELAYED,
COLLEGE FRIENDS USE THEIR LAYOVER TO GET LAID

It was somewhere over Colorado that I saw her: Holly, my long-lost college crush. My seat was in the back of the plane, so I noticed everyone walking toward the bathroom.

Suddenly there she was, sashaying down the aisle. Not only did she have a contagious smile, she also sported a perky pair of breasts and an ass that wouldn't quit. I had always lusted after her from afar, but aside from a few flirtatious comments on her end, nothing had come of it. But here was Holly right before my eyes, wearing a tight black tank top and an even tighter pair of blue jeans, looking as good as ever.

"Holly," I said, reaching to touch her arm as she passed by.

"Oh, my goodness," she said, recognizing me instantly. "Lance. It's been so long."

Holly took my hand and the sparks between us began to fly as fast as the jet. It was like no time at all had passed, and our flirting quickly took a decidedly risqué turn. Beneath our casual banter, her eyes were sizing me up, and I didn't need her leg to press against mine to know that she wanted me as much as I wanted her.

I explained I was visiting some friends in L.A. She was heading home to visit family for a few days. We talked for a bit longer, and then Holly had to get back to her seat. I watched her gorgeous ass swaying as she sauntered off, my cock totally stiff. I had to find a way to make something happen between us.

"Ever get a piece of that?" the guy next to me asked jokingly.

"I wish." If I only knew that that wish would soon come true.

We arrived in Denver, and I got ready to make my transfer to LAX. I wondered if Holly was doing the same. I waited for her at the gate, and then we walked over to the display screens to see how much of a hike we would have to make to the next gate.

"Delayed," flashed on the screen next to our flight number. Despite what you might think, it was one of the happiest moments of my life. That one little word meant we'd be stuck in Denver for close to five hours!

"Want to blow out of here for a few hours?" Holly asked with a slight smile. "Maybe go someplace private?" she added with a wicked grin.

"Definitely," I said, steering her by the elbow. My cock jolted just from that light contact, and I quickly followed her. We grabbed a taxi outside the airport.

"Take us to the closest hotel," I said.

As soon as we were settled in the backseat, Holly jumped me. There was no coy flirtation, just some major spit swapping. Holly's mouth tasted sweet and minty, and from the way her tongue tangled with mine, her erotic intentions were perfectly clear. I slipped a hand around her waist, pulling her even closer to me. My fingers caressed the upper curves of her ass. It all felt unreal, yet touching her told me that this encounter was actually happening.

We arrived at a posh hotel in only a few minutes, grabbed our luggage, and raced over to the counter.

"We'd like a room, please," I said as Holly pressed up against me from behind. It was all I could do not to take her right there in the lobby. The clerk must have sensed the urgency of our request, because he quickly gave us a key and we were off.

On the elevator ride up, I pressed Holly up against the elevator wall, kissing that perfect little mouth some more. I couldn't wait to get her into the room.

My cock was throbbing before she even grabbed it through my jeans.

"Why, Lance, it looks like someone would like to come out and play."

And play we did. My clothes were the first to go. Before I could dig into Holly's shirt, she'd dropped to her knees and had taken the full length of my dick in her mouth. I always knew that girl had pretty lips, but her tongue, now that was something else. She started licking down one side and then up the other, tickling my balls at the same time. The action began to heat up. She was moving so fast, I could feel the saliva sliding down the base of my cock, and I heard sucking sounds escaping from her active mouth. It was all I could do to keep from coming right there and then.

But I wanted more. I removed Holly's black tank top to find two very generous tits underneath. Holly's petite, but she has a fabulous rack. As soon as I felt her plump breasts, I could tell they were a hundred percent real. I pushed them together and then just had to taste them. My tongue slid over one of her nipples. It was jutting out as if we were outside in the cold. Some women have pale pink nipples, but not Holly; hers were a dark, rich brown that matched her olive-toned skin. I thought I was in heaven.

Next, it was time to undress her. Beneath her jeans, Holly was wearing a purple G-string, which only accented that perfect ass. I took two handfuls of those delicious asscheeks, pulled that little vixen tight against me, and kissed her deeply. My cock automatically found her pussy, where I could instantly feel the wetness seeping through her panties. I knew what that meant: It was time to fuck.

We backed up toward the bed. I slid off the G-string, then laid her across the mattress. With one finger in her cunt, Holly began to squirm. At three, I rubbed her clit with my thumb and the moaning started. I took my fingers out and Holly's pussy lips parted to let me in. She had just the right amount of hair, enough to give a little bit of friction but not too much. I held myself above her, sliding the tip of my cock in and out, relishing the moment of entrance by drawing it out as long as I could.

"Just give it to me," she said. "I want it all." Hearing her say those words made me have the same desire, and with one deep thrust, I gave it all to her.

Holly raised her hips off the bed to meet my thrusts. I grabbed her ass with one hand, keeping her in a raised position. She leaned forward, taking my small but firm nipple into her mouth. My cock grew even harder inside her. She grew more animated as my nipple responded to her tongue. Before I knew it, she'd flipped us over so I was on my back with Holly riding me like there was no tomorrow. She ground her cunt against my pelvis, and it didn't take much more before she threw back her head and moaned loudly. I felt every tremor of her orgasm as she shuddered around my dick.

"Oh, Lance. I couldn't wait any longer. You just felt so good."

"I loved seeing you come. It's my turn now, baby. Turn over."

"Do you want me on all fours?" she purred.

"Oh, yeah. I want to watch that sexy ass of yours."

Once again, I had Holly on her knees, but this time I was fucking her from behind. She leaned back to kiss me, and that's when the action came to a head. I placed my hands on either side of her ass and pumped into her pussy, pounding her into the bed. With every thrust, the pressure mounted and I knew that my orgasm was about to overtake me. My body tensed and then I spurted into Holly, giving her everything I had.

I never did ask Holly if she was seeing anyone back home. It wasn't about getting serious between us, but more about the physical chemistry that we had, even after all those years. I can tell you one thing, though—that was the best layover I've ever had.

—*L.K., Chicago, Illinois*

IT'S PARADISE, INDEED, FOR ONE HOTEL GUEST AND HER FAVORITE BELLHOP IN THE BAHAMAS

To think that I almost missed the opportunity to experience the best vacation and the most intense orgasms of my life.

My friend and travel companion, Jacqueline, and I were so excited about our vacation in the Bahamas, but then she came down with the flu and had to cancel. I was disappointed because I wasn't about to go alone. Jackie, however, convinced me to get on that plane to Paradise Island. I did need a vacation, so I boarded the plane the next morning, nervous about spending an entire week away by myself.

The flight was only two and a half hours long and I was at the hotel by ten. I checked in at the desk and waited for the bellhop to come and take my bags to my room. "Right this way," I heard a voice say behind me. The distinctive Boston accent surprised me. As I stood behind the bellhop in the elevator, I couldn't help but notice how his uniform pants hugged his bottom. He was ten years younger than me. I am thirty-four but I look young for my age.

He opened the door to my suite, which was much bigger than I needed since I was alone. I kicked off my sandals and went straight to the sliding glass doors and stepped out onto the terrace, letting the warm breeze flow through my brown hair. The view was great! The water was right below me, and I felt as if I could jump from my eighth-story room and land right in the blue heaven below.

Looking down the beach, I could see two lovers holding hands as they walked along the white sand. Suddenly I felt lonely. My sexy bellhop cleared his throat. I had forgotten all about him and he was waiting for his tip. Taking the money, he thanked me politely and walked out the door, my eyes following his tight butt the whole way.

I decided to head straight to the straw market I had heard so much about and save the beach for another day. Shopping always puts me in a good mood, and after purchasing a great big straw hat, I made a resolution to enjoy this trip to the fullest. Really getting into the spirit of things, I bought a sarong dress that showed off a little more of me than I usually allow strangers to see.

When I returned to the hotel I made myself a drink from the minibar and relaxed in the lounge chair on the terrace, watching the calm waves ripple against the shore. When my stomach reminded me that it was almost dinnertime, I headed for the shower to get ready, I decided to wear the sarong I had bought earlier. It flattered my figure and showed off my long legs and firm thighs. I put on a pair of high-heeled sandals and even put a red flower in my hair.

As the waitress led me to a table for one, I could feel heat on my thighs from the stares I was getting from the men in the room. I ate my meal slowly, treated myself to a gooey dessert, and then wandered outside. The hotel had an outdoor bar by the pool where at night the tourists danced and drank while the calypso band played. I sat at the bar sipping a frozen margarita, which seemed appropriate to my surroundings. I felt a hand on my shoulder and when I heard the accent say hello, I knew it was my bellhop. Dressed in a blue Hawaiian shirt and khaki pants, he asked if he could join me. When I said yes, he slid onto the stool next to mine and we started talking.

His name was Jesse and he had just moved to the Bahamas three months ago. At twenty-three, he was trying to avoid becoming part of the rat race and had decided to live in the Caribbean and take things slow for a while. As he spoke, I realized he was even more appealing out of uniform. He had wavy brown hair and dark brown eyes. His face was smooth and he had a dimple on his cheek that made me tingle.

We danced close to the calypso beat, my arms around Jesse's neck and his around my waist. He pressed his forehead to mine and ground his thigh against my mound. I was so hot I thought I would come right there on the dance floor. I knew he felt the same because I could see the tent forming in his pants. I thought about it for a second before inviting him up to my room for a drink.

I made two tropical drinks and brought them out to the terrace where Jesse was waiting. He reminded me why I like younger guys when he grabbed me with passion and intensity and pulled me down on top of him. One of the drinks spilled all over us and the glass dropped to the floor. He took the other drink from me and placed it to the side so he could kiss me. When Jesse pushed his tongue into my mouth, I moaned into his throat.

He grabbed my hand, sticky from the drink, to lick it clean. Starting with my fingers, he sucked them one by one. He traced his tongue up my arm, then stood up quickly with me in his arms and sat me back down on the chair. After untying my sarong, he licked each nipple until I moaned in total ecstasy.

Abandoning my breasts, he continued down past my stomach. He pulled my panties down my legs, over my sandals, and tossed them aside. Jesse lifted the other drink, aimed it a few inches below my belly button, and poured its contents onto me. The cold liquid flowed down into my pubic hair, over my clitoris, and down between the lips of my pussy. I jumped, then very quickly calmed down as Jesse covered my puffy sex with his mouth to lap up the concoction. As he licked my clit and sucked my labia, I started to jerk this way and that and was soon coming, wave after wave of pleasure rushing through me. When I awoke from my blissful haze and came back to my senses, I could hear the band playing down below by the pool.

I was dying to get Jesse undressed. I unbuttoned his shirt and pulled it down to reveal his well-tanned shoulders. I ran my hands over his chest and became even more excited when I saw it was hairless. It didn't take too long to remove his pants because I was in such a rush to get his cock into my mouth.

His cock was swollen with anticipation. I tasted the tip with my tongue, then engulfed the head with my hungry mouth. He tasted delicious, and before I knew it he was holding my hair and his cock was inside my throat up to his balls. I sucked him hard until I heard him moan. Thinking he was ready to come, I stopped sucking and Jesse moaned but soon cheered up when I removed my sarong and leaned over the railing of the terrace, beckon--ing him to hurry and slide himself into my pussy.

In seconds he was thrusting hard into me as I braced

myself on the iron railing in front of me. He pulled almost all the way out on each stroke, then rammed himself back into me, both of us crying out. When he reached around to stimulate my clitoris with his fingers, it wasn't long before we were both coming explosively. I felt his warm cream on my back and ass as he pulled out and came on me.

The rest of the week was just as incredible as that first night. I relaxed alone on the beach in the day and at night Jesse and I made love in every position and place possible. On the morning I left I called for a bellhop—asking for him by name—to come and get my bags earlier than necessary. My Jesse showed up in the uniform he was wearing when I first met him. We had one last hoorah, a little faster than we would have liked it to be because he had to get back to work.

We made our way outside where he placed my bags in the taxi. I gave him a tip, a big kiss, and a promise to visit when I get sick of the rat race.

—*L.C., New York, New York*   ○┼■

ADVENTUROUS COUPLE ON SECLUDED ISLAND
PUT ON WILD SHOW FOR LOCAL FISHERMAN

To Jed I was like a fruit, round and juicy, and each time he saw me naked he thought of eating me. My rounded belly, full hips, and buttocks reminded him of temple sculptures, goddesses waiting to be taken. To rekindle some of the original fire of our passion, we decided to rent a small house on a secluded island beach off the Spanish coast. It was just what was called for, and from the moment we landed I was certainly ripe for the plucking.

The big old bed stood by the glass doors on one side of the cottage's only room. Lying there you could see the long white beach and the path down to it, used only by local fishermen who were used to tourist antics. The thought of appearing naked to one of them aroused me as I toweled myself dry from the shower. Even better, suppose one chanced to be walking by as we were making love on the big bed. The thought dampened my pussy almost before I had fully articulated it to myself.

Jed lay there, and I began to play at stirring his desires by swaying my hips against the towel. His cock responded, growing even without my touch. Jed was savoring the electric distance between our bodies, prolonging it till contact would become uncontrollable. I continued my dance, for him and for my fantasy fisherman. Letting the towel slip down to cradle my ass, I bent my knees and wiggled back and forth. Jed threw back the sheet and sat up, his cock rigidly erect, his eyes glazed in a trance, fixed on my ass.

I teased him deliberately, feeling his desire and mine rise and fill the room, his cock seeming to nudge my swollen clit. I felt myself grow wet thinking of it penetrating me. I fondled my breasts, teasing my nipples erect, and turned to face him. He watched me play with my breasts, calculating the roughness with which I began to slap their curves and pinch the nipples. I wanted him to seize his cock with equal roughness, but he held back. I could feel his desire grow, and its red flush made me long to take his cock in my mouth. I turned away again and began to flaunt my ass, rubbing its cheeks, spreading them and letting go, looking over my shoulder to see his reaction telegraphed by his bobbing cock. I had set myself up with my bottom for his target.

He rose and my heart began to pound. I was no longer in control of events. I would have to submit to his desires. When his hands grabbed my ass, something seemed to tear loose in both of us. He whispered his many-layered craving to fuck, to lick, to handle all of my flesh at once.

I pushed up against him, trying to rub his erection hard. I pulled back, wanting to make it go on, but I needed to feel his hardness sliding over and between my asscheeks. He grabbed me around the waist and pulled me toward him as he fell back onto the bed. I fell to my knees, wanting his cock in my mouth, but he wrestled me up onto his lap and turned me over one thigh, his other leg holding mine down. One arm held me fast, my ass exposed. His cock pulsed against my belly.

His hand swatted hard against my butt and his cock

leaped up even harder. His slaps came hard and fast, with short pauses to feel the heat of my stinging flesh that aroused us both as if I were stroking his cock. Spanking was his own selfish foreplay, exciting, but not to the point of making him come involuntarily. As he spanked me, he reminded me that he wanted my ass bare whenever I was with him. One last swat and he told me to get up.

I grabbed my ass, trying to soothe the sting with some rubbing. Nevertheless I wiggled my red bottom at him, daring him to fuck me, bending over to display my cunt as I fingered my clit and shoved my fingers into my vagina. He looked as if his swollen cock was on the verge of bursting at the very thought of a touch.

I stopped masturbating and reached for the lubricant. Handing it to him, I again turned my bottom toward his face and moved over to the bed, stacking pillows over which I proceeded to drape my body, ass in the air. He climbed up behind where I was kneeling, loaded his palm with lubricant, and grabbed his cock to make it slippery, voicing his longing to slide it first into my cunt and then into the incredible tightness of my ass. He placed his hands on my burning asscheeks and pushed his cock into my cunt, which was offered up under him. He tried to enter me slowly, but the huge size of his erection startled me nonetheless.

He thrust in, filling me up, sliding in and out with a sure, heavy stroke that took my breath away. The heat of my ass warmed his abdomen as he pushed against me, fucking. His heavy testicles squashed against my slippery cunt as he bore down on me, pushing more and more weight to grind my belly against the heap of pillows. My genital mound rubbed against them, building up the pressure of orgasm. He thrust from the rear and I pressed into the pillows. Soon he had pinned me, pushing me forward with each stroke.

Jed bit along the line of my shoulder as he pumped. The touch of his lips on my back made heat rush through me to my breasts, which were rubbing the sheet at the same time his belly was grinding down on my sore ass and his cock was filling me. The combination broke in me with a shuddering wave, and Jed used all his control not to come when I cried out. He wanted to come in my well-spanked ass.

He pulled out of me, but neither of us was finished yet. I raised myself, scolding him for leaving me, saying I'd punish him for it. He slapped me hard to remind me he was not through with my ass and bent me back over the pillows. Then he grabbed the lubricant again and loaded his palm. He rubbed his cock, then reached for the cheeks of my bottom. As he stroked their hot surface his cock grew harder again, and he rubbed it over the handprints he had raised, promising to soothe them with lotion later. Then he reached his finger down between my asscheeks and pressed into the tiny hole, smearing lubricant and easing me open. I groaned as he slid one, two, three fingers into me, pumping them gently in and out as his cock bobbed for a chance of its own.

He moved closer, lubed his cock again, and began slowly to ease it into my ass. His shaft was hugely swollen, and he had to press hard as my tight hole began to give way, taking in his enormous girth. He began to pump in and out, increasing his pace as I moaned loudly that his cock was a little too big for me to take, and secretly prayed he keep on ramming it into me. He looked down at me, intoxicated by his view of my ass being penetrated by his cock.

Jed swatted me once again as he fucked my ass still harder, telling me what an uninhibited exhibitionist I was, showing off for all the locals. Pulling my hair, he raised my head and told me to look out the glass doors and see something that would make me come all over again. I looked down the beach that, to my astonishment, was no longer deserted. A fair distance from our cottage, a man stood down by the shoreline, watching us with a pair of binoculars! I felt completely exposed but I couldn't take my eyes off the observer.

Jed didn't mind at all, remarking that he liked our being too exciting to pass by. He was far past the point of controlling himself as he continued to drive his hard spike into me. He told me I was going to get everything I had been looking for. Suddenly his cock exploded in my ass, flooding its tightness as he pushed down hard, pressing me into the pillows. The bed rocked like the expanse of ocean before my eyes as I washed over him in waves and he sank into me.

We lay for what seemed like hours in the warm light of morning. When we looked for our secret observer, he was gone but Jed was sure he would likely see us again.

—*V.F., Parkersburg, West Virginia*

A NORTHERN COUPLE'S SPECTACULAR LUST IS EMBLAZONED ON A SOFT SOUTHERN NIGHT

My lovely wife, Darlene, was in charge of coordinating an upcoming conference in Memphis, and a year's worth of hard work and detail was finally coming together. We decided that I would go with her to offer support, escort her to social functions, and generally make a week of it.

Darlene is a beautiful woman. She's tiny, but with a body to die for and a voracious and varied sexual appetite. Her full breasts are topped with large pink sensitive nipples, and her ass is a work of art: creamy, soft, and round. However, it is her sweet pussy that is my pride and joy. She has puffy pink outer lips surrounding very large and protruding inner lips that she loves to have sucked and even bitten. Darlene keeps herself clean-shaven and has a sensitive pink clit as big as a button.

Since we've been together, I've introduced Darlene to virtually every sexual variation, and she has embraced each and every one wholeheartedly. I have a strong lingerie fetish, and I've taken her from Hanes Her Way to thong panties, and she now wears only garter belts, hose and heels, with half-cup bras that showcase her lovely breasts. Who would guess that underneath her conservative business attire is a true sexual dynamo, dressed to kill? The clerks at Victoria's Secret and even Frederick's know us by name, and Darlene's lingerie collection ranges from soft and sensual to erotic and trashy.

Darlene and I are both very oral, and she truly enjoys sucking my cock and taking mouthfuls of my creamy come. In turn, I can lick and suck her sweet pussy for hours, nibbling and biting her big lips. As a bonus, she is multi-orgasmic and can come over and over again. We regularly read *Penthouse* Variations together, and she will masturbate for me at the drop of a hat, which I find terribly exciting. She loves to play "dress up" and pose for the camera in her lingerie, and we have a sizable collection of adult videos in all genres. Our stock of sex toys is second to none.

As icing on the cake, I introduced Darlene to anal sex, and she has become a true fanatic. She absolutely adores having her lovely ass filled to the hilt with a dildo, a vibrator, or my hard cock—the bigger the better to fuck her hard and fast, the way she likes it. Then, after a day at the office, sitting and squirming on the aftereffects, she'll come home with a raging fire inside that I am only too happy to extinguish for the moment.

When the big conference arrived, Darlene was running to and fro all week. Everything was incredibly hectic, but her colleagues gave her a round of applause for her efforts at the closing banquet. We hadn't had as much time together as we'd hoped, so we decided to spend one more night in our sumptuous suite, after enjoying dinner and some of the town's incomparable music.

When we got back to the hotel, Darlene told me to lie down while she went into the bathroom to change out of her dinner dress. I must have dozed off, because the next thing I knew I was being awakened by my beautiful wife dressed in the skimpiest French maid outfit imaginable. In the tiny, sheer skirt that didn't begin to cover her lovely ass or bare pussy and a sheer top that plunged to her navel, she was stunning! To all this she had added a lacy black garter belt, black stockings, and her four-inch "fuck me" pumps that I love so well.

It was obvious she wanted to make our last night in Memphis memorable. As I took her in my arms, my cock sprang to attention and pressed against her soft belly. My hands cupped her perfect, naked asscheeks as we shared a long, deep kiss and our tongues dueled. As my hand crept around to cover her bare pussy, I commented on how incredibly wet she was, and she told me she'd been masturbating in the bathroom while I napped. I immediately grabbed the camera, posed her in numerous erotic positions, then scooped her up and carried her to the king-size bed. It was then that I noticed her favorite vibrator, a dildo, and flavored lotion on the nightstand.

As I professed my love for her, I hurriedly stripped off my clothes. By then she had pulled her top apart and was busy pinching and pulling one nipple while her other hand was sliding two fingers in and out of her slick pussy. Since I love watching her, I stood back, stroking my hard cock as I took several more photos before joining her on the bed.

Smothering her with kisses, I moved down to her breasts. Her big nipples were as hard as marbles as I sucked first one and then the other. She loves to have her nipples sucked hard, then bitten gently, so I always spend a great deal of time on them, pinching and pulling till they're bright red. Finally I moved lower to feast on her amazing pussy. As I licked up and down slowly, all around but never touching her clit, her intoxicating scent enveloped me. I began to suck and chew gently on her pussy lips as she moaned with pleasure. I moved lower and thrust my tongue deep into her wet cunt, and with a steady rhythm began fucking her with my tongue as she cupped her breasts and played with her nipples.

Darlene was on the verge now, and it was time to make her come. Reaching for the vibrator, I dipped it into her pussy for a moment before sliding it deep into her beautiful ass. She squealed in delight and was panting furiously as I zeroed in on her clit, marveling at her taste. As she was about to come, she demanded that I bite her clit, and as I did she came as only my sweet Darlene can come.

As she came down from her orgasm, Darlene wanted to be fucked, and I was certainly ready. I removed the vibrator and ordered her onto her hands and knees, our favorite position. She is such an erotic sight with her lovely ass in the air, framed by the garter belt and hose! I slid my cock the length of her wet slit several times before easing it into her velvet pussy. After a few slow, easy strokes, I picked up the pace. Because she likes it hard, I was soon slamming it into her, my balls slapping against her clit. As she pulled at her clit, it was obvious she was about to come again, which she did as soon as I reached around to pinch her nipples.

Still on her knees, she looked around and begged me to do her ass. She only had to ask once before I was lubricating my cock and pushing its head against her tight rosebud. She eased back until it popped inside, and I was suddenly buried to the hilt in her hot ass. What an incredible feeling! I knew I wasn't going to last very long, so as soon as she adjusted to my size I began to fuck her.

Darlene's hand flew to her clit and she started masturbating as my thrusts gained speed. Soon she was moaning, begging me to fuck her harder, and my balls were about to explode with come. We erupted together, and with great agility she pulled off me, flipped over, and caught my come on her breasts, which she had pushed together. I unleashed torrents of come on her pretty red nipples before collapsing beside her.

After a breather and a long, playful shower, we went out onto the balcony for a repeat performance in the soft Memphis night. If other hotel guests were watching, they got a fabulous exhibition of my naked wife first sucking my cock and then getting fucked while bending over the patio table. It was definitely a night to remember, and one that will endear Memphis to us in memory for a long time to come.

—*M.C., Philadelphia, Pennsylvania*

LOVE, ITALIAN STYLE—MUSCULAR FARMHAND INSPIRES RAW LUST IN BEAUTIFUL AMERICAN

Since I had been in Milan to cover the fashion shows, I decided to take a holiday in Tuscany, renting a farmhouse from a friend of one of the models I had gotten to know over the years. Erika is a typical Teutonic beauty, and every time we were together we ended up sharing champagne, succulent fruit, and the secrets of each other's body. It was she who teasingly suggested that I try an Italian lover, since she had a marked taste for Latin men. Since my juices were still fragrant on her lips, I laughed, but she cupped my sex with her long fingers and said, "You know what they call this in Italian? *La fica*—the fig. And Italians love to eat figs."

We rose from her tangled satin sheets and moved to the bathroom, a luxurious room with its centerpiece a warm, bubbling spa. Erika drew me into the water with her and tipped up my face for a kiss. Her hands caressed me lazily, squeezing, rubbing while her tongue played with mine. Slim fingers toyed with the soft, wet flesh between my legs, marveling at how I always seemed to be juicy and ripe as the fruit she loved.

"You see why they call it *la fica*," she said, grasping my labia between her fingers and showing me how their fleshy pout resembled the classical fruit. We sank down into the crystal water and it streamed and bubbled around us as Erika languidly offered me her full, creamy breasts.

I was happy to take them in both hands and suck the pale nipples that stiffened at my touch. I could feel my vaginal walls tighten around her finger as it searched my depths.

The hot, steaming water mingled with the heat of my own juices as she slid her finger in and out, stroking my clitoris as she passed. Her lips and tongue worked softly and surely at my nipples, and I grew weak, almost sinking below the bubbling water. Erika's deceptively slender arms enfolded me and raised me up to lie back over the edge of the sunken spa. Her fingers parted my labia and she proceeded to demonstrate once more that the Germans were also fond of the fig. Wrapped up in the miracle of each other's body, we talked hardly at all until I had to leave the next morning.

Agreeably heavy with sated lust, I emerged from the train into the hustle of Florence and hailed a cab to the bus station. I followed my instructions, and after a scenic ride, I alighted at my host's door. The old stone house stood flush with the street, with the winery buildings farther back, overlooked by cypress trees. A handsome man with silvered temples came toward me, bowed, and kissed my hand. It was Francesco, my host, who arranged for his servant, Carlo, to take me to my house farther down the valley.

When we arrived the place was bigger than I'd imagined, cool with its tiled roof and floors. Carlo took me up to the second floor and waited for me to choose my bedroom. The largest and sunniest was perfect, and he carried in my bags. We stood by the bed, electricity running between us. The raw power of his biceps inspired a primitive lust in me. He was staring back at me intently, his eyes running possessively over my body. I wanted him intensely, but I lowered my eyes and said *grazie,* thinking he would leave. Instead, he just stood there, smiling at me.

I held out my hand to shake his dismissively, but he simply grasped it and didn't let go. I was caught in an elemental spell. He spoke, his soft accent apparently pouring forth compliments, but the only words I caught were, *"Ti voglio mangiare la fica."* Remembrance of Erika's lips and lust weakened my knees and I sank to the edge of the bed. Abruptly the tension shattered as the maid bustled in with clean towels and so forth, but I knew he would return.

After supper I was alone and Carlo came in to light a fire in the great hearth. I was mesmerized by his capable hands and the strong line of his back as it joined his slender hips. As he rose and looked at me I shivered, and he asked shrewdly if I was cold. I stammered, *"Sì,"* I was. I longed to be back in Milan in Erika's hot tub, or to fall into Carlo's arms. I couldn't move. He set a match to the kindling and the fire blazed up.

He chuckled and came over to me, folding me into an embrace that warmed me more than the fire. He sat, pulling me down on his lap, kissing my eyes, my cheeks, my lips before reaching under my sweater and caressing my breasts. I could hardly breathe, feeling my cunt lips unfurl like petals, triggered by the arousal of my nipples and Carlo's slow, sweet touch. He lifted my skirt and ran his hand along the inside of my thigh as I shivered with desire.

His fingers touched my clitoris, wet and swollen. Not the fire but Carlo had lighted an inferno in my sex. He alternately pinched and stroked my labia, opening the way to my clit, peeling me as he whispered, *"La fica."* His fingers penetrated my vagina and my anus at the same time, and in a few seconds a delicious warmth, like well-aged brandy, spread from my loins and my body shook with orgasm.

Carlo lifted me up and lay me back on the long table. My orgasm still echoed through me as he pulled out his cock—long, thick, fully erect—and guided it into my aching pussy. The hard wood of the table was forgotten in an instant. It was dark when he carried me back up to the bedroom. We stood at the window, looking out over the vineyards, fireflies flickering below us.

We kissed lingeringly before he positioned me on my knees at the edge of the bed, my legs far apart, my pussy as wide open as possible, my face buried in the coverlet. He knelt behind me, licking my *fica*, driving his tongue into every fold of my cunt. As I began to come, he stood and drove his cock deep inside me again, pumping me for as long as my orgasm continued before letting go with a potent gush that filled my channel. He withdrew, basting my ass with thick strands of semen.

We threw ourselves across the bed and I fell asleep with his strong dark arm heavy across my chest. When we awoke he asked if I was warm enough. Teasingly, I tried my first bit of humor in Italian, saying that one can always be warmer and asking if he would like a breakfast of warm figs. He kissed me, his black stubble coarse against my face and breasts, his lips soft and gentle.

Carlo was a masterful lover, relentless but disarming in his gentle approach. He drew my thighs apart and slid them around his shoulders, delicately opening my nether lips with his callused thumbs. His tongue traced the map of my folds, my wetness springing up as he explored me. Equally slowly he teased at the head of my clit, coaxing it out of its folds just as I, sometime in that heated night, had coaxed his glans from the sheath of his foreskin, a small delight I had never had before.

Flames blazed up inside me again as his tongue touched my core and pursued that ravaged and tender pearl as it tried to shrink away from too much pleasure. I stood no chance; he had no mercy. Not merely warm but incandescent beneath his questing tongue, I lost all sense of anything except the glowing coal of my sex. Its red heat grew and spread through my belly, melting me until I turned to liquid fire and an orgasm rolled through me so forcefully that I was unaware that his face was now above me and his cock was searing a new pathway to my depths.

Each crest seemed the ultimate; each peak revealed another, higher one beyond. Consciousness fled, whether for a second or longer I never knew. Dimly I was aware of his body arching over mine and the torrent of his come washing through my cunt. Then his head nestled into my shoulder and his rough voice whispered, "*Sì, signorina, e bella ti mangiare la fica.*" Beautiful indeed, I thought, falling asleep once more in the arms of my Italian lover.

—*L.A., San Francisco, California*

DIARY OF A MODERN-DAY "HAREM GIRL"
IN ANCIENT CAIRO

We spent the first couple days in Cairo satisfying Oliver's desires to see the sights, including the Great Pyramid, the Sphinx, and the Mosque of Ibn Tulun. Always on the go, we usually grabbed quick meals and fresh fruit juices at the city's many sandwich bars, then headed to the next sight. We would arrive home exhausted late in the evening and fall into bed, shielded with netting from the ubiquitous mosquitoes that plague Cairo. Aroused by the sights and smells of that ancient city, we would make slow, passionate love until we climaxed and fell into a deep sleep, the sheets twisted under our sweaty bodies as the ceiling fan circled lazily above us.

On our third day in Cairo I finally convinced Oliver to skip the pyramids and accompany me to the Khan al-Khalili souk, a large bazaar built in the fourteenth century. Meandering through the narrow alleyways of the marketplace, we stopped at the tiny stalls to price carpets, leather work, and perfume. By the end of the day I was an expert, if exhausted, haggler, and was looking forward to sitting down to a meal at the famous El-Fishawi Café, which was once a meeting place for local artists.

There we enjoyed a meal of kufta, a meatball-like dish made of ground lamb, served with *aysh,* the Egyptian version of pita bread. We finished with a rice pudding called *mahallabiyya* and steaming mugs of *ahwa,* the thick, strong Turkish coffee that is served with every meal. Eating at an outdoor table, we watched the crowds of the market rush by, both of us caught up in the life of the Egyptian city streets.

Paying our bill, Oliver and I noticed that the market had begun to close, its merchants packing up their wares to head home after a long day. As we wound our way back through the alleyways, heady with heat, excitement, and the local Stella lager we had drunk with dinner, I grabbed Oliver's hand and pulled him into one of the abandoned stalls. The heavy carpets falling shut behind us, I pulled him to me in a tight embrace and kissed him with a fervor that surprised us both. The flavor of the exotic Egyptian spices lingering on Oliver's lips only served to excite me even further, and before I knew it I was groping for his belt buckle.

Deftly unfastening his pants, I let them drop to the ground as Oliver's searching hands found the buttons of my blouse. Leaning forward to lap at the nape of my neck, he inhaled deeply, drawing in the spicy scent of the Egyptian perfume I had sampled at the bazaar that afternoon. "Your scent is intoxicating," he whispered, nibbling on my earlobe. "Here in this dark stall, you could be a harem girl and I, your sultan."

Kneeling before him, I kissed Oliver's feet through the leather of his sandals and in a sultry whisper responded, "Your wish is my command, Master. How may I serve you?" Not waiting for an answer, I reached up and pulled down his boxers, then helped him as he stepped out of them. By then my eyes had adjusted to the darkness of the tent, and I could see Oliver's cock standing beautifully erect in the dim light, a drop of pre-come glistening on the tip. Resting my knees on our discarded clothes, I grasped my husband's hips and covered the head of his cock with my lips, running my tongue around its circumference. Almost imperceptibly Oliver began to thrust forward, his usual indication that he was ready for more.

Since he was my master, at least for that night, I fulfilled his wishes and quickly covered his entire cock with my mouth, swallowing him until I could feel the prodding at the back of my throat. As I sucked hungrily at his throbbing member, Oliver entwined his fingers in my hair, holding on to my head and guiding the pace of my actions. As he pumped his penis in and out of my busy mouth, I could feel the veins of his shaft running over my tongue.

A slight pulsing in his cock told me that Oliver was about to come. I tickled his balls with my fingernails, knowing that would definitely send him over the edge. In mere seconds he was grunting out my name, tightening his hands in my hair as he shot a stream of hot semen down my throat.

Pulling me back up, Oliver drew me to his chest, kissing me hard as his tongue searched for mine. He had always been ardent in his lovemaking, but the day's activities and the strangeness of our surroundings had brought him to a whole new level of passion. He seemed to be swallowing me whole as his searching hands roamed over my body. It was as though he were discovering a new delight rather than the familiar figure of his wife of twelve years.

Oliver hiked my skirt up around my waist, then pulled down my panties. I kicked them off, adding them to our pile of clothes as he felt along the perimeter of the stall, stopping when he found a rolled-up carpet that had been left behind by the shop's owner. Spreading it on the dusty floor, he pulled me down beside him, then created a pillow out of our clothing.

Soon we were kissing again, our hands exploring one another's body. When Oliver's fingers made their way between the lips of my pussy, I gasped, surprised because it usually takes much longer for me to get that turned on. His fingers ran lightly over my clit and I arched my hips, guiding him to my waiting cunt. He inserted first one, then two fingers, and began to thrust, fucking me slowly.

Keeping his fingers firmly inside me, Oliver scooted back on his knees as he kissed and licked his way down my belly. He tenderly pressed his lips to my quivering mound, sending shivers up and down my spine. As he sucked my tender flesh between his lips, he continued fucking me with his fingers, causing my moans to grow even louder. I was glad that there was enough bustle outside that no one would hear my utterances, because at that moment Oliver took my clit between his teeth and nibbled gently and teasingly. He then resumed his lapping, periodically flicking my hard nub with the tip of his tongue.

I grabbed his hair as my body began to quake uncontrollably, my climax almost at the breaking point. Then, with his free hand, Oliver reached up and began fondling one of my nipples, rolling it between his fingertips and pinching it lightly. The added attention to my breast sent my arousal into overdrive and I immediately exploded, my body bucking against Oliver's face as I came.

As the spasms of my climax subsided, Oliver shimmied back up, covering my body with his weight.

Cradling my face in his hands he kissed me deeply, and I could taste the tang of my honey on his lips and tongue. A slight pressure at my groin told me that he was hard again, so I opened my legs wide, wrapping them around my husband's waist. Wet with my juices, Oliver positioned his cockhead at my opening and I tightened my legs around him and pulled him toward me. As he slid in slowly, we both savored the feeling of his cockhead skimming along my canal, a sensation that has always given us both great pleasure. When he was fully embedded in my pussy, Oliver pulled most of the way back out, then thrust back in, this time more quickly.

Oliver began to fuck me in earnest now, his thrusting cock filling me again and again. Repositioning my legs so that they rested on his shoulders, he drove into me with great force, his balls slapping against the backs of my thighs. Knowing from experience that this signaled his oncoming orgasm, I reached between my legs to finger my clit so that we could come at the same time.

Drops of sweat from his face spattered on my breasts as our temperatures rose even higher in the hot Egyptian night. Feeling my orgasm start to wash over my body, I moved my hand away from my clitoris and grasped Oliver's balls. My husband's body tensed. Drawing in a short breath, he muffled a cry as with a few more strokes he emptied his load into my pussy. I quivered below him, overcome by my own powerful orgasm.

Our energy returned a little while later and we quickly put our clothes back on and sneaked out of the stall, hoping no one would see us. We grabbed a taxi and returned to the hotel. When we got to our room, Oliver lay on the bed while I bathed him with a cool, wet washcloth, still in my harem girl mode. Sighing contentedly, Oliver murmured, "Mmm, I like this. You can be my slave all the time." As I ran the washcloth over his flaccid member, watching it once again begin to rise, I laughed.

"I may be your slave this time," I said, "but for our next vacation we're going to the Amazon, and you're going to have to answer to me!"

—*L.E., Portland, Maine* ⊙┳■

NAKED IN THE JUNGLE—
BOLD TRAVELERS HEED CALL OF THE WILD

You might remember me from a letter my wife wrote a while back, about a vacation we took to Cairo. Well, we had so much fun on that trip, especially finding all sorts of exotic locations in which to fuck each other silly, that we were well and truly bitten by the traveling bug. Lucky for us, it wasn't long before we embarked on another sexual adventure. As you may also recall, Lauren had threatened to release her wild Amazonian side on our next trip, payback for playing my subservient harem girl in Cairo. Well, that was fine by me, so I did some research and planned a week's stay deep in the Brazilian rain forest.

After the long flight, we took a three-hour boat ride from Manaus, a small city on the Negro River, to our hotel. We stood on the top level of the double-decker boat, so we had a great view of the scenery along the Negro, which flows right into the mighty Amazon. The river was beautiful, but what really amazed me was our hotel. It was built on stilts high in the treetops, so it felt as though we were living right in the trees. Comprised of a number of buildings joined by long, meandering catwalks, it even has two swimming pools and a heliport up there! That first night we joined all the other guests of the hotel for a delicious buffet dinner in the dining room, then followed a catwalk to a ninety-foot-high observation tower to meet some of our jungle friends. The hotel provides local fruits to entice monkeys and parrots from the trees to come and eat out of your hand, which, as Lauren and I soon learned, is not at all difficult to do.

Afterward we retired to our room, which was built of native wood and was, in effect, our very own tree house. I was standing by the window, feeling the warm, damp air on my face, when Lauren came up behind me and wrapped her arms around my waist. "Hey, Tarzan," she whispered, "wanna come swing on my vine?" Spinning around, I swept my five-foot-eight, 130-pound wife off her feet and threw her over my shoulder in a fireman's carry. She giggled and squirmed as I brought her over to the bed and threw her down on the mattress, then proceeded to rip off my clothes.

"Me Tarzan," I grunted as Lauren's clothes joined mine in a pile on the floor. "You naked!" I jumped into bed on top of her, almost crushing her with my weight. Stimulated by the call of the wild, we kissed, our tongues dancing as they met. My cock throbbed insistently, begging for release as it pressed against Lauren's upper thigh. I broke our kiss only to lick and nuzzle my way down her body, inhaling the musk that arose from the nape of her neck and the crevice between her breasts.

Lauren sighed and arched her back as I took an erect nipple between my lips, biting it lightly. "Harder," she moaned, so I gave it a little nip, loving the sound she made as she sucked air between her teeth. I switched to her other breast and repeated the process, then kissed my way down over her stomach. She giggled when I swabbed her navel with my tongue, then gasped in expectation when my lips reached her mound.

When I continued my way down, traveling past her pussy to her thighs, Lauren did something that surprised me. She reached down and grabbed my hair, pulling my head back to her sex. "I want you to eat me, slave," she commanded. "Now!" I thought this was out of character for Tarzan's woman until I remembered Lauren's desire to be an Amazonian queen. Smiling at her change of roles, I did as I was told.

I slid my tongue between her puffy outer lips and searched among the slippery inner folds for her clit. And it wasn't difficult to find, as her hood was peeled back, her hardened nub yearning to be touched. I gave it a few broad strokes with the flat of my tongue, feeling her body tense every time I brushed over her sensitive center. Then, sucking her clit between my teeth, I flicked at it with the tip of my tongue as I inserted a finger into her cunt.

Lauren cried out, the twin assaults on her pussy sending her immediately over the edge. Her body bucked as she clamped her thighs against the sides of my head, pinning me to the bed like a true Amazon woman. I continued my ministrations on her clit as she began to wheeze above me, and only when she was satisfied did she let go of my head and pull me up on top of her.

"Fuck me, slave!" she cried, guiding my cock to her wet and ready hole. "Fill me with your big, hard dick." Not one to disobey, I rammed into her, shoving my cock into her dripping cunt again and again. I was more than eager to come, aroused to heights even higher than the mightiest tree in the rain forest, but Lauren had a few other ideas for me, and she was, after all, my queen.

After grasping the base of my cock firmly, she somehow managed to flip us over without dislodging me from her pussy. Now she was on top, riding me like a cowgirl as she bounced up and down over my shaft. I didn't have to do anything but lie still and let her take control. At one point I even popped out of Lauren and she immediately grabbed my cock and shoved me back in. I had never seen her so red-hot, and my temperature soared as well in the Amazonian night air, a small electric fan doing little to cool us down.

My balls tightened and threatened to burst, so I warned Lauren that I was going to come soon. "You'd better not do it without me!" she warned, so I bit down on my lower lip and tried my hardest to hold back the impending explosion. I reached out and placed my hand on her mound, thumb down, and drew circles over her clitoris, knowing it would send her over the top. Her breathing quickened and grew louder until finally she came so hard she could no longer lift her body up and down over my prick. That was all right, though, because her pussy muscles tightened and released around my shaft, pumping me like a fist, and I let go as well, shooting my cream deep into her cunt. She collapsed on top of me and we embraced tightly, both of us covered with sweat, until she gingerly lifted herself off my spent prick. We fell asleep shortly, exhausted from our long day.

The next morning the alarm went off at dawn, waking us for an early breakfast and a day of jungle trekking, piranha fishing, and alligator spotting. I noticed that Lauren wasn't in bed and found her standing by the window. When I started to speak, she shushed me impatiently. Listening carefully, I heard the light rain that was falling on the leaves outside. When Lauren turned to beckon me over, her face was covered with a light sheen of moisture.

Taking my place behind her, I looked down to see what had my wife so entranced. It was a couple of large pink dolphins gamboling in the Amazonian waters below.

I stroked Lauren's breasts, squeezing them in my palms, and she pressed against me, her ass grinding against my cock. She bent against the windowsill and then opened her legs even wider.

Positioning my cockhead at her wet pussy, I gave one hard thrust and was buried to the root. I then slowly pulled out and pushed back into her tightness. Lauren pressed back to meet me, and our movements became short and quick, both of us racing toward orgasm as the rain drenched our heads and shoulders. I reached around to finger her clit, and she cried out after just a few strokes. The sensations drove Lauren wild and she writhed about on my cock. I pumped harder, my balls slapping against her firm ass, and soon I was ready to come. Holding Lauren tight against my body, I shot volleys of semen into her pussy. Just then the rain ebbed to a drizzle and we realized we were famished.

We took a quick shower, then made our way down to the dining room, where we helped ourselves to a huge breakfast from the buffet. The tables were filled with other guests from the hotel, and we sat down with a couple who looked to be about our age. When they asked us if we were ready for a day of jungle adventure, Lauren and I just looked at each other and smiled, thinking about the jungle adventure we'd already had.

—*O.E., Portland, Maine*

SUMMER VACATION BRINGS OUT THE
EXHIBITIONISTIC SIDE OF A PLAYFUL COUPLE

I look forward to the last weekend in August all summer, because that's when my wife, Angela, and I have our annual getaway. For the past five years, we've rented the same cottage, right on the beach. From the front deck, you can see the ocean, but it's the view from the backyard that's really amazing.

It was only two days into our first summer there that I first saw our next-door neighbor, Rikki, a petite, sexy brunette with an amazing ass. Rikki planned all the big beach parties in town, but it was the private shindigs she threw that made me reserve the same cottage every year. My wife is hot, but Rikki is something else, and my cock gets hard just looking at her.

From the beginning, it was clear that Rikki was sexually adventuresome. More than once, I saw her seducing a college boy, not caring who might be watching as she let him fuck her in her backyard or sucked his cock. It was clear just from the skimpy clothes she wore and the sassy way she walked that she was up for anything.

One day, while I was looking out the window, I saw her cavorting with a tanned, muscular guy. He was clearly enthralled by her, judging from the grin on his face and the massive erection jutting out of his swim trunks. She peeled them down and took his entire length down her throat in one gulp, getting his cock slick with her saliva. Then she wriggled out of her own bathing suit, pushed him onto the grass, and straddled him, plunging his dick inside her and thrusting her hips back and forth.

As he played with her tits and moaned, I slid my hand into my briefs and pulled out my own already-hard dick. I stood there, watching her bounce up and down on his shaft while I stroked my cock. I rolled my thumb around the head and imagined what it would feel like to have Rikki's cunt wrapped around me. As I pictured her writhing above me, her breasts bouncing, I came in a fast, intense climax. I quickly composed myself and joined Angie downstairs. I couldn't stop thinking about what I saw, and as it turns out, I didn't have to wait long for a repeat performance.

That next night, Rikki was in her outdoor hot tub. This time, she was sucking on the nipples of a gorgeous blonde woman. I retreated upstairs and relished the performance as Rikki led the blonde out of the hot tub and over to a chaise longue. When she laid the curvy babe out on the chair and began licking her pussy with long, slow strokes, it was more than I could stand. My cock exploded and my hot come dribbled onto my hand. I kept watching, in a state of continued arousal, as Rikki fingerfucked the blonde in time with the music blasting from her stereo.

After watching their sexy show for a few more minutes, I headed downstairs and found Angie in the bathtub. She was surprised to see me, but when she saw my raging erection, she didn't protest. I joined her in the bath, getting on top of her in the small space. I rubbed my dick against her pussy until she moaned and clutched my back. Then I lifted her out of the water, laid her wet body across the plush bath mat, and fucked her deep and hard. As I slid my cock into her tight cunt, she thrust back against me, clearly as horny as I was. She wrapped her legs around my back and crossed her ankles, making her pussy tightly grab my cock. I didn't last long after that, shooting my load into her while she climaxed beneath me.

"What brought that on?" she inquired once we'd both recovered.

"Come here, I'll show you." I grabbed her hand and brought her upstairs. She gasped when we reached the window, looking from Rikki to the other woman, who was now eating Rikki with absolute abandon, her blonde head practically buried in her cunt.

"You've been up here watching her?" she asked.

I nodded. "Angie, you know I'm totally hot for you, but one day I was up here and saw her with this hunk and my cock just got hard and—"

She cut me off. "No, baby. I asked because, well, I've watched her, too." Her cheeks were flaming red at this confession.

"You have?" I smiled at her, then stood behind her, and together we watched Rikki have an explosive orgasm. I'd never imagined that I'd be able to watch my sexy neighbor while also touching and kissing my gorgeous wife—this was truly the best of both worlds and the start of many voyeuristic afternoons for the two of us.

This year, I saw Rikki almost as soon as we pulled into the driveway. Our hot neighbor greeted us fondly and invited us to a party she was having that very night. After unpacking all day, we were ready for a party. We dressed in skimpy attire: a light white shirt and khaki shorts for me, and a bikini top and gauzy sarong skirt for Angie.

When we got to Rikki's place, neither of us were surprised that her party had already turned into an orgy. Couples were making out, groping and having full-on sex all over her living room and backyard. Rikki greeted us wearing only a tiny pair of panties, her breasts jiggling. "Welcome!" she exclaimed, throwing her arms around us and leading us inside. "As you can see, things have already gotten off to a wild start. Join the fun!" Then she scampered off to meet some other guests. We each got a drink and then settled onto a love seat in a corner, taking in all the action. Angie was sitting on my lap, and from the way she kept squirming, I knew she was getting turned on by the sight of so many naked, horny people.

I reached between her legs and fondled her through the thin fabric of her skirt, then whispered in her ear, "I want to fuck you right here and have everyone watch us the way we've been watching Rikki. Maybe she'll watch us this time." As I spoke, I slid my fingers under her waistband and along her slippery entrance. I felt her pussy twitching, throbbing with the need to be penetrated, so I pushed my fingers inside her. The minute I felt how hot and tight she was, I got even harder and pulled her closer, so her cunt was pressing directly down on my cock. As she wiggled against me, my body responded in a major way. I couldn't wait any longer, but I wanted to get closer to the action—and to Rikki.

I lifted my wife into my arms and carried her around until I found an empty space in the living room near our hostess. She quickly got up from where she'd been perched and moved closer to us. I kissed my way down

Angie's body, from her lips, over her sensitive nipples, before I reached the main course—her pussy. I dipped my head between her legs and shoved my tongue into her cunt, tasting her savory juices. Then I pulled back a little to savor her sensitive slit, teasing her by toying with her labia. I briefly glanced up and saw Rikki intently watching us, riveted on my wife's beautiful body as her fingers flew beneath her panties, her hand moving back and forth. Her nipples were tightly beaded, and watching Rikki touch herself in response to our display made my cock even harder. I once again renewed my efforts, twisting my head back and forth as my tongue lapped at Angie's clit, pulling the small, hard nub into my mouth. By then, my cock was raging with the need to be inside her sweet cunt, and I lifted my head up. I looked at Rikki, who brought her face down to mine, kissing me and tasting the delicious flavor of Angie's sweet pussy on my lips.

Then, without saying a word, I took off my shorts, revealing my bare cock in all its hardness. I saw Angie shiver at the sight of my erection, and keeping my eyes pinned to hers, I entered her, pushing into her deeply to let her know how much licking her had turned me on. She was so close to coming already. All I had to do was push her breasts together and nuzzle her nipples, slapping my tongue against them in a frenzy before nipping at them with my teeth. That set off her orgasm, and she trembled beneath me. I put my arms around her, hugging her close to me. I continued to fuck her as the vibrations spread through her body. Even when she was done, her hot pussy still clenched me securely.

"Angie, I'm gonna come!" I shouted, and I tried to

pull out, but my sexy wife held my cock like a vise as I shot my hot load into her cunt.

"Me, too!" called out Rikki, and I looked up to see her, now totally nude, flicking her clit with one hand while plunging her fingers inside her cunt with the other. Then her whole body tensed and relaxed, and I watched her pull her soaked fingers out of her pussy. When she offered them to me, I licked them clean. We'd had a fair trade, watching her and getting off, then having her watch us and get off. That adventure was only the beginning of many glorious summer escapades with the wonderfully insatiable Rikki.

—*H.M., Scottsdale, Arizona*

GOLFER AND HIS WIFE FIND THAT
COSTA RICA SUITS THEM TO A TEE

It was fairly late at night by the time I arrived in Tortuguero on a boat. I was exhausted from the long flight and too tired to care about scenery, so once onshore I rushed my wife to our room and immediately hit the bed.

The following day was sure to be a long one. I had flown all the way to Costa Rica for a special golf tournament at the premier golf course, Melia Cariari, in the San José area, the site of two PGA tours. I considered this a monumental event.

My wife carped about the fact that we had to come so far just so I could play golf. She reminded me over and over about the proximity of the equator and how hot she feared it would be, repeatedly asking me why we would travel to a rain forest in the height of the summer.

However, the following morning my wife had the drapes drawn and she appeared to be singing a different tune. "Would you look at that view?" she said quietly as she gazed out the window in a seemingly catatonic state. Claire is a stubborn one, and I was sure that she had not intended for me to hear that. I know that even if she loved Costa Rica after all, it would kill her to admit it.

In an hour's time we were out the door and driving around in our rental car. I have never really been one for sightseeing, and I was really not interested in very much besides golf at this point, but I was immediately overwhelmed by the idyllic vision of countryside that stretched out before me.

I tried to concentrate on the road as I drove around, quickly scanning lush rain forests that spilled down steep mountains, which eventually greeted both the Pacific and Atlantic oceans. Surrounded on either side by the two deep-blue seas, Costa Rica is a land bridge between the continents of North and South America, with mountain ranges forming its spine.

You won't find any tall buildings blighting the fabulous beaches, which remain unspoiled even by footprints. Instead, only multiple bays, inlets, and two large gulfs indent the surface. In fact, there appear to be few tall buildings anywhere, allowing Costa Rica to proffer more beauty per acre than any place I've ever seen. Even the city with its old-fashioned cozy homes and antique cathedrals was a feast for the eyes, and by afternoon my eyes were certainly full, but my belly was aching with need.

Turns out, I wasn't the only one with an appetite. While I had been thinking about grabbing a quick burger, my wife had been thinking about grabbing a quick bite of man-meat in the backseat.

When I felt Claire's hand in my lap, I looked over at her for the first time since being awed silly by the sights before me. She was smiling mischievously and began to run her hand up and down the crotch of my khaki shorts. I smiled back, my eyes as wide as two saucers, wondering what exactly had got into my wife, but not breathing a single word of complaint.

We toured for a little bit longer, then found a place to have some lunch. Afterward, Claire pointed me back in the direction of the hotel. "I still have jet lag," she said with a hearty yawn that had me believing sleep was all she craved. But I was certainly wrong.

I was feeling kind of sleepy myself by the time we got back to our room. It was already pretty late in the afternoon, and I was glad that we had decided to arrive a day early so that I could be well rested for the tournament.

I had golf on the brain again as I slowly began taking off my shoes and then folded my shirt neatly into the chair beside the bed. It wasn't until I turned around and discovered my sexy wife waiting for me buck naked on the bed that I was able to momentarily forget about tomorrow's game.

Knowing my one-track mind all too well, Claire said, "I know a sure way to get a hole in one," as she began slowly running her hand down her throat, stopping at each breast. She lazily caressed her nipples before continuing her journey down to her belly where she traced her navel with one manicured fingertip. My cock was immediately rock-hard, and I tore off the rest of my clothes and jumped onto the bed to join my very naked and very horny wife.

As soon as I was nestled beside her, Claire turned over on her side and pulled me toward her so that my cock was pressing against her pelvis. I was delighted by the feel of her wiry hairs against my cockhead, and as our lips met, Claire placed my hand on her chest before lowering her hand to my shaft.

We kissed and fondled with the passion of two new lovers, with Claire's demanding kisses sending shock waves throughout my body and supercharging my penis.

Desperately wanting to be inside her, though, I grabbed her asscheeks and pressed her against me, squishing her breasts into my chest and attempting to angle my penis toward her already-wet cunt.

Sensing my urgent need as well as her own, Claire guided my throbbing cock directly inside her hot pussy. We held each other like that momentarily, my cock pulsating inside her, our quivering arms wrapped tightly around each other's back.

I stared lovingly into my wife's eyes as we continued to enjoy the feel of being joined together as one, and then I kissed her sweetly on the lips. I wanted the honesty and intensity of the moment to last forever, but when Claire reached down to cup my balls in the palm of her hand, all sentiment was lost and I was propelled to move. With both of our bodies lying sideways, it was a bit of a challenge to keep my cock inside her, so I had to begin slowly, pumping my cock in and out of my wife's cunt with a steady thrust of my hips.

We kissed with raw abandon, the friction of my cock sliding in and out of her cunt and the pressure of her pussy clenching against my shaft becoming almost too much to take. The easy rhythm and my wife's soft moaning were driving me totally insane, and I quickly found myself bucking frantically, clutching at my wife's ass, back, and hair.

Our bodies ground against one another as Claire wrapped her thighs around my back, welcoming me even farther inside her. Slow and gentle lovemaking had been long forgotten as we gave in to our primordial needs, and I engorged her pussy with my ready-to-explode cock.

I tried to visualize the following day's golf tournament in an effort to stave off my orgasm for a few seconds, wanting Claire to come before I shot my load. It didn't seem to be working all that well, though, because all I could see when I closed my eyes was a naked image of my sexy wife—sprawled out on the golf course naked, driving in the back of the golf cart naked, standing at the tee naked.

Luckily, though, with a few thrusts Claire was writhing in orgasm, contracting her pussy muscles around my cock as she climaxed. The pulsing combined with the heat was about all I could take, and within a nanosecond of my wife's crisis I was shooting my load inside her, my body quivering and my eyes nearly popping out of my skull from the intensity of it all.

I played fairly well in the tournament, but I am certain I could have done better. Claire and I had stayed up a bit too late the previous night, fucking like honeymooners, and the skimpy little number that she wore that day didn't make matters any better. I couldn't help but think about fucking her right then and there on the eighteenth hole. Even that morning, before we headed to the golf course, I got down on my hands and knees to lick my wife's pussy. The tongue lashing had almost made us late, but it had been worth it.

—*D.S., Cambridge, Massachusetts*

TRUMP CARD—EXCITING WEEKEND IN
ATLANTIC CITY REVITALIZES A MARRIAGE

Melanie is a beautiful woman, but the pressures of every-day life can make it hard to keep the flames of desire lit in any marriage. We decided that what we needed was a weekend away from it all, so I booked us into the most luxurious hotel in Atlantic City for our own "Romantic Reunion."

We drove down, classic rock on the radio, windows open, and Melanie's black hair blowing in the wind, making her look like a young Cher. Her long, tanned legs and sandaled feet were driving me crazy the whole way there, and I was all choked up with the sense that she really was the love of my life, and the sexiest woman alive.

We checked in and went directly to our room, whose lofty vantage point gave us a view of a spectacular sunset and the gaily twinkling lights of the boardwalk strip. I opened a bottle of champagne and we toasted ourselves. At that moment I wanted her unbearably, but I had planned the whole perfect evening and intended to follow through.

Going to my suitcase, I presented her with a bra and panty set in an outrageous tiger stripe that suited her perfectly. She insisted on slipping it on immediately and modeled it for me before she put on her slinky, sleeveless black dress. I could hardly keep my hands off her. She looked like a goddess, and I saw that image reflected in the gaze of every man we passed as we walked through the casino. Having her on my arm seemed the most erotic moment of the whole trip.

While we dined, Melanie did everything in her power to drive me crazy, including rubbing my crotch under the table with her prehensile toes. We headed back to our room without dessert. Both of us were so overwhelmed with desire that we knew we'd never be able to concentrate on anything else.

We both entered the room and I took Melanie in my arms, crushing her body against mine and kissing her passionately. My hands roamed over her delicious figure as I whispered once more how much I loved her. Returning the sentiment, she confessed she could wait no longer.

Reaching behind her, I unzipped her dress and watched, mesmerized, as she stepped out of it, letting it fall in a heap on the floor. Looking at her standing there in tiger stripes, bathed with the city's neon glow, I felt goose pimples break out all over me. The moment we'd waited for had arrived.

I moved to put a CD in the portable player, and moments later soft saxophone music filled the room. It was a little lush, but perfect for the way we felt. When I turned back to her, Melanie was already stretched out on the bed, writhing on the multicolored comforter like a cat in heat. She beckoned to me, her other hand playing with her pussy through the panties.

Not that I needed much tempting. I walked over to the bed and she sat up and began undressing me as I knelt on the edge of the mattress, stripping me down to my briefs. When she ran her fingertips along the bulge under my clothing, I shivered again.

I told her to lie on her stomach, and she rolled over. I lit a scented candle and carried it over to the nightstand, then took out a bottle of scented body lotion to match the mood. I straddled her and tenderly placed a kiss on the small of her back, delighting as she flinched a bit from the ticklish sensation. I kissed all the way up her back, undoing her bra en route.

Pouring some of the lotion into my hands, I began massaging her shoulders, working the lotion into her soft skin. She murmured something I couldn't quite decipher, and I worked my way down her back, rubbing lotion all over her luscious body. With another handful of lotion I massaged the backs of her legs, and then her thighs, noting with pleasure and pride the solid muscles in her slim legs. I worked back down to her ankles and raised each foot, planting a kiss on each sole before licking and sucking her toes, relishing her mews of submissive delight.

I kissed my way up to her tiger-striped panties, my fingers caressing her asscheeks through the silky fabric. With my face against her I could easily smell the strong, musky scent of her arousal, and I could hardly wait for my first taste. I slipped off her panties, exposing her magnificent bottom. I sat there captivated for a moment, watching as Melanie flexed the muscles in her asscheeks, reveling in that perfect round ass glowing in the candlelight.

I lowered my face and kissed first one cheek and then the other. Sliding my hand beneath her, I cupped her small patch of pubic hair, pressing my hand against her aroused pussy and thrilling to the heat and moisture emanating from within her. With no effort, I slipped my thumb deep inside her warm, wet pussy, then withdrew it and began rubbing her clitoris gently, using her musky juices as lubricant.

She purred as I continued to stimulate her. I blew lightly on her ass, moving lower until my breath was directed at her pussy. That must have sent her over the edge, because the next thing I knew she had rolled over onto her back and was bucking her pussy right up into my face. I lifted her ass and licked my way around every bit of her sweet sex. Reaching down with her own hands, she spread her lips open for me, allowing me to slip my tongue deep inside her and savor the sweet taste of her lust. Taking her clit in my mouth, I sucked gently on it before releasing it to lick her widespread labia.

Melanie's hands gripped the back of my head, pulling me closer between her legs. I covered her entire pussy and sucked before taking her clit in my lips once more and sucking for all I was worth. In seconds she was moaning and gyrating wildly, her crotch grinding into my mouth. When her orgasm finally hit, she closed her thighs firmly around my head and her entire body bucked beneath me.

She released me before my head exploded—barely. Reaching down, I removed my briefs and began kissing my way up her still-trembling body until she took my face in her hands and kissed me, our tongues mingling amid the taste of her desire. My cock found its own way between her thighs and slid easily into her warm, waiting pussy. I shuddered with pleasure, feeling the woman I love close around every inch.

When I was in as deep as I could go, I stopped and lay there for a few seconds, cherishing the nearness of my soul mate. The feel of Melanie's lips on my throat brought me back and sent another erotic shiver through me. I began a rhythmic thrusting in and out, and as we made love I let my hands roam over her body, caressing her breasts before I lowered my mouth to suck one nipple and bite it gently.

I found her clit with my fingers and slowly began to massage it as I continued to pump into her. My passion was incredibly high, and I wanted to make her come again. Covering her mouth with mine, I kissed her, her tongue entering my mouth as I did so. I pressed a little harder on her clit and she wrapped legs around my back tightly as the kiss ended.

She moaned, pulling me deeper within her. I rubbed little circles on her clit, increasing my tempo as her breath became more labored. She was nibbling my ear when her orgasm began and she let it go, crying for me to fuck her hard.

My arms held me up as I slammed in and out of her, our bodies slapping together and Melanie's nails digging into my back. We made love with a frenzied passion, not stopping until our bodies were slick with sweat.

Amazingly I still hadn't come, having tried to prolong our oneness as long as I possibly could. Senses reeling, I slipped out of my lover and asked her to roll over. She did so eagerly, hugging a pillow to her chest as she raised her buttocks high. I knelt behind her and guided myself between her soft pussy lips once more, eliciting another loud moan of pleasure as I sank back inside her.

I began driving in and out, knowing I had little resistance left. Her pussy was as tight as a blood pressure cuff, and I felt the familiar tingling in my balls that grew to a rush as my beautiful wife came once more, her cries pulling me along as I shot my load into her.

Collapsing on top of her, I kissed her sweat-soaked neck before flopping down next to her. She rolled into my arms and we kissed as we held each other tight. We fell asleep that way, agreeing later that it was the deepest and most relaxed sleep we'd shared, after the most intense lovemaking of our marriage.

—*M.T., Lakewood, New Jersey* ⚬━■

MY BLONDE WIFE, HER BLACK LOVER, AND ME—
NAKED IN THE ISLANDS

My wife and I have just returned from an amazing Caribbean vacation. We loved the islands. The landscape is lovely, the people are friendly, and the atmosphere is very sexy. Our resort had a pervasive air of eroticism, with nakedness and open sex everywhere we looked. My wife, Claire, fit right in, with her petite but curvaceous blonde beauty and truly memorable breasts. She's one hot woman in and out of bed, and even among the tanned lovelies of the resort she attracted more than her share of attention.

We met lots of people and enjoyed several sexual adventures, but one stands out in particular. We were hanging around the nude hot tub before dinner, drinking frosty rum concoctions and talking to new friends. I was chatting with a black guy named Nick, a lawyer from California, and we were putting the final touches on the idea of his having sex with Claire. She's often been attracted to black men, and it was obvious that Nick had a cock that would please any woman.

After a bit we left the hot tub and went up to shower and get ourselves ready. We'd already talked over the details with Nick, and Claire was so excited that her shaved pussy was glistening wet. Our ten-minute head start gave me a chance to get the video camera in place.

Nick arrived right on time and joined Claire on the bed

without much preliminary conversation. She was already naked and he was clad only in his swim trunks. They began kissing and nuzzling each other, with Nick sucking eagerly on Claire's pert nipples. His large body—linebacker size—made quite a contrast with my petite blonde wife. I sat naked in a nearby chair, stroking my cock and running the camera, as they got to know each other's body.

Claire pulled off Nick's trunks and began slowly licking his cock and balls. I had seen he was well endowed, but we couldn't appreciate his true size until he began to get aroused. His cock was so long and thick Claire had trouble holding on to it. She paused in her tasting session and just looked at it in awe. Then, as if taking on a challenge, she began to suck his cock.

Claire is an expert cocksucker, and it's one of my favorite bits of foreplay, but I had never seen her so absorbed. Nick had incredible control and she'd let up every time he seemed close to coming. She could only swallow about half of him, but she stroked the base of that massive dick so it wouldn't feel left out.

Nick was fingering her pussy as she sucked him, and she had to pause several times to gasp as his caresses took her over the edge. My favorite shot was of her lying back with Nick straddling her chest, feeding her his cock and reaching behind him to rub her clit while fucking her face. She began to moan and squirm and tried to take him deeper into her throat. Although muffled by his cock, her moans heralded another tremendous orgasm. She bucked wildly as her orgasm overtook her body.

After she got her breath back, she let him go long enough to say she had to have him inside her. Nick lay on his back and let Claire straddle him and impale herself slowly on his shaft. When it was all the way inside her it stretched her pussy to the limit, and her eyes were wide with wonder and excitement. She rode him with abandon and came again almost immediately. At that point I lost it and came all over myself.

Claire had been on her knees riding Nick, but he pulled her legs up so she rode him more like a horse, which seemed appropriate. That also allowed for maximum penetration—as if she needed more cock! She handled it well and soon she was moaning and squealing her way through another mind-blowing orgasm. They kept murmuring to each other about how good his massive dick felt in her hot, tight pussy.

In one swift move Nick picked Claire up and tossed her onto her back. He put her legs over his shoulders and began fucking her hard and fast. She was moaning again, begging him to fuck her longer and harder. The whole resort must have heard their cries as they came together. They rested for a moment and then Nick kissed her and left to get ready for dinner.

I was hard again, and my cock felt like a heat-seeking missile that had locked on to its target. I was obsessed with getting a feel of my wife's well-fucked pussy for myself. I rolled on top of her and drove into her come-laden cunt, feeling Nick's seed squish up around us as we came together. I pounded my hard shaft into her over and over again until we were both groaning and whimpering with the sensory overload. Then the rush started in my balls and I gushed my come to join Nick's inside my wife.

We clung together until my cock softened and slid out,

then we got up and showered. Dressed for dinner, we went downstairs, greeting Nick as we passed the bar. It was a toss-up whose grin was bigger, and we looked forward to another round later in the evening.

Yes, if you want to recharge your sex life, I recommend a Caribbean holiday—especially with a handsome stud to help out. You won't regret it.

—*S.B., Via E-Mail* O+■

GRECIAN BURN—DARK-HAIRED TEMPTRESS SMOLDERING WITH LUST INFLAMES ADMIRER

I scanned the usual tourist scene swarming in front of me. I was in this idyllic Greek seaside town, having taken a few weeks off from my hectic schedule solving software problems for big-city clients, and wanted to just relax and enjoy myself in this land rich in mythology. I was lounging by the pool overlooking the Mediterranean, with the usual mix of Europeans dispersed around the pool and enjoying drinks at the bar.

Tanned, svelte bodies with nipples pert with desire surrounded me. Some were by themselves and others with the usual fawning boyfriend or bored husband. I was somewhat curious about one lady sitting two lounge chairs away.

She was probably in her thirties and had this smoldering sexual *je ne sais quoi* emanating from her body: delicate, soft skin tanned with an Italian olive complexion and a slender body with taut buttocks and perfectly proportional breasts. She had a nice oval face and a sharp nose with nostrils tilted just a little upward to give a flared, feral look that suggested she was inhaling exotic sensual scents. Her lower lip was naturally rose red, and her upper lip was framed by an arrogantly taut Cupid's bow. Her icy cool blue eyes suggested she could fathom and take in any situation. Shoulder-length black hair fell lazily in soft waves at her temples.

She was relaxing, stretched out in her European-style bikini, which showed her waist and smooth thighs with a down of very fine hair that shone like soft, beaten gold.

I felt a warm, buzzing sensation in my testicles and my penis slowly started to swell as I sharpened my gaze and could make out the soft mound of her pubis outlined beneath the thin material of her bikini. Suddenly I felt someone was watching me and looked farther up her torso to see her blue eyes looking at me. Those eyes momentarily dipped to acknowledge my growing erection, and when we locked eyes again there was an encouraging smile on her face and a twinkle in her eyes that suggested she was well aware of my gazing caress of her private parts.

I smiled back at her and saw her ever so gently arch her waist a little to push her mons up a little. My cock became even more engorged with pure, instinctual desire, protruding up through my tight swimming trunks.

Just then a tourist wearing loud boxer shorts jumped into the pool near her and a splash of water landed on her thighs. It startled her out of the eye lock she had on my crotch and I watched her fumble around for a towel, but she had none on her chair as she must have forgotten to get one from the concierge at the front desk. I grabbed my towel and quickly walked over to her.

She reached up for the towel, saying, "Thanks a lot. My name's Elizabeth." I crouched beside her so that we were at eye level and introduced myself. I looked down to the gap her bikini made with her thighs and I could make out some fine, soft brown hair. I thought I could even make out a faint outline of labia at the vertex of her thin bikini. Not wanting to waste any time, I asked, "Are you having dinner here at the hotel tonight? I saw a nice little tavern by the water around the corner. Would you like to have dinner with me?"

I could see that she was pleased at the way things were developing as she acquiesced—"Shall we meet in the foyer, around sixish?"

"Sounds good to me," I said, feeling pleased as punch.

The tavern was dark and cozy. The native maître d'— dark hair combed back like a flamenco dancer—seated us at a square table in a sweet corner. Elizabeth sat perpendicular to me instead of across from me. As we settled in, the waiter stepped up and recommended the locally brewed lager, Aegean, and then went away to get us some.

We enjoyed a mashed eggplant prepared in olive oil, lemon juice, and garlic. I was pleased that she was not afraid to eat garlic, and as I commented upon it, she coyly responded, "If both of us eat it, then it's all right." I kissed her soft warm hand and we both ate a good amount of the wonderful Greek contribution to the dips, the custardlike *tzatziki*.

It seemed only natural that after our meal, washed down with the traditional ouzo, we walked arm in arm back to our hotel and ended up in her room. I was incredibly curious about her and utterly delighted to find her rather assertive. She pulled up my shirt as we were entwined in a hot embrace and deftly undid my belt. Her hand slid into my underwear as her tongue slid into my mouth and began dueling with mine, sending electric waves of pleasure through my whole being. We collapsed into the bed where Elizabeth removed my pants and underwear.

With a mischievous twinkle in her eyes, she said, "It's fascinating, this cock of yours, with its little turban of foreskin." Holding it in her palm, she retracted my foreskin with her thumb and index finger and bent down to engulf the exposed cockhead with her mouth. Her tongue gently ran around the rim of the crown and my buttocks tightened with lust, arching my groin deeper into her face.

Her hands were shockingly knowledgeable as they caressed my buttocks and came to rest near my anus. She used her slender finger in a delicate circular motion all around my asshole that made me mad with desire. Her teeth clenched lightly on the base of my shaft and she began to slide her teeth up to the glans and back to the base of my cock.

She performed this pleasurable oscillation at a steady and insistent rhythm, occasionally lingering at my cockhead, sucking as if she wanted to swallow me whole. I felt my semen building up and clenched my thighs tight around her head. When my cock throbbed and exploded with a volcanic eruption of semen into her mouth, she held me tight, sucking up every creamy spurt. She held me gently in her mouth as my erection subsided.

Afterward, I pulled her face to mine and kissed her softly, almost in gratitude for the supreme pleasure she had given me. Slowly, I turned her around so that her crotch was near my lips. Her pubic hair was soft and it gave me a nice feeling as I gently ran my tongue across it, moistening it with my saliva. My tongue probed lower and I could taste a little of her excitement. My tongue found her clitoris and I licked it, then took it between my lips. When I gently sucked on it, she began to tighten her thighs around my head.

I sucked and licked her until she bucked up into my face in a violent spasm of pleasure. I inserted three fingers into her vagina and felt the incipient rhythmic contractions of her release. Orgasmic ripples spread all over her body. She shuddered and lapsed into a languorous swoon of pleasure and hugged my head.

I rolled away from Elizabeth and lay beside her, lazily watching the softly whirring blades of the rotating fan overhead. And then she was at my cock again. I looked down to see her mass of black hair cascading over my belly and through it Elizabeth's lips forming a snug caress around the shaft of my penis. She was good—very good. She was sucking on it just tightly enough to send icy hot flames of pleasure searing up my shaft and make it swell with desire.

The tip of her tongue grooved around my cockhead, and I felt a tingle of liquid pleasure ascend into my cock and my testicles tighten with lust. As her lips slid up and down my shaft, I lay back with contentment. My eyes went back to the fan making that slow but insistent rhythm and I came in a long, slow gentle surge, almost as if I wanted to keep time with the lazily rotating fan blades.

Feeling dry and thirsty, I gently rolled Elizabeth to one side and asked softly, "Fancy a beer? I'm thirsty. You have completely drained me." She brought her hands under her head and smiled. "Sure," she said.

When I returned she was lying on her belly. I could not help marveling at her slender torso, the gentle undulation of her back into her exquisite buttocks. I could see delicate wisps of soft brown hair peeping out and her rose-petal-pink leaf of pleasure tissue. I bent to kiss her nape and she shuddered with pleasure. We parted the next day, saying fond farewell to a matchless vacation experience for the both of us.

—*E.T., Milwaukee, Wisconsin* ⊶∎

OF GOLDEN SUNSETS, THE BLUE PACIFIC, AND LOVERS CONSUMED WITH RED-HOT DESIRE

We both needed this Hawaiian vacation so badly we could taste it, and when I told Jason I'd arranged for us to stay with Mia, he couldn't believe it. She's my closest girlfriend from college, and she now manages a pineapple plantation on Oahu. I thought it would do him good and I knew Mia liked Jason very much.

We both managed to extricate ourselves from our offices and prepared to let go for a few days. Upon arrival in Hawaii, we found our bags and Jason spotted Mia. She looked sexy as usual, wearing a tight halter top, revealing much of her voluptuous breasts. Her cutoffs showed the firm, well-tended ass that all the guys craved in college. Everybody thought we looked alike, but her tresses were golden from working outdoors and mine deep auburn.

After welcoming hugs and kisses we got into Mia's Jeep, and a few hours into the trip I noticed Jason beginning to relax, the sun and sea air of Hawaii taking effect. A slow smile curved his lips as Mia drove farther down single-lane dirt roads. They sat in front, chatting, while in the back I was thrilled to be away from the rat race.

Suddenly Mia asked Jason to take the wheel. She undid the halter top, releasing her breasts to the sunlight. Looking back at me, she yelled over the sound of the engine, "Go ahead, Annette, it's okay! This isn't Columbus!" Jason's eyes glazed.

"Go ahead, baby!" He grabbed my hand, squeezing it, and smiled. "We're on vacation!" I slipped off my shirt, unhooked my skimpy bra, and for the first time since college felt really liberated. The wind rushed around my breasts, patterns of shadow and light on them created by the foliage flying by. Jason was in his glory, riding high in Hawaii with two beautiful half-naked women! I noticed him staring at Mia's breasts, and it excited me to see him lusting after her.

After we settled in, Mia suggested we take a walk out back to see the view. We set out into the forest and in no time came to a spectacular lookout. Jason and I stared in awe at the cerulean blue Pacific below. We walked down the path and once out of sight I reached for his cock. He kissed me. My tongue answered his as he hardened under my grasp. I wanted him in my impatient mouth, but instead his mouth flicked over my exposed nipples, warm in the Oahu breeze. As he sucked, I worked open his zipper, shoving my hand in to find a throbbing prick I could hardly grasp. It sprang to attention, knocking up toward his navel. Dragging him off the path, I got down and licked the underside of his hard penis, working my tongue over its whole length.

His eyes rolled back, ecstatic, as I took the purple glans into my mouth and began pumping on his cock, shoving it far down my throat. His balls tightened as I massaged them. He grasped my hair, pushing himself into my mouth with each stroke.

Suddenly, glancing up, I saw Mia watching us through the leaves. Jason yelled, loud enough for Mia to hear. I greedily consumed every drop of his spurting semen and continued sucking until his cock softened. Finally I zipped him up, and he whispered in my ear, "I'm gonna give you a fucking later like you've never had!" I couldn't wait, and on we went, back to the house, stopping for a cool drink at the side water faucet.

As we drank, Mia appeared again, her face flushed. Stepping right up with us, she dunked her long blonde locks under the stream. The water flowed down her perfect upturned tits, causing her nipples to grow erect. The bulge in Jason's pants grew noticeable again. The thoughts going through my mind were incredibly lustful.

The sun began its descent, growing crimson near the horizon. Jason and Mia stood in silhouette, watching the sunset in the delectable heat. How many times had he told me of his fantasy of two women making love to him? Why did it excite me? Was it because I harbored the same fantasy?

I walked toward them, casting all inhibitions aside, and nudged between them, putting my arms around their shoulders, an uncontrolled sultriness in my voice as I pulled them close and admired the sunset. Mia's breasts pushed against mine, our mouths nearing one another's.

I put my mouth full onto Jason's, giving him a passionate kiss, still holding Mia near. When I turned toward her, we stared into each other's eyes. Since college we had joked about making love, but never acted on it. Now our lips met. For the first time I felt the softness of another woman's lips on my own and it made an intensity rise between my legs. I remembered how sexy she said she thought Jason was, and now I was bringing the three of us together.

Jason stepped back, removing his shirt so he could feel our breasts against his chest. Mia knelt down and undid his fly, letting his pants fall to the ground. Jason looked over to me as if asking for a little support.

I leaned forward, whispering in his ear, "We're both yours tonight, lover." He smiled in appreciation as Mia pulled his pants off, revealing yet another erection from my lusty husband. She took it into her mouth, voraciously gorging herself on his thick meat.

It fascinated me to watch another woman sucking my husband's cock, to see the difference in her technique. Mia seemed to be enjoying it immensely, and I knelt down beside her and began swirling my tongue around Jason's balls, kissing his cock. I flicked my tongue over her outstretched lips as they descended to his root, her eyes glimmering with thanks.

How I wanted to be fucked, and as I watched them I shoved two fingers up my willing slit. But just as much I wanted to see what lay beneath Mia's shorts.

"Please, Jason," I cried. He knew what I wanted. In moments Mia's shorts were tossed aside, removed by my husband's strong hands as I removed mine. He pulled the wedged panties from the fig of her sex, their wetness clinging tightly to her smooth, unblemished skin. What lay beneath was a well-manicured bush of light blonde pubic hair. His prick throbbed at attention, ready for penetration. Mia whimpered quietly, wanting him, and I gave them the okay.

Drawn to her wet pussy, Jason's cock was already well greased, and he groaned as he slipped his full length carefully into her. He began pistoning slowly there under a eucalyptus tree, its shadows accentuated by the warm colors of the setting sun. As he pumped, I got this truly outrageous idea, and I moved my head underneath

Jason's scrotum, watching his rock-hard cock squeeze into Mia, stretching her pouting cunt lips.

I put my tongue, timidly at first, to the point where his shaft met Mia's pussy and held it there. Jason slid back and forth over my moist tongue, increasing the pleasure of their fuck, a first for us in so many ways. Growing bolder, I made a swirling motion with my tongue while Jason increased his speed, assailing my friend with his sexy blade. The muscles of her pussy clenched down, beginning to spasm as she moaned for me to keep going. My face was drenched with both their juices as I lapped away at their genitals grinding together.

"God, I could come any second, but I want to feel you both at once," Jason sighed. Mia met me face-to-face, whispering, "I've dreamed about this a thousand times." Then she kissed me deeply on the lips and I could taste the stickiness of arousal, hers and Jason's, which had been plastered all over my mouth and chin.

I pushed back her hair, lovingly caressing her face, and pulled her body to mine. So Jason could have us together at the same time, she lay atop me, full contact, breasts pressed against breasts, bush to bush. When Jason entered her, she gasped as if the wind were knocked out of her. I embraced her tightly and we kissed like young lovers wanting to consume each other. Her body rubbed into mine with Jason's pounding, our cunts grinding together, her juices running over his cock and my own wet labia. I held Mia stable, helping him to maintain his steady strokes.

This was his fantasy realized. Our pussies being so close, one atop the other, gave him easy entrance into either, and he took full advantage. A simple change in direction had him pounding my cunt, and four or five strokes later his cock slithered back into Mia's pinkness. Between us we got a delicious fucking, the smells of our sex intoxicating us more than those of the tropical flowers around us. Jason watched his cock slide in and out of each of us, sweat pouring from his brow.

The fevered pitch of his thrusts led to a triple climax. Mia's thighs clasped tightly around mine, her orgasm pushing me over the edge. While Jason rammed into her cunt, balls slapping against my pussy, he exploded a bucket of hot sperm inside her, but before spending himself entirely he gave me a few final thrusts as well. And then Jason slumped over Mia's back. Our sweaty bodies writhed in the ecstatic afterglow of sex and sunset. Mia lifted her head, saying, "Welcome to Oahu."

—*A.N., Columbus, Georgia*   Oᴛ◼

JOYOUS GERMANS ABANDON ALL DECORUM AS THEY CUT LOOSE AT STREET FESTIVAL

Call it Carnevale, Mardi Gras, or Fasching, we human beings need to let go of our buttoned-up workaday personae and let our primitive side loose. The more repressed the culture, the more startling its wanton abandon. Tops in my book has to be Fasching, because after months at work in a major automotive firm, I was finding German stodginess chafing like a straitjacket. Dieter blew that away by inviting me to spend Fasching with him in Mainz. I couldn't imagine that staid city letting rip like the Big Easy.

Arriving at the station, we wound our way into the crowded heart of the medieval city. Everyone around us was wearing clown makeup, and even more startling, the usually overformal Germans were using the familiar *"du"* reserved for spouses, children, and pets. We climbed a narrow staircase and dropped our minimal luggage. Dieter's girlfriend was soon smearing clown white makeup across my face and telling me it was important to let go and play the fool at Fasching. She was painted like a Tyrolean house front, hearts and flowers rioting across her cheeks. She was the first woman to talk to me familiarly, and my whole body tingled as her fingertips reddened my mouth and nose and made whimsical patterns on my cheeks.

The apartment overlooked the parade route. People lined the narrow streets and hundreds more hung out of windows like ours. Couples kissed and groped in door-ways. Floats sailed by, their occupants tossing party favors. A float recalling the city's Roman past inspired me to yell *"Ave Caesar!"* to the toga-clad patrician on board, who grinned and slung me a cheap beaded necklace.

Hunger drove me into the street, toward a square that Dieter assured me held all manner of goodies. I munched as my eyes roved the crowd. A girl on a bench nearby seemed to be watching me with a look both salacious and predatory. I grinned. Why not? In my clown face I was as disguised as she was, and wasn't the whole point of Fasching to let go and fool around?

Her white face sported generous red lips and dark, comic circles around her eyes. Blonde hair flowed onto her shoulders. I sat down next to her, my thigh warm against hers. Long legs in jeans tucked into cowboy boots promised other interesting features. Unfortunately a down jacket and scarf muffed her upper body. Before I could figure out an opening line, her cool fingers pressed my lips. My throat constricted and we just stared at each other. She smiled and her hand dropped to my leg. Apparently she wanted me, but she wanted me silent.

She stood up in front of me and I got a better look at her long, gracefully curved legs before she took my hand and pulled me to my feet. Her next move was totally unpredictable. Taking the scarf from her neck, she turned me to face the cathedral—and the Dom was the last glimpse I caught before she brought the scarf up over my eyes.

Blindfolded, I was led into what must have been a less-frequented back street. Caution set the hairs on my neck upright, but desire had already produced its own erection. From the sound of things, nobody seemed to be following us, so I relaxed a little. Keys rattled and a door opened on creaking hinges. The air from inside was warm, with a scent that was familiar but unplaceable. The door swung shut and my excitement increased. The improvised blindfold showed me a sliver of dim light, and I could hear my companion's movements before her arms enfolded me and her body pressed against mine.

Her lips touched mine, softly at first, then with an exploratory kiss and questing tongue. I raised my hand to her shoulders and my cold fingers met warm, naked skin. I stroked her flesh, under the thick fall of her hair and down the delicate articulations of her back. My palms felt her shiver as my hands cupped a beautifully rounded ass.

Slowly she broke off the kiss, lifting my jacket to unbutton and pull down my pants. Her hands on my hips, she seemed to be crouched with her face centimeters from my cock. Her warm breath felt like sunshine on the tip of my rapidly cooling member as it bobbed in time with my racing pulse. My fingers sought her hair as she finally ended my sweet anticipatory torment by taking my cock in her mouth. Warmth bathed my taut skin; the edges of her teeth reminded me where I was; her tongue rasped softly on sensitive tissue. Pulling my pelvis forward, she forced me deep into her throat as if she were bent on consuming my cock.

Drawing back a fraction, she slid her left hand over my flank and cupped my balls, the chilly fingers causing them to draw up in surprise. It was a move calculated for its effect—the juxtaposition of warm mouth and cold hand was marvelous. Like a consummate musician, she brought the first movement of our little symphony to a close with a delicate flourish of her tongue on the tip of my instrument.

She stood and pulled off my blindfold. The smell I couldn't place was now identifiable—we were in the back of a furniture store, surrounded by new upholstery. That awareness fled as my eyes took in the sight before them. The woman stood there naked except for her clown makeup and cowboy boots. I had never seen so perfect a form in my life—long legs, exquisitely formed breasts with tight, erect nipples, and well-manicured golden pubic hair. Still, her most astounding feature was her painted face. The lavishly red mouth gave her a tawdry look. Her eyes smoldered within their dark circles. Her hair was now a wickedly tangled nimbus. She backed up to a desk and motioned me to finish undressing.

Only when I was completely bare did she remove her boots, leaving us exposed but for our greasepaint masks. She moved her right leg up onto the desk and her hand spread the finely formed lips of her glistening sheath. No further invitation was needed. I pulled a chair forward and she threw her calves over my shoulders, bringing me close to breathe her musky scent. Her juices were flowing freely, tasting like honey on my tongue as it ran up and down her slit before settling on her clitoris. I let my tongue hover like a hummingbird above a succulent flower. Then, without warning, she was coming, grasping my head and drawing me closer with her legs as she let out a deep groan—the first sound I had heard from her.

As her climax slowly waned, she relaxed and put her feet down, pulling me with her to a couch that opened up to reveal a bed. She climbed onto it and rested on forearms and knees, tilting her pelvis to display her shining pussy. I took my swollen cock in hand and pointed. She was so wet my aching erection slid easily into the folds of her vagina. Each stroke was rapture. I picked up my tempo and she arched like a bow being strung, grasping the mattress with futile fingers. She came again, convulsing and letting out a tiny cry.

She leaned forward, uncoupling us, and stretched out, beckoning me to lie beside her. Once I was stretched on my back she swung her leg over my hips and mounted me. Looking deep into my eyes, she seized my cock and sank down on me till her clit rubbed in my pubic hair. Each motion increased our delicious friction until she began to tremble again, her climax bringing me irresistibly to my own, as my creamy come flowed into her.

Neither of us spoke as we lay there. Eventually a mutual urge got us dressed. Standing before the door that separated us from the outside, I took her scarf and rebound my eyes so that she could lead me back to the square. Amid the crowd she removed the blindfold, gave me a kiss, and disappeared.

I worked my way back to the apartment, relaxed and satisfied. Dieter and his girlfriend had been joined by several others, and my entrance occasioned some curious glances and a couple of grins. Only when I glanced in the mirror did I see what caused the stares. My face, like that of my anonymous companion, had lost its tidy paint job in our passion, just as I had lost my inhibitions in a perfect Fasching celebration.

—*H.P., Detroit, Michigan* ⚬━▪

BUSINESSWOMAN ROYALLY PLEASURED IN MEDIEVAL CASTLE BY HER CREATIVE MATE

My husband, Paul, and I are successful and very busy people who often forget how important it is to get down to the basics and just love each other emotionally and physically. But in late August of last year my husband did something I never expected. He created a magical weekend that most women only dream about.

He had been in Europe on business for over two weeks when he called to tell me that he would have to stay there a little longer. I tried not to be upset, knowing that he had no other choice, but when we hung up he knew I was not pleased. The next day, while at the office, my husband's assistant delivered a bouquet of wildflowers and a sealed manila envelope. In the envelope was an airline ticket to Italy where we would spend a long weekend together.

I called him at his hotel and warned him that if this was going to be a weekend of me sitting in a hotel room in Rome while he was in meetings, he could forget it, but he assured me that it would be wonderful.

Arriving in Italy, I was highly impressed by the Rolls my husband had waiting for me. The driver helped me in. "Your husband eagerly awaits your arrival, my lady," he said in a thick Italian accent.

As we left Rome, I started to ask the driver questions about our destination, but he would reveal nothing. My curiosity was killing me as we climbed high hills into a heavily wooded area. The trip was long and I eventually grew tired and fell asleep.

I awoke to the sound of the driver calling me: "*Signora! Andiamo!* We have arrived." I blinked a few times, trying to shake off the sleepiness and see where I was. There in front of me was the most magnificent building I'd ever seen, a giant medieval castle. I was in awe, feeling so tiny beneath its shadow, and I turned around to watch the iron gates close behind us.

One of several people waiting outside the castle stepped forward and kissed me once on each cheek. Her name was Rose and she welcomed me, assuring me that Paul would be back later. In the meantime, she would show me to my room where I could freshen up and change before dinner. I think I was still in shock as I walked through the large doors into the castle. The floors were oak parquet and the ceilings were high. As we walked through the rooms, I wondered where it would end. Was this castle being rented out as a hotel? Did we have one room?

"Feel free to explore all of the rooms," Rose said, as if reading my thoughts. She then led me up two flights of stairs. She was out of breath when we reached a door, which like the others had a Renaissance arch, and she opened it for me.

It was the bathroom, and it was as big as our entire bedroom at home! In the middle of the room was a giant tub made out of the same marble used for the floor. Rose pointed out where everything was and then turned on the tub. She picked up a bottle of bubble bath and I was just about to stop her when she paused and smiled, saying, "Whoops, I almost forgot. Your husband said you prefer your baths really hot without the bubbles." I smiled, happy that he still remembered the small details.

As the bathtub filled, Rose opened another door that went directly into the bedroom. She opened the shuttered windows and I got an even better view of my surroundings. The furniture was dark wood, which had gently aged over hundreds of years. I slipped off my shoes and let my toes be tickled by the bear rug alongside the king-size four-poster covered by white netting. I peeked in and gleaned the satin sheets and velvet blanket. I felt like a princess.

Rose whispered for me to take my time, then said, "Dinner will not be for at least an hour and a half. There is a robe hanging behind the door and I will lay your clothes out on the bed."

I took off my clothes, letting them fall in a heap at my feet, then tied my hair up in a bun. As I lowered myself into the water, my muscles immediately began to relax, the tension just lifting away as I picked up a washcloth and submerged it in the water before running it over a bar of soap.

I started behind my neck, the excess water dripping down my shoulders and back as I ran the cloth over my flesh. I pleasured myself, gently making circles around my full breasts and down my belly. The washcloth disappeared under the water again and found my pussy.

I basked in the glory of all that was around me: the stack of fluffy towels by the side of the tub, the cage housing two little birds in the opposite corner of the room, the sound of the washcloth lifting out of the surface and spilling water back onto my relaxed body. At that moment, I hadn't a care in the world and I enjoyed my half-dazed, half-aroused state until the water began to cool and it was time to get out.

In my robe, I sat at the vanity to brush out my hair. It seemed I would not have to go into my suitcase for anything. I did my hair in long, soft curls, just the way Paul likes it, and then went to the bed to see what I was to wear. There was a note from Paul. He hoped I liked the dress he had bought for me in a little town not too far from the castle. It was wine-colored and fit tight around my chest, pushing my bosom together and up. It had a waist girdle that tied tight down the middle. The sleeves were long and hung like giant bells and the bottom of the gown was free-flowing. It fit perfectly and I stared in amazement at my reflection in the silver-framed mirror.

A short while later, a butler was sent upstairs to guide me to the dining room. I was grateful because I had no idea where it was. I was announced as I entered the room and that was when I got my first glance at Paul. Though he looked incredibly handsome, I almost giggled at the sight of him. He had really gone all out, trading in his suit for a white shirt, leather jerkin, baggy pants, and knee boots. He rose from his seat and bowed, pointing to the seat that the butler was holding out for me.

We ate our dinner, at opposite sides of the table, served to us by wonderful servants wearing white gloves. Throughout the meal, we made love with our eyes over and over again. My flesh burned and I knew that his cock was throbbing. After dinner, he offered me his arm and led me through the castle to the high tower. It was a bit windy up there, but in the darkness we danced by lantern and moonlight, a violinist playing a soft melody. I whispered a thank-you in his ear and in response got a passionate "you're welcome" kiss. The violinist's music grew more passionate and Paul suggested we make our way to our quarters.

We went a different way than Rose had led me earlier, actually exiting the castle and walking through an enchanting garden. Our path was guided by gas lanterns, illuminating trees that must have been hundreds of years old. We stopped at a stone bench to enjoy the cool night air. My heart raced as Paul knelt on the grass before me and buried his head between my breasts, sucking on them hard. His absence these two weeks suddenly flooded my being. I wanted him to devour me.

Paul moved downward and buried his face under my dress, biting on my thighs as he tugged on my lace panties. He pulled them down around my ankles, then spread my legs. His mouth was so warm as it covered my pussy. I wiggled a little from the intense pleasure as he licked me over and over again.

Pleasure flooded my whole body as I came, thrashing about on the stone bench, Paul fighting to hold me still. When he emerged from under my gown, his breathing was ragged and the look in his eyes was one of a man who needed to be fucked. Quickly now, we made our way to our quarters.

Once there, I went into the bathroom and put on the white chemise nightgown that had been left for me. Paul positioned me so that I was bent at the waist, holding on to one of the bedposts. I heard his pants drop and then felt the warmth of his cock on the back of my thigh as he pushed my long hair to one side and began to nibble on my ear and neck. "Put it in me," I begged.

Paul positioned the head of his cock at my opening

and slid right into me. I moaned along with him as he slowly fucked me from behind. His arm was around my waist while he used his other hand to lean against the post, keeping his balance. I felt as if my feet would come off the floor each time he pulled me back onto his shaft. Paul's grunts and groans grew louder and more insistent. His pace quickened and I held on tight to the post, imploring him to play with my clit so that I could come with him. It was only a few more thrusts and a few more rubs on my clitoris before Paul pulled me as hard as he could onto his cock. I felt him pulsing inside me as he filled me with hot come and I shuddered through my orgasm. After a nice hot bath we retired for the evening to our satiny bed for a wonderful night's sleep.

The rest of the weekend was just as exciting, although we didn't get into costume every single night. We did, however, spend much of our time making love in the beautiful garden, the watchtower, and in the dimly lit staircases of our medieval castle nestled in the hills of Italy.   —S.L., New York, New York ○┼■

EVENTS COORDINATOR: HOT-LOOKING COUPLES GET SPECIAL TREATMENT AT MY RESORT HOTEL

As someone who loves to experiment with sex, I read *Penthouse* Variations because it gives me lots of great ideas. I am the events coordinator at a small resort hotel in Barbados, and I am sometimes approached to set up a "special" event. Couples come to the islands for a little rest and relaxation, and occasionally dare to do things they would never consider doing at home. An island vacation seems to be tacit permission to experiment, and I'm just happy that I'm here to help.

Julie and Martin were looking for that kind of adventure when they arrived. She was gorgeous, in her midtwenties, with long, blonde hair and a perfect figure. Her husband was older, with hair just beginning to gray at the temples. Checking the register, I discovered that they would be staying for a week.

I saw them again in the bar that night. He was boldly playing with her thighs through her long dress, spreading the slit apart to expose her legs to the other patrons. She would giggle and push his hand away, modestly covering up, only for him to do it again a few minutes later. Soon they got up to dance, his hands roaming over her body.

I knew right away that I wanted to meet them. Approaching their table with a round of drinks on the house, I casually commented on their displays of affection. Instead of acting embarrassed, they told me their story.

They had gotten married five years earlier, soon after he had been cashiered from the navy, and they were now on their second honeymoon. Martin had been around the world and known many women. Julie had only been with her husband, and now she wanted to experiment a little. They thought that this vacation would be the perfect opportunity for her to explore one of her sexual fantasies. What Julie wanted to do was fuck another man while her husband watched and possibly joined in.

Not one to shy away from an opportunity like this, I flirted with Julie openly for the rest of the evening. Running into them the next day by the pool, Julie's skimpy bikini only reconfirmed my desire to be their sexual guinea pig. It didn't look as if they had found anyone else yet, so I broached the idea and they quickly agreed. "Come to my suite tonight," I said, giving Julie's hand a little squeeze. "I promise that you can leave at any time if you change your mind."

That evening, I sent flowers and a bottle of champagne to their room with a note saying that I would be in my suite all night, awaiting their arrival. I changed into my robe and sipped a scotch as I waited. They arrived around nine-thirty, and when I opened the door I noticed that Martin was carrying a video camera. Seeing my glance, he commented that this was one sightseeing excursion he definitely wanted caught on tape.

He went in to set up his tripod as Julie stood in the doorway for a moment, giving me a chance to take a good look at her. She was dressed in a long white skirt and a sheer top that just barely exposed her rosy nipples. We talked for a moment as Martin made himself comfortable in a chair by the bed.

While Julie was in the bathroom, I dimmed the lights, put on some soft music, and set a glass of champagne on the nightstand for her and poured two more for Martin and myself. I sat down on the bed and made small talk with Martin as we waited for his wife's return. The door soon swung open and Julie stood framed by the light from the bathroom. She was wearing a full-length nightgown, but the sheerness of the silky fabric made it seem as though she were wearing the skimpiest piece of lingerie.

I beckoned her to the bed and she sat down on the edge, for the first time seeming a little nervous. While her back was to me, I opened my robe and slipped it off. Leaning forward, I brushed her hair aside and nuzzled the back of her neck, whispering for her to take the champagne. She seemed startled by my closeness but gradually eased into the sensation of my mouth on her warm skin. She tasted so sweet. As she sipped her drink, I caressed her through the gown, the silky negligee whispering against her smooth flesh.

I moved toward her earlobe and took it gently between my lips. Her breathing became heavier and I sensed that she was starting to relax and respond to my attentions. Easing her back, I sought out our first kiss, barely brushing her lips, then opening my mouth wider to search out her tongue with mine. As she fell back into my arms, she began exploring my naked body. Her hand stroked my thigh with a soft, almost imperceptible touch.

Gently placing her down on the bed, I kissed her throat, shoulders, and her breasts, slowly and methodically. Very slowly, I nuzzled down her cleavage, exposing more of her breasts as I unbuttoned the front of her gown. Her hand lazily caressed my face as I journeyed downward. She gasped with surprise as I caught her nipple between my lips and teased it to attention, then moved to her other breast and repeated the tonguing.

I slipped my hand down to her mound, stimulating it through the silk of her gown. Soon she had her legs spread wide, yielding every inch of her most intimate depths to my probing fingers. I flipped up the nightgown to expose her wet pussy as I glanced at her husband to see his reaction. I could tell he was enjoying the scene before him, because he had removed his pants and was stroking his erection with the hand not holding the video camera.

At my bidding Martin approached the bed. He and the camera were capturing every intimate detail, and as he zoomed in on us I buried my head between Julie's legs and found her clit with my lips. I fanned my tongue rapidly over that tender button as she pressed her pussy into my mouth. Martin zeroed in on her dripping cunt as it gaped open under my tender attack. Small groans escaped her lips as I brought her close to orgasm, then backed off before she could come. Her frustration grew as she forgot Martin and the camera and knew only her intense need for release.

My mouth was dripping with her juices as I worked my way back up her body. She moved into position below me, arching her hips so that her cunt was directly beneath my cock. I teased her for a moment, just barely sliding the tip between the lips of her pussy, then pulling back out. I moved higher, positioning my cock over her mouth while I began to stimulate her clit with my hand. She swallowed me hungrily, and soon I was cradling her head as I slowly fucked that hot mouth. By this point,

Martin had removed the rest of his clothes and was on the bed with us, catching every minute of the act on tape.

I felt my orgasm beginning to build, but before I came I wanted to put on a good show for Martin and his camera. I pulled out of Julie's mouth and moved between her legs, placing her hand on my firm cock. "Guide me in," I whispered, my cock several inches above her pussy. She angled me toward her opening and lifted her hips high.

When she had slipped her wet pussy over the head of my cock, I held that position for a moment, savoring the feel of her warmth around me. Looking deeply into her eyes I thrust home, and immediately her first orgasm of the night washed over her. All the while Martin was at the foot of the bed, his camera tightly focused on this intimate act his wife was committing. Julie came again and again before I let go, flooding her with my sperm. Our juices ran thickly down the crack of her ass, mine and hers, commingled for the camera.

As I rolled over, Martin immediately slipped into my place and I picked up the camera to continue filming. The rolling motion of Julie's hungry hips hardly missed a beat between the thrusts of my cock and the newly energized thrusts of her husband. She was lost in a sexual frenzy that kept the three of us going until well after midnight.

The next night we watched the videotape, an erotic tribute to Julie's awakening, and I don't think any of us was surprised when we all ended up back in bed. In fact, we spent almost every night of their vacation together, and I was as sorry as they were when it came time for them to leave. Fortunately for me, new guests arrive at the resort every day.   —*J.Y., Via E-Mail* ○┱■

COUPLE FALLS IN LOVE ALL OVER AGAIN
DURING WEEKEND IDYLL

Four years ago, after a decade of living and working in what my husband often referred to as "urban chaos," he and I decided to abandon the corporate rat race and go into business for ourselves. As we both loved books of all kinds, we decided to open a small bookstore in a quaint village upstate we had visited several times and enjoyed immensely. We knew we'd be working hard, longer hours, perhaps, than what we'd had to put in with our city jobs, but we would be doing something we both enjoyed in a clean, quiet community. We were giving up frantic for relaxed, trading in hurry-up-and-do-it-now for take-it-nice-and-easy.

More important, we'd be spending so much more time together. No more would we have to practically schedule an appointment to see each other. "We might get sick and tired of each other," my husband would sometimes say with a grin. "After all, we'll be together twenty-four hours a day, seven days a week. Can we stand the strain?" I would respond with, "Well, we'll just have to cope as best we can, darling," thinking how great it was going to be having my man around all the time. Little did we know that we would eventually come to understand that it is indeed possible to have too much of a good thing.

In the beginning everything was great, with Thomas and I having fun learning to be small business owners while at the same time getting comfortable in the small house we had purchased after unloading our city condo. It was all so new and exciting, we hardly even knew we were tired at the end of each long day. But then, as time went by and we settled into a comfortable routine, a certain uneasiness crept into our relationship. Thomas and I were together all the time, and while familiarity certainly didn't breed contempt, it did, much to our dismay, cast a pall over how we related to each other. Where once we would have tackled a problem with good cheer, now we tended to blame each other for it. Hours would pass in the store when we did not say a single word to each other, and this pattern carried over to home, where we would each go our separate way as if thankful for the time alone. Our lovemaking, like our relationship, became routine, with both of us going through the motions in a seeming hurry to get it over with.

I was becoming increasingly concerned where all this was headed when fate stepped in to save the day—perhaps even a relationship. A promising young author we had befriended published his first novel, and while not a runaway best seller, it did well enough to earn him a nice book contract with a major publisher. By way of thanking us for our support and encouragement, he offered us the use of a beach house he had purchased with his newfound prosperity. Thomas brightened considerably at this opportunity, as did I, thinking that it could only help to get away from things for a weekend.

The following Friday morning we tossed our luggage into the SUV and began the three-hour drive to the Hamptons. Thanks to our author friend's detailed directions we had no trouble finding the beach house, which, to my amazement, was more like a mini-estate off the Atlantic Ocean than the cozy beachfront property we had expected. Beautifully, if sparsely, furnished, it had a deck that wrapped around three sides and large windows offering magnificent views. There was a sunken living room, a decent-size kitchen, a bathroom, a dining area, and a large bedroom that overlooked the Atlantic. And to top it off, our author friend had stocked the refrigerator for us and left several bottles of wine for our enjoyment.

"Wow!" was all either my husband or I could say.

After a bite to eat, Thomas and I donned our swimsuits and went for a dip in the ocean. Within minutes of swimming and frolicking in the ocean, I felt like a new person, invigorated by this total change of scene as well as the refreshing chill of the water. I could tell from the look on my husband's face that he, too, was enjoying himself. As we splashed each other, I tried to remember the last time I'd seen him this frisky.

We spent the balance of that afternoon lazing on the beautiful deck, not talking all that much, really, but every so often turning to smile at each other as we sipped our wine coolers. For the first time in a long time I was getting genuinely turned on by my mate. Seeing him there, stretched out on the chaise longue, I renewed my appreciation of his fine physique and the special appeal of his bearded face. "This is really nice, isn't it?" he said at one point. "Very," I answered, returning his little smile.

That evening, on the deck, Thomas grilled the swordfish our author friend had left in the fridge for us while I prepared a complementary salad, all of which we washed down with a fine white wine. Later, more relaxed and at peace with the world—and each other—than we had been in some time, we took a walk along the beach. Almost tentatively, as if he wasn't sure I'd appreciate it, Thomas reached for my hand.

My heart jumped a bit as I accepted it eagerly, and hand in hand, we continued our walk. Conversation, which so recently had seemed a formidable task, flowed easily, as did the smiles and laughs, and by the time we started back to the house I was more than ready to make love. It had been ages, I thought, since I'd wanted my husband so bad.

Still holding hands, we entered the house wordlessly—two minds with but a single thought—we quietly made our way to the bedroom.

Our pace quickened considerably as we started removing our clothes, and by the time we fell into bed we were like a pair of newlyweds on their honeymoon, moaning and gasping with pleasure as we groped and kissed each other with a passion neither of us had felt in so long.

Thomas went down on me, licking, sucking, and kissing my soaking pussy as if tasting it for the first time, which is pretty much how I tended to his mighty hard-on some twenty minutes later, after I'd come not once but twice from his magical tonguing of my cunt. I'd almost forgotten how much I enjoyed sucking on him, how thrilling it was to take him deep, until his hairy balls were resting on my chin and he was making these funny little sounds in his throat.

The fucking that followed was wonderful, spirited and joyous, not at all like the mechanical, let's-do-it-and-get-it-over-with sex we'd engaged in during the previous months. We started off missionary style, with Thomas alternating between long, slow strokes and short, fast ones, and then I got on top, riding my man like a rodeo cowgirl, relishing every inch of his cock as I bounced up and down in it while he held fast to my heavy breasts.

We finished doggy-fashion, our favorite position, with Thomas giving my round butt a good smack every so often as he plowed into me from behind, which is something he knows only propels me closer to orgasm. We came within seconds of each other, Thomas announcing his climax with a guttural moan while I let loose a shrill shriek of total delight, my happy pussy contracting wildly around my man's spurting cock.

Already we were coming back, I thought happily as I drifted off to sleep in my husband's strong arms. Here in this idyllic setting we were rediscovering each other, learning anew what it was we found so special about each other in the first place. And we had two days to go!

Saturday and Sunday were just as satisfying, with lots of hand-holding, kissing, and enthusiastic sex. After a day spent relaxing on the deck and swimming in the ocean, we drove into East Hampton for a delicious steak dinner at a charming little restaurant. Then it was back home for a nightcap on the deck under a full moon as in the distance the ocean waves lapped at the shore. Later, in bed, we went after each other as if possessed. So aroused was I that I let my husband penetrate me anally, something we seldom did even in the early years of our marriage. I came so hard I thought for a moment that I'd pass out.

Sunday we drove to Southampton for brunch and to browse among the many charming shops on Main Street. We bought ice cream cones and enjoyed them on a sidewalk bench as we people-watched. And then it was back to the beach house, where we changed into our swimsuits for a dip in the ocean before dinner, with Thomas again playing chef by grilling our food on the deck. Then, as a fitting conclusion to this magnificent holiday, during which dormant feelings of love and desire had been reawakened in my husband and me, we had sex on the beach. Right on the beach, mind you, on a blanket, under the stars. It was so romantic yet exciting at the same time.

Thomas and I returned home refreshed, rejuvenated, and eager to get back to our little business. Yes, we'd be together twenty-four hours a day, and wasn't that just grand.   —*E.M., Wilton, Connecticut* ⊶◼

SMALL-TOWN COUPLE SAMPLES A VARIETY
OF BIG-CITY THRILLS

When I handed over the dollar bill for the raffle, I never thought that I would win anything. At least I'm helping out the needy, I told myself, and then didn't think of it again until about a week later, when Carol called me and told me that I'd won.

"Won what?" I asked, in the middle of cooking dinner for myself and Sam and having no idea what she was talking about.

"The raffle," she replied. "An all-expenses-paid weekend in New York City, including airfare. Don't tell me you forgot!" After I'd hung up with Carol, I called Sam into the kitchen and told him to start packing. We were going to New York City!

On the flight there, Sam and I argued almost the entire way about what to do our first day. I wanted to go shopping, especially at all the big department stores, but he was set on seeing the sights. However, when we got to the hotel, our argument was put on hold, since we were both so overwhelmed.

We were on the twenty-first floor, with a beautiful view of the skyscrapers and the river to the west. Windows lined one entire wall, so from the king-size bed it was like we were floating in the air. I couldn't believe that there were buildings even higher than ours, but Sam was most fascinated by the bathroom. At his beckoning,

I went in to check it out. It had a huge whirlpool bathtub that was big enough for the both of us, and the room even had its own phone extension. Now that's luxury!

Deciding that New York could wait, Sam and I filled the tub instead. We climbed in as the warm water swirled around us and settled back, glad to relax after the long, uncomfortable flight. I sat between Sam's legs and he massaged my shoulders and upper arms, occasionally bringing his hands around to caress my breasts. As my nipples hardened so did his cock, which I could feel prodding the small of my back.

I turned around in the tub so that I was facing Sam, my legs bent over his thighs and my feet flat on the bottom. I reached for his cock and pumped it a few times in my fist, watching as my husband closed his eyes and pursed his lips. Then, with my hand firmly around the base of his shaft, I lifted myself and managed to guide him into my slick cunt.

I slid down his member until I reached the root. Then I balanced myself on Sam's shoulders and began bobbing up and down in the water. I felt the soft pouch of his balls flatten against my ass on each downward stroke, and his glans scraping along the inner walls of my vagina. Sam grasped my hips to guide me, and we built a steady rhythm that grew faster and faster.

Water splashed over the side of the tub as our movements grew more frenetic. My large breasts bounced as we fucked, and Sam leaned forward to suck a nipple into his mouth. He bit down slightly and I gasped, feeling that slight pain race straight to my pussy. My orgasm loomed closer and closer as he moved his mouth to the other breast to lick, suck, and nibble that nipple. Finally I tensed, my knees pressed against his sides as I was gripped by my orgasm, and I leaned against Sam and bit down on his shoulder. This triggered Sam's release, and within seconds I could feel warm liquid inside my body as well as around it. He pumped me full of his sperm, clasping my body tightly to his until his cock was totally spent.

Our coupling in the bathroom had left us happy but tired, so we chose to stay in that night and take advantage of room service rather than dress and find a restaurant. Besides, our package included reservations at the recently renovated world-famous Russian Tea Room the next night, so we figured we'd wait until then for our gourmet meal.

The next day we were up bright and early, ready to explore the Big Apple. Everything was just so romantic. We went to the top of the Empire State Building and the view just about took my breath away. You can't see anything like that where we come from! Then I wanted to see a Broadway play, but Sam talked me into the Circle Line tour, and I'm sure glad he did. It was a beautiful spring day, and the boat trip was a definite treat. After that we were starving, so we headed to the Russian Tea Room for dinner. We ate Chicken Kiev, washed down with lots of vodka. Everything was wonderful, but looking at the prices on our menus, I was glad that this meal was included in our prize!

After dinner we went to Central Park for a hansom carriage ride under the stars. Sam thought it was silly and sentimental of me to want to do that, but once we got going, I could tell that he enjoyed it just as much as I did. But that may be because when the driver wasn't looking,

I reached over and fondled Sam's cock through the front of his slacks. Soon we were necking in the back of the carriage, oblivious to the world around us, and it felt a little like a scene in a movie. I caressed Sam's erection as we rode, and he squeezed my breast in his hand, bringing my nipple to life with a stroke of his fingertips. By the time the ride was over we were both hot and eager to get back to the hotel.

We hailed a cab, and after a few passed us by, one finally stopped. Sam gave the driver the name of the hotel and then we got back to our kissing, not caring what the cabby saw. I explored Sam's mouth with my tongue as he thumbed my nipples, making me wet and ready for his invasion when we got back to our room. Reaching between his thighs, I cupped his balls in my palm and felt them throb, and I hoped we'd get to the hotel soon. The trip was taking longer than I expected, and I wondered if the driver was lost.

We finally got to our hotel, and by then I suspected that we'd purposely been driven out of our way, but I didn't care, I just wanted to get Sam into bed. The wait for the elevator was agonizing, and when it finally came we were the only passengers, which was lucky because we were able to keep the flame of passion alive by kissing and fondling each other for the twenty-floor ride. At the door to our room Sam fumbled with the card key, and as soon as the light turned green we fell inside, leaving a trail of clothing behind us as we made our way to the bed.

The bedspread had been turned down, so we threw it to the floor, along with the mints that had been left on our pillows. Once the bed was clear Sam and I got down to business. He pushed me back, then dove into my pussy with his tongue, licking and sucking my moist folds and my clit until I was writhing in ecstasy. Then he filled me with his fingers, pumping what felt like at least three of them in and out of my cunt as he lapped at my sex. I pinched my nipples, gasping, as I raced toward my climax, desperate to come.

Finally, my husband pulled his fingers out of my cunt and slid them into my asshole. They were moist enough from my pussy for his easy entrance, and he only had to thrust two or three times before my body was jerking all over the bed as my orgasm finally hit me like a ton of bricks.

I slowly came down from my sexual high and unclenched my fingers, letting go of the handfuls of sheet that I hadn't even noticed I'd been grasping, and pulled Sam up on top of me. I opened my legs wide for him, eager to have his cock inside me. To my surprise he flipped me over, so I got up on my hands and knees so he could fuck me from behind. I felt him line up his cockhead with my sopping canal and push through my opening. Then, with one strong thrust, he sank his cock home, burying his shaft to the root.

Sam kneaded my fleshy buttocks as he pumped into me. His shaft ran along the walls of my vagina and stimulated my clitoris with each forward thrust. Soon my cries were mingling with his grunts, our orgasms climbing simultaneously. His movements quickened as he slammed into me, his balls bouncing against my thighs. Just then he stopped, his fingers pressing holes into my asscheeks, his cock swelling and pumping inside me. As he filled me with his cream I came as well, my pussy milking him of the last drops of warm semen.

Sam slid out of me and we lay back on the large mattress. "Whew," Sam exhaled, "this city sure is invigorating. What do you want to do tomorrow?" I just smiled and said that I didn't know. My thoughts hadn't been on sightseeing, or New York at all. I had just realized that the next morning someone else would have to make the bed!

—*D.W., Norman, Oklahoma* ⊶▪

AN AMERICAN GIRL WITH HER CUTE NEW PAL KEEPS WARM IN ICELAND

My best friend, Sam, a travel agent, offered me a week-long vacation to anywhere as a birthday gift this year. When I chose Reykjavik, Iceland, he looked at me like I was crazy, especially since I wanted to go in January. "What are you thinking, Viv?" he asked. "Why would you go somewhere called Iceland in the dead of winter?" I just shrugged, unable to explain my fascination to him. Well, it turned out I'd picked the right time to go, as Reykjavik had been chosen as one of nine European cities of culture for the year 2000, and its festivities would be kicking off just as I arrived.

Our overnight flight arrived on Friday morning. I checked in, then after a hearty breakfast from the hotel buffet I bundled up and headed outside. Finding that some sort of warm spell had hit, I stuffed my hat in my bag and hopped on a bus. As part of the celebration all bus rides were free that day, which was good because one of the first things I had discovered about Iceland was that it could be really expensive. I took a seat next to a woman dressed as a clown doing magic tricks. Seeing the confusion on my face, a guy behind me dressed as a troll explained that they were art students who were there to entertain the passengers as part of the day's festivities.

I spent that day seeing the sights. There were goings-on everywhere, including the opening of a fifty-year-old

time capsule and open houses at many museums and
artists' studios. By dinnertime I was exhausted and decided to head back to the hotel for a nap before hitting
some clubs that night. The troll I'd met that morning was
on my bus again, and he was just heading home, so we
started to chat. Aron was funny and nice, a little flirtatious, and when he took off his mask I was delighted to
discover that he was also cute.

When the bus stopped in front of my hotel, Aron got
off with me and invited me to dinner. That week also
began the ancient festival of Poori, and Aron said that I'd
be remiss if I didn't pay a visit to a feast. As much as I
wanted to rest, there was no way I was going to pass up
the chance of attending a traditional Icelandic celebration
with an adorable Icelandic guy. Aaron said he had to run
home to drop off his mask, so I invited him to leave it inside my hotel room.

Once there we had barely dropped our stuff on the
floor and taken off our jackets when Aron wrapped his
arms around my waist and pulled me in for a kiss. As I
kissed him back, Aron slipped his chilly hands down my
back and under my pants to cup my asscheeks, causing
me to shiver. He laughed, saying, "Here in Iceland we
have many ways to keep warm."

Deciding that "when in Rome," I slid my hands under
his waistband and caressed his firm ass. After that, things
got hot very quickly as Aron backed me over to the bed
and we fell on it. He found his way under my sweater,
pushing my bra up over my breasts to play with my nipples, then heading back below the belt. As he made quick
work of my jeans, I unzipped his fly and pulled out his
cock, warming it in my hands.

Pulling away, I shimmied down the bed to take his prick between my lips. He groaned as my tongue swabbed the crown, then slid all the way down his shaft. My nose was soon buried in his pubic hair and he moaned my name as I bobbed up and down over his erection. Then, hardly missing a beat, I swung around so that my pussy hovered over Aron's face.

Aron reached up and grabbed my ass to pull me into his mouth. He teasingly sucked on my labia, then swirled his tongue lightly over my sex. Needing more, I ground my pussy against his mouth as I continued sucking on his cock and massaging his balls in my palm. In response, Aron's tongue finally found my clit. My body jerked and my thighs pressed firmly against his ears as he helped trigger my orgasm, then sent me even higher by fucking me with his stiffened tongue.

I shuddered through my climax as I sucked Aron's cock even harder, though I barely managed to retain a hold on it. Through my orgasmic haze I noticed Aron tense almost imperceptibly, and seconds later I was rewarded with a mouthful of warm come. His fingers bored into my ass as I swallowed shot after shot, and when he was finished he turned me around so that I faced him as we cuddled.

We relaxed together for a moment, until Aron noticed the time. We had about half an hour to get to his friend's house, so we took a quick shower together, bundled up, and then hit the streets again. As we walked, I was amazed at the clear, starry night sky, already dark although it was only about six o'clock.

Gunnar and his wife, Helga, had laid out a huge buffet of Icelandic delicacies for their feast, which I had learned was called a *porrablot*. Luckily I'm not a very picky eater, because many of the dishes were really unusual. I sampled *skyrhákarl,* putrefied shark meat, and *slátur,* which is sort of like Scottish haggis, and washed it all down with a caraway schnapps called Brennivín, known to the locals as "black death." After a sip I understood why, and finished the rest of my meal with a glass of Coke. The only dish I passed over was something called *svio,* which was a singed sheep's head cut in half lengthwise. I just couldn't get past those eyes staring up at me.

The night was a lot of fun. Everyone ate and drank a lot, and we sang and danced. After we'd had dessert and coffee Aron invited me back to his house, just a few doors away, for a final shot of Brennivín. Once again I pretended to like the stuff, but was glad when Aron put the bottle aside and pulled me onto his lap.

We started kissing, slowly and passionately. Aron slipped his tongue between my lips and mine met his eagerly. In front of a blazing fire we caressed one another, becoming better accustomed with each other's body. I loved Aron's slender form and the layer of pale curls that covered his chest, and he seemed to delight in my small breasts, which fit perfectly in his hands. He rubbed my nipples softly, gently, his touch growing more intense when I reached down to fondle the growing bulge between his legs.

I undid his pants and pulled out his erection, cradling it in my hand as I slipped down to the floor. Taking Aron's cock into my mouth, I gave it a few good sucks before releasing it and standing up. As I hiked up my skirt, Aron slipped off my shoes and drew down my tights, putting them both aside. Then we each removed our sweaters and I straddled his lap.

Balancing on my knees in the large armchair, I lowered myself onto Aron's cock as he suckled my nipples. When I was fully impaled on his length, he grasped me by the hips and helped me move up and down. My speed built as my juices slickened his shaft. Throwing my head back, I gasped, loving the feel of his cock deep inside of me as his tongue danced over my breasts.

We established a rhythm, my body bouncing over Aron's as he rose up to meet me on my descent. When my orgasm began to boil I moved faster, spurring it on. Our movements became frantic, though still not swift enough for Aron. Holding me tightly around the waist, he picked me up, and while I was still posted on his cock, he laid me down on the rug in front of the fireplace.

I threw my legs over Aron's back as he covered my face and neck with kisses. Reaching between us, he found my clit with his thumb and rubbed little circles over it, faster and faster, until my body exploded like a ton of dynamite. I grabbed hold of his waist as though it were the only thing tethering me to earth, screaming as my cunt contracted around his dick. The look on Aron's face as he pounded into me, his balls slapping against my ass and his sweat spattering across my breasts, is one I will always remember. It was a mixture of concentration, extreme pleasure, and frustration, and I knew he was close.

Grabbing his sac, I gave it a squeeze, inducing the beginning of the end. He thrust in once more, hard, and his entire body went rigid. Inside me, his cock remained still for a split second as a liquid warmth shot deep into my body. As he came he quickly pulled out, and then the sticky semen dripped down the crack of my ass as he plunged back in. Finally, he collapsed on top of me, sated.

We dozed off in front of the fire, and at some point during the night he must have woken and carried me to his bedroom, because the next morning I found myself in a large feather bed under a patchwork quilt. Aron brought me a steaming mug of coffee and a plate piled high with pancakes, made from an old family recipe.

I couldn't believe my luck. I'd traveled all the way to Iceland and found a man who was not only a terrific fuck but also a fabulous cook. Later that morning we went over to my hotel where I checked out and picked up my stuff, and I spent the rest of my stay with Aron. I was sad to leave, but after a year's worth of long-distance calls and short trips abroad for both of us, I am now married to Aron and happily settled in Reykjavik, living out all my fantasies. And lucky for me, I can still get *Penthouse* Variations by subscribing to it online!

—*V.T., Via E-Mail*

MAN VISITING MEXICO SPENDS AMAZING
NIGHT WITH THREE HOT GIRLS

The last thing I expected to hear in a Mexican beachfront cantina was a young female voice calling my name. I looked up from my book to see a remarkably beautiful woman with coal-black hair waving her arms. She was sitting a few tables over with two equally attractive ladies, all of them clad in micro bikinis and flaunting the bronze glow that spoke of hours under the tropical sun. She jumped to her feet and ran over, chirping happily. I decided that if I did not know this sexy wench, I certainly wanted to.

She was all smiles, giggles, and gams—long, sexy, golden legs that drew my eyes like magnets and steered them to unseen treasures barely hidden behind the bright yellow thong of her bikini. I was suddenly thankful my lap was concealed by the table. She grinned at my inability to remember her name and helpfully gave me a hint. She shamelessly shoved her bare, curvy hip in my eager face and moved aside a piece of nearly nonexistent bikini.

A flood of warm blood and warm memories rushed in as I recognized the little pink birthmark on her buttock. "Jenny!" I growled happily.

I suggested that she better explain to her friends, but she laughed that they already knew about the birthmark and me. We traded stories, discovering that we were both still single. Then Jenny's two tasty companions joined us. Envy darkened every male eye in the place. I was surrounded by three of the most gorgeous females on the beach.

Zoe was a statuesque brunette with hair down to her tight, round buns, and Debbie was the petite blonde with breasts that were earnestly struggling to escape her bikini top. It was more temptation than any mortal should have to endure. It appeared they were all down here because Zoe, a travel agent, got a lot of free perks and had invited the other two along. We talked for an hour before we parted company, promising that we would get together before our holidays were up.

I slept badly that night, probably due to the incredible hard-on produced by the thoughts of the three beauties and the memories of my first acquaintance with Jenny's famous birthmark. I finally got up, showered, and decided to go out for a walk.

Like resort towns everywhere, this one was still lively well after midnight. I wandered down to the Plaza Mayor and then toward the beach. Suddenly hands were over my eyes and a leg was wrapped around mine. Soft lips were kissing mine and another pair of arms was circling my waist under the hem of my loose shirt. No, I wasn't being mugged by an all-girl gang. It was Jenny and her friends, still up and having fun, delighted to see me.

There I stood, flabbergasted, in the midst of loud tourists and Mexican bars, with a hard-on that was doing its best to poke out of the leg of my shorts. My mind reeled. I wanted all three of these beauties—badly. Apparently they wanted me, too. My hands were as busy as theirs, cupping Jenny's warm mound as several hands groped for my raging cock.

Zoe had already flagged down a taxi, and in moments we were all piled into it. Jenny and Debbie and I were in the backseat, and Zoe was up front, charming the socks off the rotund driver with her fluent Spanish and her gorgeous bosom. He dropped us off at the hotel, refusing a tip but trying to grope Zoe's ass as she alighted.

Things got hot in the elevator. Zoe and Jenny were exchanging frantic, libidinous kisses while Debbie, on her knees in front of me, was nuzzling my hard cock through my shorts. Before we reached the third floor she had slipped her talented hand inside and taken a firm grip on my pulsing shaft.

The door to the girls' room had scarcely opened when Jenny wiggled out of her tube top, cupping her firm breasts in both hands. She offered them to me, aiming both stiff nipples at my face. I wordlessly obliged, taking one firmly between my lips, then the other. Jenny's breath caught and she seemed to shudder as I sucked and kneaded her soft flesh. Meanwhile, a pair of hands traveled up my bare thigh, pausing at my zipper, then tugging at it, and my fly fell open.

Moments later my shorts and briefs were around my ankles. The tip of my stiff cock suddenly entered something warm and moist, and I glanced down to see Debbie's blonde head bobbing as she sucked my cock. As I turned back to Jenny's rigid nipples, so responsive to every flick of my tongue, I heard Debbie say I could come in her mouth if I wanted to.

As my sensitive glans disappeared into her mouth, I became aware of other soft lips nibbling at my balls. Zoe tugged us toward the bed, and all three girls broke position long enough to shed their scanty clothing and escort me to the king-size bed, where they shoved me down roughly on my back.

Debbie's hot lips once again encircled my cock, and Jenny squatted over my face, her fingers spreading wide her moist pussy lips. I eagerly licked her slit and drove my tongue between her labia. She ground her cunt into my mouth, groaning and writhing. I sealed my lips around her swollen clitoris and sucked softly. She was lost in her spiraling passion and I was almost delirious with my own. My cock was deep in Debbie's throat, her nose hitting my pubic bone. She was kneading my balls with both hands, and I knew I would soon be pumping a huge load of creamy come down her throat.

Jenny craved Zoe's pussy, and the bed shook as Zoe straddled my head, standing to receive Jenny's tongue. Jenny was the first to come, her cries of pleasure muffled by Zoe's cunt, but unmistakable. They drove me over the edge, and Debbie must have recognized the signs, because she pulled my cock from her mouth and curled her fingers around its base, thwarting my ejaculation. I was suspended in that incredibly arousing instant just before spurting out my come. It was electrifying.

Suddenly Jenny scooted backward, pulling away from my mouth. I could feel Debbie's hand repositioning my cock and then it plunged into Jenny's hot, wet vagina. I threw back my head and howled as my balls ached to discharge their load, but Debbie still held it back. Jenny pumped up and down like a madwoman and I rammed my hips upward as Debbie began squeezing my scrotum.

Zoe took up Jen's place over my mouth and began to

suck Jenny's nipples. As her delectable sex settled over my tongue, I reached upward and found her full, round breasts. I tweaked her nipples as I drove my tongue into her, her musky juice anointing my face.

In spite of Debbie's finger clamp, I was seconds from a colossal orgasm. I was almost screaming, but Zoe's cunt had sealed itself over my mouth. Debbie released my cock and I exploded into Jenny's pussy, pounding away, my balls slapping up at her crotch even as I was moaning helplessly into the pink abyss of Zoe's warm cunt. Jenny stiffened and shuddered, her knees tight against my sides. She sat down hard, impaled on the whole length of my spurting cock, coming like crazy. At almost the same moment Zoe cried out and came, almost shaking herself off my avidly sucking mouth.

Jenny pushed herself off my slightly flagging penis and plunged it into her mouth. She flicked the tip with her tongue, lapping up the last of my come, and in almost no time I was hard again. One last lash of her tongue and it was replaced by Debbie's lush pussy. I could tell she was close by the way she rode my cock, her muscles working it with wicked precision.

Seconds later she burst into an impassioned cry that mingled with Zoe's as I brought her to another climax with my tongue. I pulled her down as Debbie rolled off me and sat her on my still-throbbing cock, bouncing Zoe up and down until I came in yet another torrent and collapsed, thoroughly spent.

What an amazing chance meeting with Jenny, and what an amazing climax to the whole vacation!

—*B.D., Butte, Montana*

SWAPPING IN THE TROPICS:
WHAT A WAY TO SPEND A VACATION

My new girlfriend, Sheila, and I recently went on our first vacation together. We boarded a plane for a chain of small islands in the South Pacific, and after a long flight and a short drive, we arrived at one island's largest and fanciest hotel. The trip had been tiring, so we decided to eat something light and have a drink in the hotel bar.

We showered and changed in our suite. Sheila wore a lightweight green dress that caressed the outline of her shapely body. It draped over her beautiful breasts, revealing the exactly location of her nipples, especially when they were hard.

We entered the bar and picked a table near the dance floor. A talented local band was playing as we shared a seafood salad, drank piña coladas, and talked to the couple seated next to us. Their names were Scott and Elise and they were from New Orleans. They invited us to hit some clubs with them, but by then my attention was focused totally on Sheila. The last time we'd danced, we'd kissed passionately, and my cock was fully erect. So we said good night to our new friends and walked out to the beach.

I thought my cock would burst by the time we found an isolated stretch of sand. I removed Sheila's dress and massaged her swollen nipples, causing her to throw back her head and sigh loudly. She then got on her knees and unfastened my shorts, letting them fall to the ground. Taking my cock in her mouth, she swallowed as much as she could. The sensation of the ocean breeze on my body as I watched her suck my dick was delightful. While kissing me passionately, Sheila pulled me down and pushed me onto my back, guiding my hardness into her wet pussy.

I fucked her slowly for a short time, and as our pace quickened, our climaxes raced forward. Our hearts beat rapidly as I pushed my cock into her tight cunt. As we exploded together, our moans were long and loud, almost drowned out by the surf. We kissed as we lay in the fine sand that felt cool beneath our hot bodies.

We caught our breath and then walked into the water to wash off before dressing and heading back to the hotel. We slept for the next nine hours, exhausted from the trip and our lovemaking. It was a wonderful way to start a vacation and it only got better from there.

The next morning we dressed and went downstairs for coffee and breakfast. Looking out the window, we could see the early sunbathers strolling along the beach, some wearing swimsuits, some not. We finished our coffee and then walked along the water's edge, holding hands and touching. Back on the beach, we chose a spot near Scott and Elise.

The sun was strong but a gentle breeze kept it from being too hot. I rubbed oil on Sheila's body, watching her nipples harden. As I massaged her breasts, we noticed that Elise was rubbing oil on Scott's cock, and they gave us a knowing smile. Aroused, I pulled Sheila from the blanket and walked with her into the blue-green water. As we kissed, our wet, naked bodies touching, I slid my fingers into her pussy. With one hand on my shoulder to steady herself, she stroked my cock with the other.

Scott and Elise were in the water not far from us and we knew they were doing the same thing. The ocean was calm, which helped me keep my balance as Sheila wrapped her legs around my waist. I pushed my cock into her cunt and moved in and out of her with a slow, sensual motion. Then I relaxed and let Sheila take me whatever way she wanted, enjoying each stroke of her pussy.

We heard Scott and Elise moan, and knowing that they had reached their climax excited us even more. Sheila's rhythm quickened as our arousal mounted. Unaware of anyone else around us, I was kissing Sheila passionately as we exploded together in an earth-shaking climax. After holding her for a few minutes, I pulled out and we walked back to the beach, rather shocked by what we had done. We took a nap on our blanket and before we left, we invited Scott and Elise for lunch the next day.

We met them the next afternoon at an outdoor café. As we ate, they told us about a boat that carried passengers to an island for a luau. We told them we were interested, so Scott used his cell phone to make the reservations.

We split up so that they could sightsee while we shopped. Then we met at the pier at seven o'clock and boarded the large boat. As we sailed, we drank mai tais while sitting in lounge chairs and watching the sunset. As the sun slipped below the horizon, Sheila's eyes sparkled in the final glimmering of light. Her hair blew softly in the gentle breeze and I could see the outline of her body through her sheer sundress.

We were soon in sight of the island and I could see what looked like a huge bonfire. As we got closer, we heard island music being played. The boat slipped into a dock where we eagerly disembarked and were led to the luau. Sheila and I walked with our arms around each other's waist and I could feel her warm body pressing against me.

The four of us were seated at a table and served a rather strong, sweet drink in coconut shells. The show consisted of ten male and female islanders dancing to the music in front of the fire. The night was beautiful—the sky was crystal clear and the stars sparkled like diamonds. After a while, the movements of the dancers became more sensuous, their bodies glowing in the firelight as they touched. You could feel the electricity in the air. I kissed Sheila's lips and could feel her pointy nipples through her silken top. Looking over at Scott and Elise, I could tell that they were affected by the highly erotic show. By the end of the evening, my cock was so hard that I thought it might burst.

We sailed back to the hotel and Scott and Elise invited us back to their room for a nightcap. I was anxious to get Sheila into bed so that I could fuck her silly, but she accepted before I could turn them down. From the gleam in her eye and the way she looked at Scott, I could tell she was thinking about doing more than just having a drink. To be honest, the thought of fucking sexy, blonde Elise had crossed my mind once or twice.

Luckily, we weren't the only ones feeling that way. As Scott poured drinks, Elise came over and sat very close to me on the couch. She brushed her large breasts against my arm, and when Sheila smiled her assent, she reached between my legs and rubbed my cock. Sheila took that as an invitation to do the same to Scott, so she walked across the room to where he stood at the bar and wrapped her arms around his waist from behind. Drinks were forgotten as Sheila ground her pussy against Scott's ass and Elise massaged my hard-on through my pants.

Elise and I began kissing, and over her shoulder I could see that Scott had turned around to embrace Sheila. He had slipped the straps of her dress off her shoulders and was beginning to unzip it. Meanwhile, Elise had undone my fly and was pulling out my cock. Her fingers felt great as they pumped my shaft, and I let out a low moan. My hand found its way up her dress, only to discover that she wasn't wearing any panties! I buried my fingers in her wetness, eliciting a groan from her.

Scott and Sheila had moved to the bed, and my girlfriend was completely naked by now. He was between her thighs, eating her sweet pussy. From the way she was crying out I could tell that she was enjoying it very much. I undressed Elise and began sucking on her nipples. Then she helped me out of my pants and I mounted her, positioning my cockhead at the opening of her cunt. I thrust inside and was swallowed to the balls in one quick motion.

I fucked Elise hard and fast, and my balls slapped against her ass as I looked up to see that Scott and Sheila were doing the same. Only Sheila was on top, bouncing up and down over his erection. His hands were on her tits, squeezing and rubbing, and the sight of that made me go crazy so I quickened my pace, which brought Elise to a tremendous orgasm. Her pussy clutched my cock and I came a minute later, filling her with come.

I finished just in time to see Sheila and Scott reach their climaxes as well. It was thrilling to see her so excited to be fucking another man. She moved faster and faster over his dick until finally she was coming, too. Then she pulled off and quickly moved down so that as Scott came, she could catch his come in her mouth. I could tell that was for my benefit, and let me tell you, I definitely appreciated it!

We went back to our own suite to sleep, but met them for breakfast the next day. In fact, we spent most of our vacation with Elise and Scott, and it couldn't have been more fun. When we left at the end of the week, we made plans to travel with them in the future. New friends and great sex—this trip turned out to be even better than we'd planned!   —*D.C., Greenfield, Ohio* ○┵■

FOR AN AMERICAN CUTIE IN COSTA RICA, SURF'S UP—AND SO IS HIS COCK

I was excited about traveling to Costa Rica with my friend and her boyfriend, but wasn't sure how I'd feel watching Pam and Rick canoodling during our vacation. Luckily, I got to do some of that myself with a hot Costa Rican surfer, whose strong hands and dexterous tongue made me shudder in orgasm after orgasm as we made memories of Costa Rica that I'll cherish forever.

Pam, Rick, and I arrived in the early afternoon at Juan Santamaria International Airport just outside the capital, San José. Eager to get to the beach, we picked up our rental car and began driving south on Route 2 toward Dominical, a small surfing town on the Pacific coast. I relaxed in the backseat as Rick drove along the two-lane roads. Just smelling the rain forest air from my rolled-down car window and seeing the lush greenery of the junglelike woods made me feel more peaceful already.

Pam and Rick are big-time surfers and Dominical beach is known for its strong rip currents that make for excellent, but dangerous, surfing conditions that only serious wave riders attempt. Not much of a surfer myself, I was looking forward to lounging on the beach and working on my tan while my friends waxed their surfboards and paddled out to sea.

When we pulled into town that night—after driving by the dirt road exit a few times, since there were no signs—we found a small hotel that offered us an apartment-style suite with two bedrooms, a kitchen, and hot water. Perfect. We checked in and then walked across the unpaved street to a *soda,* a cheap kind of lunch counter that was open all day. We ordered *casado,* a set bargain meal that is the Costa Rican specialty, consisting of rice, beans, chicken, and vegetables, that we washed down with *guanabana* shakes. *Delicioso!*

Then we freshened up and asked the hotel owner where we could get some beers. She explained this was a one-strip town, so we walked down the road until we came upon a bar decorated in a surfer theme. The tables were made out of surfboards, and there was some Elvis memorabilia to complete the scene.

We sat at the bar and ordered Bavarias, a Costa Rican brew, and toasted to a splendid vacation. Rick and Pam kissed passionately for a good few minutes as I sucked back my beer and tried to forget that I'd be sleeping alone. Luckily, that was about to change.

Since I've got very dark hair and eyes and have a year-round tan, I was easily mistaken for a *tica*—a native Costa Rican woman. So when a very sexy man—a *tico*—filled the empty seat next to me and started chatting in Spanish, I did my best to keep up the ruse that I was a native.

My Spanish didn't last long, but I found out that this hot stranger's name was Desi. That was short for Deside-rio, which means "desire," and this handsome stud couldn't have had a more appropriate name. He was tall with a lean, muscled build and a white-toothed smile that melted my heart. His white tank top and hunter-green board shorts illuminated the richly tanned skin of his arms and legs, which were both covered in downy, light blond hairs. He had soft brown eyes and curly, sun-bleached blond hair.

His English was good from having spent time in California, checking out the surf. Now Desi lived in Dominical, working in bars off and on to support his surfing lifestyle. I introduced him to Pam and Rick and we all drank another *cerveza* before Desi led me out onto the dance floor. Normally I'm reserved when it comes to dancing, but heck, I was on vacation, and Pam and Rick were urging me on.

First there were a couple of fast songs, but then some Spanish music came on and things started heating up. Desi pulled me close so that he had one thigh between my legs, rubbing along my inner thighs, inching up my short skirt a bit. I got flushed as the heat of his flesh brushed against my smooth, bare skin, making me wet with desire. It had been a while since I'd had a good fuck, and I knew it wouldn't be much longer until I got laid good and proper, Costa Rican style. Staring into my eyes, Desi asked in sexily accented English where I was staying and if we could go there, now.

Without thinking, I decided to go for it, my pussy weeping with need. I told Rick and Pam that I was leaving, and though it was barely a five-minute walk back, it took us nearly an hour since Desi kept stopping, pulling me close to him, pressing his body against mine, and kissing me. I could taste the ocean salt on his skin and smell the sea and sand in his hair, and it drove me wild.

I ran my hands under his tank top and pressed them against his chiseled chest. When he enveloped me in his strong arms the ache in my lower belly grew more intense. My whole body responded with chills to every touch of his hands and mouth as he groped me over my clothes, making me desperate for direct skin-to-skin contact. He kissed small circles on my neck, and despite the heat, chills ran up my spine.

When we made it to the room, I shoved all my stuff to the floor and pushed him onto the bed. Smiling, he looked up at me with those sweet brown eyes and held his arms out wide. I pounced on him like a wildcat, smothering his body with mine. Writhing against him, I felt the hardness of his cock pressing against his trunks. I eased off and pulled down his shorts, releasing what had to be one of the most perfect specimens of manhood I had ever seen.

My mouth watered at the sight of Desi's cock—long and thick and complete with fleshy foreskin. I moved up to kiss him on the lips and suck his tongue for a moment and then stripped off my T-shirt and skirt so that I stood before him in my thong and black bra. Reaching back, I unhooked my bra to release my large, full-nippled tits for his viewing pleasure. He groaned at my near nakedness as I slowly peeled off my thong and tossed it to him. He brought it to his nose and inhaled deeply, telling me in Spanish how much he loved my scent. His sexy words drove me crazy as my pussy dripped juice down my thighs.

I rubbed my cunt in wide circles against his thigh, dampening his flesh. He groaned, raising his head to stare into my eyes as I ground my clit into him.

"Mi amor," he breathed as he tossed back his head. I kissed him once more on the mouth, then lowered my lips over the head of his uncircumcised cock. Feeling the

fleshy hood slide back, I slithered my tongue all over the crown, slickening it with saliva. His callused hands reached for my hair, smoothing it down my naked back as I moaned over his cock and slowly slid the meaty shaft down my throat.

Desi's cock filled my face and I pursed my cheeks tightly around its width, suctioning as I wrapped my fingers around the base and then glided them up and down. He sighed when I loosened my grip to take him down my throat, and then I pulled off him to slather the head with long, hot strokes of my tongue.

I ground my clit hard against his thigh, rubbing my juicy pussy over him. "Come on me," he whispered, and I obeyed, riding his leg as I planted kisses on his cock. It felt so good to rub along his knee, my clit pounding each time I moved it over the hard part of his joint. Close to coming, I sped up my movements, thrusting my hips faster while urging his pole deeper down my throat.

Desi pressed his hands to the back of my head as an explosion burst from my cunt and I cried out around his twitching shaft. I pursed my lips around his cockhead as a rush of boiling hot come flooded my mouth and I drank it down, my pussy quivering through a mighty release.

When I'd swallowed all of his tasty cream, he lifted my head from his dick and pulled me to his face for a mouth-probing kiss. He sucked his juice off my lips and then flipped me onto my back, gliding his tongue down my body to my seething-hot center. With a few licks I came again, a deluge of my nectar gushing over his lips as I gripped his head tightly with my thighs, holding him there as I quaked through several orgasms.

We rested and must have fallen asleep because I remember waking to the sounds of my friends returning and seeing Pam poke her head through my door. Her face broadened into a smile when she saw the blissful look on mine.

The next day we—my new Latin lover included—went to the soda for *cafés con leche*. Desi explained that the best surf was in the afternoon, so that morning he took us in his Jeep a few miles out of town to a hidden waterfall only the locals knew about. We had to hike, but it was worth it when we saw the water cascading over a stone cliff into a pool sparkling in the sunlight. We went swimming and Desi showed me how to make a clay mixture that he spread over my face like a mask. We lay on the rocks with clay baking on our faces, our fingers intertwined, and I couldn't think of a moment when I'd felt more relaxed.

Washing off the clay, we joined Rick and Pam at the waterfall and cheered as we each took a turn climbing up the rocks and jumping in. It was an amazing morning followed by an incredible afternoon of surfing. I'd never realized how sexy surfing was until I watched my new lover get up on that board and ride waves like a hero returning to shore.

We treated Desi to dinner that night at a restaurant in town decorated with shiny, glittery mobiles in all different shapes that made it look like we were dining among the stars. After dancing, Desi took me back to his tiny apartment in the back of a surf shop where he fucked me all night long. The first entry of his cock into my soaking pussy nearly made me come, and each stroke kept me hovering on the brink of ecstasy until he pushed all the way inside my hot tunnel. I came on his gorgeous cock over and over again until the morning sun burst through his window.

We had to leave Dominical that day in order to make it to Manuel Antonio, our next destination. I'd been excited to see the monkeys and beaches, but I was reluctant to leave my surfer love behind. I promised Desi that my next trip will be to visit him, and as I count the days until I return to Dominical, my desire for him only grows stronger.   —*K.S., San Diego, California* ⚷■

JOURNALISM STUDENT GETS A LESSON IN SEX FROM AN OLDER, MORE EXPERIENCED REPORTER

I had been saving up my vacation days so that I could spend two weeks in Prague. I rented an apartment in Nove Mesto, or "New Town," which was cheaper than staying in a hotel and turned out to be nicer than my place at home. When I arrived I dropped off my stuff and set right out, determined not to let jet lag get the better of me. With my guidebook in my bag and a map in my hand I headed for the Old Town Square, which was ringed by outdoor cafés and completely packed with tourists. Needing some caffeine, I sat down at a table and soon a waiter came over to take my order.

"Kava?" I asked, pointing at the menu that was written in both Czech and English.

"American?" he replied, smiling at my attempt to speak his language. I nodded and he left, soon returning with my coffee, which I sipped as I took in the scene before me. It was just about noon, and the Astrological Clock was what had brought the crowds—every hour as the clock chimes, windows open to reveal small figures that spin by. Local legend has it that the clock's creator was blinded so that he couldn't make a similar one for another city. I know this because my waiter, Martin, felt a strong need to give the American a history of the area.

It was nothing I couldn't have read in my guidebook, but I didn't mind the intrusion because Martin was cute, with sandy-blond hair that fell in his eyes and a warm smile. Realizing that I was alone in a city where I did not know the language, I asked him for recommendations of things to see and do. Instead of giving me an answer, he offered to show me around. I accepted his invitation.

The next morning Martin met me at my apartment for my tour. The medieval castles and churches he took me to see were all beautiful and full of history. During our walk, we picked up sandwiches and ate lunch as all the locals seemed to do—on the go. We wandered around the city until I pleaded exhaustion. Still not entirely adapted to the time change, I definitely needed a rest. I asked Martin how close we were to home.

"To here," he replied, showing me on the map. It seemed extremely far, so he told me he had an idea. We'd crossed one of Prague's seven bridges to the other side of the Vltava River, not far from Kampa, a beautiful park with tree-shaded patches of grass. It was closer than the apartment, so I agreed it would be a good place to stop.

As Martin led me to a desolate area of the park, it occurred to me that he might have ulterior motives. I hoped so, because in addition to being attractive, he was funny and charming. Well, I was in luck—it appeared Martin's attentions weren't entirely innocent.

When we were comfortable on the grass he reached over and touched his fingertips to my cheek. It was an obvious move, but the romantic in me fell for it hook, line, and sinker, though I wondered how many other female tourists he had brought to this very spot. No matter, I thought to myself, because the wetness of my arousal was seeping through my panties and my pussy was starting to tingle.

Leaning forward, Martin brought his lips to mine, which opened, and his tongue slipped into my mouth. Our long, deep kiss turned my tingling into an ache, and I rolled over so that our bodies were touching. I mashed my cunt against the hard bulge in his pants to communicate my need. He pressed back and I could just barely detect the throbbing of his cock.

It was a weekday and not quite the height of the tourist season, so the park was practically deserted. Therefore, no one was around to see Martin slip his hand into my shorts to finger my wet pussy. I groaned into his mouth as his digit slid inside me and began pumping in and out. Meanwhile, my own hand had made its way into his pants and onto his stiff dick.

I wrapped my fingers around the thick shaft and pumped. Martin groaned as he finger-fucked me with more urgency and greater speed. We were both racing toward climax, writhing in the grass under the warm afternoon sun. I could see the spires of Prague above us and the statues of the Charles Bridge off in the distance. It doesn't get much more magical than this, I thought to myself as Martin slipped his hand under my shirt to caress my breast.

He nibbled my earlobe and neck as his fingers flew over my cunt. When they finally centered on my clit I bucked up, moaning and gasping for breath. I reached down to cup his balls and felt his body stiffen against mine as I gave them a good massage. Then I pumped his shaft again while caressing the tip of his cock with my thumb. He went wild, and his movements on my cunt came to a stop as he filled my hand with cream.

When that was done I moved impatiently against his

hand, demanding more attention. Martin kissed me and apologized before picking up where he'd left off. He stroked my clit just right and I was coming in mere seconds, drenching his hand with my juices so that we were both a sticky, sweaty mess. We cleaned up with some tissues that were in my bag and then walked back to my apartment.

We parted ways to shower and change, but made plans to meet up for dinner and drinks. I followed Martin's directions, which included a ride on the metro, and somehow managed to meet him on time at the spot he'd chosen. I felt way overdressed in my little black dress when I discovered that it was a traditional Czech beer hall and almost all of the other patrons, mostly men, were wearing jeans and work clothes.

We drank cheap—but good—beer and ate sausages and fried cheese. It seemed that every time I put down my empty mug, a waiter was right there with another to take its place. I'm not sure how many I had, but I was feeling pretty good by the time we left. Martin picked up the check, which I allowed him to do without my usual end-of-date argument because a tankard of pilsner costs the equivalent of thirty cents American, and our food cost only a little more, making this—and me—a pretty cheap date.

Afterward, we went back to his place, which was conveniently right around the corner. Once there, I again put up no argument as he led me to the bed and started to undress me. I let him strip me completely, and then I did the same to him. I ran my fingers over his muscled torso as I pushed off his shirt, then smiled when I pulled his pants down over his hips and his erection sprang right up in front of me. He was as ready to go as I was.

Martin kissed me for a moment before moving me onto my back and getting between my legs. Then he slid down until his mouth hovered above my pussy, and before I knew what was happening, his tongue was on my clit. I jumped at the contact and grasped the sheets as he began lapping at my cunt. He sucked at my lips and clit and pumped two fingers in and out of my hole. Soon he had me screaming with orgasm, his face awash in my juices.

It was his turn now, so I flipped us over to reverse our positions. With one huge gulp I swallowed his entire length and Martin threaded his fingers in my hair as my head bobbed up and down. His spongy cockhead repeatedly hit the back of my throat, and when I felt him swell inside my mouth, I knew he wouldn't last long. He was groaning and panting, yelling out my name, so I sucked harder, my chin brushing his balls on the downstroke. I deep-throated him with ease, and when his shaft throbbed against my tongue I prepared myself for the deluge. But instead of feeding me his load, Martin pulled his hard cock out of my mouth.

He grabbed me by the armpits and pulled me up so that I was on top of him and straddling his thighs, which left no question as to what he wanted next. I was so wet and his cock was so covered in saliva that my pussy enveloped his length easily as I sank down. When he was buried to the balls I began moving in a slow, rhythmic style that quickened as he began thrusting his hips upward to drive his cock into me. He grasped my asscheeks to guide me in the pace that he desired, our bodies slapping together.

Smiling up at me, Martin moved his hands from my ass to squeeze my tits and run his thumbs over my sensitive nipples. "Oh, God," I whispered as I was brought to the brink of orgasm. Then one breast was abandoned and a thumb pressed to my clit sent me over the edge. I threw back my head and groaned as my cunt contracted around Martin's cock. He followed suit a moment later and I could feel the warmth of his creamy release as his cock pulsed inside me.

I rose off of Martin's dick while he was still coming and quickly moved down to catch the rest of his load in my mouth. Then I licked my lips, settled in beside him, and fell asleep, still a little jet-lagged. I woke in the morning to the smell of fresh coffee, or *kava*, and then Martin dropped me off at my apartment before heading to work at the café.

Martin and I hung out a bunch of times while I was in Prague. As well as being a wonderful lover, he was also a very good tour guide, showing me parts of the city most tourists don't get to see. Meeting him made my trip to the Czech Republic even better than I had imagined, and I hope to get back there soon.

—*E.S., Baltimore, Maryland*

YOUNG LOVERS TRADE CHILL OF THE MIDWEST
FOR THE SENSUAL HEAT OF MARTINIQUE

Will and I had been planning on taking a warm-weather vacation together for months. We decided on Martinique when we heard of its incredible sailing and snorkeling, the island's active volcano, Mount Pelée, and its European flavor—a little bit of Paris in the Caribbean Sea. Will was also particularly intrigued by the thought of me sunbathing topless alongside stretches of other topless women on miles of soft, sandy beaches. And, I have to admit, I was excited by the idea, too.

We arrived at Martinique's only airport in the city of Lamentin—about twenty minutes from Fort-de-France, the capital—at midday and began the drive in our rental car to the resort along the southern coast. The immediate impact of the hot sun against our chilled Midwestern skin was almost overwhelming. We took the top down to get the full effect of the warm breeze, and then to get in the spirit of the island, Will convinced me to take my top down as well and expose my breasts to the sun for the first time.

We'd been traveling since early morning and this was our first chance to relax and be alone, and the drastic rise in temperature was causing a very obvious rise in Will's pants. Sitting bare-chested beside my handsome boyfriend, thousands of miles from home, made me excited and restless at the same time. I couldn't wait to feel his naked body pressed against mine, and I was squirming in my seat in anticipation.

Will took one hand off the steering wheel, which made me a little nervous considering the snakelike roads we were driving on, but then placed it on my exposed breast, and I felt soothed by his touch. We realized that there was no way we'd make it to the hotel without a pit stop, so Will pulled over to a row of frangipani trees on the side of the road and feverishly buried his face in my tits. He hungrily sucked on my nipples, teasing them with quick flicks of his tongue and then slower circles on the surrounding areolas. I was getting so wet, I reached for his zipper, ready to unleash his cock. Realizing what I was planning to do next, Will lifted his face from my chest and kissed me on the mouth while unexpectedly thrusting his hand between my legs, which made me gasp.

Under the shade of the frangipani, Will delved into my panties, deftly parting my slick labia and finding my already-throbbing clit. He pressed on it with increasing pressure as it hardened under his fingers. I was already almost coming when Will suddenly pulled down my jeans and panties and dove face first into my hot pussy. I nearly exploded when he positioned my clit between his teeth. He sucked and sucked on it as I covered his face in my overflowing juices as waves of pleasure deluged me. He slid two fingers inside me, and my vagina pulsated around them as my orgasm peaked and then gradually subsided, leaving me panting, quivering, and eager to make Will come, too.

I could taste my nectar on his lips as I licked them clean, and then the sea air that clung to his neck and the tender spot under his ear. Will moaned in delight when my tongue trailed its way down his lean body to his naked cock, and I took it wholly into my mouth. It quickly stiffened to full erection between my lips, and I sucked it with long, deep throaty motions that kept him groaning while he smoothed down my hair that was being blown around by the wind.

I rubbed his balls while humming my way up and down his shaft and nibbling at the cockhead. I could feel that last bit of expansion of his cock and then the stream of thick come that shot down my throat. I drew the last drops of it out of his member and then kissed him, mingling the taste of him with the fresh Caribbean air. We were in paradise.

When we finally arrived at the resort, after our delicious detour, we took a short nap, then a walk along the beach as the sun was setting. The pinks and golds of the sky met the turquoise blue of the water in a fantastic color display along the horizon. It was amazing feeling Will's arms around me and his warm breath on my neck as we gazed into the seemingly endless sea.

We were tempted to strip off our clothes and dive right into the water, but decided that we should get some dinner. Our sexual appetites had been temporarily sated, but we were still ravenous for food! So we shared a long passionate kiss and then headed to the dining room of the resort to satisfy our hunger.

And the island sure did offer us a feast—freshly caught fish, fruits in a rainbow of colors, free-flowing wines, and an array of French cheeses and warm baguettes. Will smeared a chunk of bread with Brie and slowly fed it to me. His fingers brushed against my lips as he eased in the large morsel, then dipped into my mouth, moistening themselves on my tongue. After I swallowed, I caught one of his fingertips between my teeth and bit down on it, savoring its buttery flavor. My tongue played with it, encircling it with wet warmth, sucking on it firmly. When I finally let him go, I breathed into his ear that I couldn't wait to have him inside me again.

As we headed back to our room to continue where our sensual eating game left off, Will pointed out the luminous reflection of moonlight on the water. We stopped to stare, and suddenly he had swept me up into his arms and was running into the water. He stopped when we were submerged to our waists and quickly stripped me of my drenched sarong and tank top. His own clothes seemed to fly off him, and soon we were completely naked and he was pulling me in deeper until only our heads and shoulders bobbed above the water's surface.

I wrapped my legs around his tapered torso and pressed my breasts tightly up against his chest, breathless and exhilarated from Will's spontaneous act. We kissed deeply and I started to devour the skin of his neck, sucking on his sensitive spot, hearing him moan in delight. I could feel his stiff cock slide against my slit, and easily, he slipped inside me. He began thrusting away at my cunt and I closed my eyes and arched my back so that my breasts were above water and bobbing in his face. He bit my nipples and I kept arching back so that his cock could go in deeper. It felt so incredible fucking him right there in the water.

I reached down and rubbed my clit while his shaft kept pounding me with pleasure-filled strokes. I was carried away by the moment and so close to coming. I dug my heels into Will's ass and gripped his waist firmly with my thighs, pulling him deeper and deeper into my open pussy.

As my orgasm was building, my pussy was getting hotter and hotter even in the cool water. While Will's demanding cock was pushing its length into my cunt, it ground against my engorged clit with each stroke in and out. Soon I erupted in the most overpowering orgasm of my life, forcing me to grab on to Will's back for support as my body started to shake and screams of ecstasy came out of my mouth.

My hot pussy contracted and clenched around Will's cock as it shot its hot load in a series of quick final thrusts that kept reigniting my fiery clit. When he finally slowed down, I relaxed the vise my legs had made around him and opened my eyes to the sky, noticing the moon glowing above us. Will looked up, too, and then directly at me and smiled. We kissed again and then entangled ourselves in a wet embrace. Martinique had already been explosive for us, even though Mount Pelée has not erupted in almost a hundred years!

We spent the rest of the days of our vacation sunbathing—topless, of course—and eyeing the other bare breasts on the beach, and then running off to our room when the sight of naked skin got us excited. And the rest of our nights? Well, we spent them pretty much reliving the first, all under the glorious light of the Martinique moon.   —*E.M., Dubuque, Iowa*

PASSION IN PORTUGAL—BACKPACKING BEAUTIES, JACKIE AND PAMELA, MEET MUSCULAR MARIO

Right after we'd graduated college, my friend Jackie and I spent our last few months of freedom backpacking through Western Europe. We'd been roommates for the last two years of school and shared almost everything: notes, clothes, and even the occasional lover. We were that close.

That was why our trip to Portugal was such a blast. Since we'd already done many of the major European cities—London, Paris, Madrid—we decided it was time for something a little more low-key, namely a beach. Our guidebook recommended the Estoril coast of Portugal, which boasted "Europe's largest casino." And, the book went on to mention, since the season was still off-peak, accommodations would be available and affordable.

We stayed in the town of Cascais, which was just a short walk up the coast from the town of Estoril. During the day we sunbathed on the beach. It was too cold to go in the water, but the sun was warm and quickly tanned our bodies and made us more relaxed than we'd been in weeks. Sightseeing and pub hopping can take a lot out of a girl. Our nights, however, were entirely different. We donned our finest clothes (which, since we were living out of our backpacks, weren't all that fine) and hit the casino for an evening of eating, gambling, and dancing. Casino Estoril has a number of rooms for dining and entertainment, complete with pretty showgirls, in addition to the gaming rooms.

On our second night on the Portuguese coast, we ate a late dinner at a Japanese restaurant and then hit the casino. We both started out in the slot machine room, then I decided to check out the roulette wheel while Jackie went to dance. So we split up, making plans to meet up later for a drink.

I didn't have much money, so my gambling for that evening didn't last long. I decided to head over to the Wonder Bar and find Jackie and hang out with a drink for a while. When I got there, I grabbed a martini and then found her on the dance floor and caught her eye. She gave me a smile loaded with meaning, so I took a close look at her partner. He was gorgeous, the embodiment of tall, dark, and handsome. As they danced, he grabbed her ass and pulled her against him. I could tell there was more going on there, so I gave her a signal that said "see you back at the hotel . . . maybe." Jackie signaled for me to stay. Maybe he has a friend, I thought, and found a place at the bar.

At the end of the song, Jackie and her friend came over to me. She introduced him as Mario and said that we'd been invited back to his place for a nightcap. He was even more attractive up close, and I could see his muscular arms and chest through his tight-fitting T-shirt. I wanted to go, but not if it meant that Jackie would not be getting laid that night. However, she gave me a wink that said there was more to this invitation than a round of drinks for us both, so I grabbed my purse and headed out with them.

Mario lived a few miles away from the casino, and he

drove us to his apartment. Once there, he poured us each a glass of port and we all got comfortable on the couch. After chatting for a few minutes, I got up to use the bathroom and when I returned, Jackie and Mario were making out on the couch. I cleared my throat to make my presence known, and without breaking the kiss, Mario patted the couch next to him, so I went and sat down.

Mario finally pulled away from Jackie and drew me toward him. Our open mouths met and his tongue searched out for mine. As the two of us kissed, I reached out to feel his bulging crotch and met with my friend's hand there. Together we caressed his dick as it hardened and grew, taking turns kissing him while he searched out our pussies. We were both wearing short skirts and had opted to go pantyless that night, so his was a pretty easy task.

By this point I was already wet, and I was sure that Jackie was as well. It had been a while since either of us had gotten laid because we'd been wrapped up in finishing college and then traveling. We'd discussed how good it would be to experience a nice hard cock once again, and now it looked like we'd get to do that, and together.

We both took off our shirts and then I unzipped Mario's jeans while Jackie pulled off his T-shirt. His chest was smooth and broad, and I watched my friend lean forward to tongue his pointy nipples. As she was taking care of the top half of his body, I turned to the bottom. His cock was now in my hand, warm and pulsing, so I lowered my head to take it into my mouth. It tasted a little salty from the sweat he'd worked up dancing, and I savored the taste as I covered each and every inch with my tongue. Mario just groaned as he thrust between my wide-stretched lips, soon hitting the back of my throat with his dick.

After I'd been sucking him for a few minutes, Mario tangled his hand in my hair and yanked my head up off his dick. He moved me onto the floor and roughly pushed up my skirt, then mounted me. Jackie helped him work off his jeans and soon his cock was poised at my slippery cunt. Taking his cock in her hand, Jackie guided it in, then played with my clitoris as Mario began to thrust. Sliding a hand up her skirt, I returned the favor, stoking her fire with my fingers while my Portuguese lover pounded into my pussy. It wasn't long before I was screaming out in ecstasy.

As soon as I'd finished coming, Mario withdrew from my cunt, then pulled Jackie on top of me so that our breasts were squashed together and our pussies touched. We kissed passionately as Mario took his place behind us, lining his cock up with my best friend's dripping hole. She moaned into my mouth as he slowly impaled her, and I could feel her whole body shake when his movements quickened.

Suddenly the movements stopped and Jackie was still, then a groan rose from deep in her throat and I knew that he was filling her ass with his cock. He couldn't possibly have known that anal sex was my friend's favorite, but I could see by the look on his face that he was also an aficionado of that act. His eyes were closed tight, sweat poured down his brow, and his mouth was open wide as he gasped in deep breaths of air. It seemed that he was going to come soon as well.

Jackie could barely hold our lip-lock now, so overwhelmed was she by the sensations Mario had created by shoving his hard dick in her ass. Her body was heavy on mine and it rubbed up against my clit, and soon I found myself once again reaching climax. I bucked up against Jackie, hoping to induce her orgasm as well. I guess it helped, because soon she was moaning her pleasure and then screaming for Mario to fuck her harder and come in her ass.

There was no way that Jackie's snug ass squeezing around his pistoning erection wasn't going to make him come, but he had other ideas as to how to do it. Pulling out of her, he rolled her off me so that we were lying side by side on the floor, our breasts heaving from our exertions, our legs wide open and ready. "Finger each other," he said in his wonderfully accented English, and as we complied he began pumping his dick in his hand.

With our arms crossed over our bodies, our fingers were hard at work on each other's clit, sometimes sliding down into each other's wet hole. Mario watched intently, his own hand busy at his cock, which looked angry and red as it jutted out from his washboard stomach. We put on quite a show for him, moaning, writhing, and licking our lips as we finger-fucked each other almost to completion. Without having to say anything, both Jackie and I knew what we were waiting for before we would come.

Mario moved up a bit so that he was on his knees, straddling Jackie's left leg and my right. His fist flew over his cock until finally he let out a huge groan and come shot from the tip. His pearly semen splattered all over our breasts and stomachs, and I even got a little bit in my hair. As this liquid warmth covered us, Jackie and I let go as well, gasping through clenched teeth as we came together. Then Mario collapsed on top of us, pulling us into his arms for one last embrace.

After a short while we got up and cleaned the come off our bodies. We dressed, and Mario gave us a lift back to our hostel. Exhausted, Jackie and I hit the sack immediately, though we stayed up late into the night talking and giggling about our experience with the Portuguese stud. Later, when we'd returned from our European adventure, we both agreed that our night in Estoril had been the best of the entire trip.

—*P.E., Los Angeles, California*

FISHERMAN MAKES SURE LOVELY ISLAND NATIVE IS NOT THE ONE WHO GOT AWAY

My buddy Bill and I had saved all year for what we expected to be our greatest fishing excursion to date. We were headed to Belize, a country the size of New Hampshire, in Central America. We arrived in Belize City early Monday morning, then boarded a small plane to the island known as Ambergris Caye. As we flew over the Atlantic, Bill pointed out how clear the water was. We could actually see an eagle ray swimming from the plane!

When we checked into the fishing lodge, we were so eager to get out on the water that we asked if there was a guide available for a couple of hours. It was as easy as that: We dropped our bags, grabbed our rods, and jumped on the boat. Heading straight out to a reef, we baited our hooks with the live yellowtail snappers we found in the boat's well. About sixty feet from the reef we began to see some action. Whatever was down there was biting our bait right in half!

My heart pounded as I finally snagged something. I battled with the fish for some time, with Bill and the guide cheering me on, as I landed my first barracuda of the week. We quickly learned that the waters were full of many amazing sea creatures, including jellyfish, conches, octopi, and starfish. We caught some snappers and another barracuda before heading back to the lodge.

Exhausted from our travels and our day spent in the

steamy Belize heat, we showered and turned in knowing it was going to be an eventful week.

We got an early start the next morning, opting to stay in the shallow water and fish for tarpon. The day proved even better than the last as we fly-fished, casting our lines about eighty feet into the clear water and pulling in what we had come for. The guide made us lunch right there on the shore, grilling fish straight from the ocean so we wouldn't miss any good fishing time. Bill got the biggest catch of the day, a forty-four pounder.

Back at the lodge we cleaned ourselves up and then ate an early Creole dinner. We made it to the small bar just in time for happy hour. This was my kind of place, decorated with dark paneling, fishing net, and plastic crabs and lobsters. The bar stools were filled with sunburned men drinking beer and trading fishing stories. Each man had an incredible tale about the one that got away.

I had just ordered another beer when I noticed an island beauty enter the bar. She had long black wavy hair and a deep, even tan. I checked to be sure I had remembered to put on a clean shirt. The last thing I ever expected was that I'd meet a woman on this trip. I hadn't even shaved in three days and my beard was growing in heavy. She walked up beside me and leaned over the bar to kiss the bartender on the cheek, then ordered a drink and sat down.

Her dark eyes were friendly as she nodded her head at a couple of guides sitting at a nearby table. Then she noticed my gaze. She smiled, knowing that I was staring at the shark's tooth that hung between her cleavage. Clutching the tooth in her hand, she leaned closer so that I could get a better look. My face was so close to her neck when she asked me if I had any luck at sea. It was all I could do to keep from licking the soft skin of her neck, but I controlled myself and sat back. I learned that her name was Marianna and she was a scuba instructor on the island. Belize has the largest living reef in the world, which makes it a popular spot for divers.

We talked for hours about our love of the sea and all the places we'd traveled. I noticed that she was really warming up to me, getting closer with every giggle. I had completely forgotten about Bill when he tapped me on the shoulder and told me he was turning in for the night. "Don't stay out too late," he said with a knowing smile. "We'll be getting up at dawn."

Marianna was wearing a loose-fitting tank top and a long sarong. As she sat back on the stool, her thigh peeked out through the slit. I ran my hand over her skin and was suddenly aware of my callused, stained hands, but she put me at ease by covering it with hers and inviting me for a romantic walk on the beach.

We walked along the sand, holding our sandals and each other's hand. The water washed over our toes in the darkness and my cock throbbed. I wanted to make love to her in the worst way. I looked around to see if we were alone, but she already knew we were. Pressing her body against mine, Marianna kissed me gently. I could taste the salt from the misty air on our lips as I slipped my tongue into her mouth.

Marianna pulled my shirt from my pants, took it off, then let it fly a few feet away from us. She kissed my neck and chest, sucking my nipples into her mouth and nipping at them with her teeth. I moaned my appreciation but then, without warning, the beauty before me stopped her licking and stepped back. She untied her sarong to reveal her swimmer's body. Her belly was flat, her thighs hard, and her calves thin and muscular. She was wearing a little black G-string that made her tan lines visible. I could tell that her bathing suits weren't much bigger.

With the sarong flattened out on the sand, she lay her half-naked body on top of it and offered herself to me. In one motion I pulled off my shorts and boxers, then dropped to my knees to remove what little she was still wearing. When she was naked save for the shark-tooth necklace, I explored her whole body, starting with the nape of her neck and working my way down. I kissed the curve of her breasts as she lay on her back, her nipples erect between my fingers. I sucked one into my mouth and pulled my head back. She seemed to like that and pulled my head hard against her bosom.

My hard cock was throbbing against her thigh and she was trying to shift her hips in a way to align it with her pussy. Reaching between her legs, I ran my fingers along her slit. She was so wet that I easily slid two fingers into her. Marianna was quick to follow my lead, reaching down to grasp my hard-on.

She mimicked my speed, working my cock as slowly as I was finger-fucking her, just enjoying the sensations of a new lover. When Marianna began to grind her hips hard against my fingers, I sped up my motions, fucking her harder. I knew she wanted to come as she pumped my cock faster. I grunted, trying to hold back my climax and rolled my thumb over her clit. Marianna began to shake uncontrollably and I knew she was coming hard. Her orgasm was so powerful that she released my cock and raised her hands to her head, pushing her hair away from her face, then wrapping her arms around my neck.

The side of my face was pressed against her chest as she came down. We were both sweating and I gave her a second to relax. As soon as her breathing slowed, Marianna pulled me up to face her. She took my cock in her hand again and aligned it with her pussy. Thrusting my hips forward, I was enveloped by her sex, her wiry pubic hairs tickling my shaft as I moved in and out of her. Marianna wrapped her legs around my back and met me thrust for thrust. She was sinking deeper into the sand, so I placed my hands under her head to make her more comfortable.

We were locked together on the beach, the ocean lapping at the shore behind us. After a while Marianna flipped me over and began to ride my cock. I reached up and cupped her breasts in my hands, pinching her nipples and spurring her to move faster. I was right on the brink and she was moving faster, slamming herself down against my pelvis on every stroke.

Lost in my lust, I took hold of her hips to manipulate her movements. My balls tightened and I shot my come into Marianna as she shook and came on top of me. She collapsed on my chest and I thrust two more times into her to get the last of my come out.

After a little rest we got up and attempted to brush the sand off one another. It was still stuck to our skin, but I was so tired after I walked her home that I just fell into bed back at the lodge. It seemed as if I had just hit the pillow when Bill woke me. As I got dressed, Bill laughed at all the sand in my bed.

I fell asleep on the boat a couple of times that morning, but it didn't matter. After all, I was on vacation and I wouldn't have wanted to recount another story about the one that got away.

—*K.D., Tallahassee, Florida*

A SPARK OF DESIRE BECOMES A RAGING FIRE
WHEN OLD FRIENDS REUNITE IN ENGLAND

It had been about eight years since I'd seen the University of Oxford and my friend Edward. He was an old friend from my post-college days when I spent a year doing research at Oxford. We had remained casual friends and kept in touch via quippy postcards and e-mail. Since we'd both become college professors of literature, albeit on opposite sides of the Atlantic, we had a lot in common, and often discussed our various research projects along with exchanging anecdotes about our course loads, students, and the other faculty.

I had been very attracted to him when we were students together, and our friendship managed to survive into our more settled adult lives. So, when I told Edward about a trip to Paris to visit a girlfriend, he insisted, in a most gentlemanly way, that I take an extra couple of days and visit him and our old haunts around Oxford.

I had to admit that the thought of sipping Pimm's and lemonade in the pubs of Oxford was deliciously appealing, as was the thought of seeing Edward again. All through the five-hour plane ride and then the hour-and-a-half coach ride from Heathrow to Oxford—driving on the opposite side of the road, of course—I was imagining how he must have changed in the past few years. When I stepped off the coach, I recognized him instantly: tall and lean, with a neatly trimmed goatee, longish brown hair that befits a British professor, and a contagious smile that stopped me dead in my tracks. I remembered the slender man in my memories and was pleased that time had been more than kind to him.

When he caught sight of my long blonde hair, which hasn't changed much in the years we've been apart, he rushed toward me and immediately swept all five feet eight inches of me into his arms so that my feet were high in the air. He kissed me long and deep, the way I had secretly always hoped he would, sending a shiver of excitement up and down my body. A delightful tingling of sexual anticipation lingered deep in my pussy and I was so glad I had decided to accept his invitation.

Edward picked up my bags and grabbed me by the hand, eager to get our visit under way. Recognizing that I was probably tired from the flight, he led me the few blocks to his house. Every stone-faced building and every brick-lined street seemed to hold a wonderful memory for me, and I was embraced by a romantic sense of nostalgia, as if I were stepping back into my past.

We entered his charming three-story house, and Edward carried my bags up the stairs to his bedroom. There was a vase full of red roses by the bay window, and an enormous four-poster dark wooden bed handsomely made with stark white sheets, two large fluffy pillows, and a thick, white downy duvet. It looked so romantic and inviting after my long flight that I just dove, head-first, right into it. Edward laughed, watching me roll around in the plush bed, and offered to leave me alone so I could get some rest.

Admittedly, I was tired from my journey, but the excitement of seeing him and being back in Oxford, with all

of its history and many wonderful memories, had my
mind reeling. I knew that sleep was just about impossible
for me. Instead, as Edward walked through the door and
closed it behind him, I got up on my knees and called out
to him to come to me. I reached out my hand and he
clasped it in his, smoothing his thumb over mine. It was
a delicate gesture that made my juices flow wildly with
desire for him. I pulled him closer to me and continued
where our first kiss had left off.

His tongue gently prodded mine, but after a few moments a surge of passion swelled through us and the soft
prodding quickly became a hard and deep probing of our
lips, tongues, and mouths. He eased me back on the lux-
uriant bed and covered my face and neck with passionate
kisses. He took my face in his hands and told me in his
most sexy English accent to relax and enjoy every second
of the pleasure he was about to give me. He said that he
had been waiting years to touch me and had played this
very moment over and over again in his mind.

I was consumed with lust for him, so overwhelmed
that I could only nod my agreement. He slowly unbuttoned my blouse and slid it off my shoulders, revealing
my lacy white bra. My nipples pointed sharply through
the lace and he pinched one between his fingers through
the thin fabric. I arched my back as he slid his hands beneath me and undid my bra, letting my large breasts spill
out. He cupped them together with both hands and slowly
licked up and down my cleavage, then teased me with
flicks of his tongue on my hardened nipples, alternating
between them. Still holding my breasts together, he
buried his face between my mounds of flesh, rubbing his

soft goatee against my tender skin, the prickles of which made my nipples almost ache with stiffness.

Edward now leaned back and stripped off his clothes, revealing a smooth chest and a trim waist. I was pleasantly surprised to see that his cock was both long and thick, and I felt my pussy drip for want of it.

I slid off my jeans and my damp panties and he tossed them aside, sliding his whole naked body tightly up against mine until our eyes met, only inches apart. He slowly traced my lips with his fingers, then dipped them into my mouth for me to suck. After coating them heavily with my saliva, he kissed me again while sliding his moistened fingers down my flat stomach to the soft fur of my pussy. His fingers met the hot wetness of my vagina as he spread my labia and rubbed my honeyed slit. His mouth was firmly pressed against mine as he fondled my pussy lips and then centered his fingers on my aroused clitoris. I squealed as he slipped two fingers into my cunt while resting his thumb on my clit, and then slowly rubbed my ruby gem as his fingers explored my wet tunnel.

I felt the climax building within me, and my breathing grew fast and heavy. His fingers thrust in and out of my pussy as I was overtaken by an orgasm that left me shaking. Edward smiled at me as I came, and before I had fully recovered, he moved down my body and kissed my clit, holding it between his lips, sending me right away into another crashing orgasm. He stroked my pussy lovingly and kissed my thighs as I came back down to earth.

I had come so hard I could barely move, but my desire to taste his cock gave me energy I didn't know I had. I slid out from under him and put him on his back, hoping to give him as royal a treatment as he'd given me. I licked his ears, and the sides of his neck, nibbling on his smooth skin as I worked my way down his body to the hairless expanse of his chest. I lingered over his nipples, taking each of them into my mouth as he groaned deeply with every movement of my tongue.

I felt his cock hard against my leg, almost begging for attention, and as soon as I moved down and took it in my warm mouth, the head spread even wider, filling my face with delicious cock. I grabbed his balls with my hand and lightly scratched them with my fingernails, feeling his member swell even larger in my mouth. Soon, I was sliding my full lips up and down the length of him, taking as much of his cock as I could deep down my throat, then sucking upward and licking long circles around the cock-head, dipping my tongue tip into his slit.

As I took him deep in my mouth again, I reached my hand under his ass and stroked between his asscheeks until my finger slid into his asshole. I thrust my finger in and out of his ass in sync with him fucking my face, and together our fucking got faster and more intense until he lurched forward and shot a huge load of creamy come down my throat, while letting out an animal cry of ecstasy. I swallowed down his sweet liquid, but a little bubble of it dribbled onto my lips and he leaned forward to gently lick it off me.

We drifted off to sleep wrapped in each other's arms. Several hours later, when I awoke, my pussy quivered, still wanting the feel of Edward's cock plunging into its warm depths. I roused him from sleep by climbing on top of him and stroking his shaft to a rock-hard erection. I lowered my juicy cunt over his cock and eased myself down on it as his newly opened eyes met mine. It felt incredible as his large member filled me up as I rocked back and forth on it, rubbing my engorged clit against him with every movement. Fully awake, he grasped me by the hips and pulled me harder down on him, speeding up the pace of our fucking, surging deeper into my hot, squishy pussy.

I was riding him hard, bringing us closer and closer, and feeling him grow bigger and harder inside me as he thrust away at my hungry pussy. Our moans of pleasure collided, filling the room with the sounds of sex. Edward reached up and clutched both of my breasts in his hands, playing his fingers gently over my nipples, giving me exactly what I needed to send an orgasm surging through me. I felt my pussy walls grab hold of his cock and squeeze it as I came. The tight embrace of my pussy around his shaft sent him into a frenzy, his stomach muscles tightening as his cock shot streams of hot come deep inside me.

I fell over onto his chest, exhausted and completely satisfied. We slept all the way through teatime and supper, not actually rousing ourselves from bed until our hunger got the better of us and we rushed out for some jacket potatoes and kebabs from the street vendor on the corner.

Edward and I spent the rest of the days of my visit exploring around Oxford. First off was visiting a few of the more beautiful colleges, making it to about five of the thirty-nine, and walking around enjoying the magnificent architecture and landmarks of the "city of dreaming spires," in particular, the incredible Radcliffe Camera and the world-renowned Bodleian Library. We went to the

Covered Market for fresh sandwiches and a number of pubs for fine ale and cider, including one where C. S. Lewis spent much of his time. We revisited places from our friendly past and created new special places for our romantic future. And our nights were spent with even more fun exploring each other in bed.

When I finally made it to Paris to see my girlfriend, I was too tired and too much in love with Edward to meet Frenchmen. I did, however, have a wonderful time shopping for sexy French lingerie, which I plan to wear on my next visit to Oxford, which can't happen soon enough for me. —*J.P., Cedar Rapids, Iowa* ⊶▄

G'DAY, MATE! SEASONED TRAVELER HAS
SPLENDID TIME IN AUSTRALIA

I needed a vacation. Working six, sometimes seven days a week trying to put my latest venture, a dot.com retailer, on solid footing had left me with jangled nerves and turned my usually pleasant disposition into something bordering on evil. Oh, yeah, I needed a break, all right. But where to go to lift my spirits and rekindle my love of life? That was the question. And the answer didn't come easily.

Fortunately, my success in the business world at an early age has given me a certain financial security, permitting me to indulge in interesting risky ventures, like the dot.com, and enabling me to travel extensively. Down through the years, whether it was for business or pleasure, I've visited almost all of Europe, many of the more popular tropical islands, most of Asia, and much of North and South America. Which is why I couldn't decide where to go when I realized I simply had to get away from it all for a while.

And then, quite by chance, I got a call from a friend I hadn't spoken to in a while who, in the course of our conversation, told me of the fabulous time he'd had in Sydney, Australia, during the Olympic Games in 2000. "It's the most beautiful city in the world," he opined enthusiastically. "And the beaches in Australia are just fabulous.

And the women? Pal, we're talking drop-dead gorgeous. You've got to check it out sometime."

My old buddy made a trip to Sydney sound so appealing that by the time we hung up I was already mentally arranging my work schedule so I could take ten days off in January, which I now knew was summer in Australia. In the days that followed I grew more and more excited about my first-ever visit to the land "down under," as I recalled the inviting views of Australia from telecasts during the Olympics. Yeah, this was going to be all right, I thought.

All right? Man, it was nothing less than fabulous. Perhaps the best time I've had anywhere in all of my travels. From the moment my plane touched down at Kingsford Smith International Airport to the day I had to fly home, I was kept enthralled by the beauty and charm of Sydney and its magnificent harbor, in particular. Out and about soon after checking into my hotel, I strolled along Circular Quay for a bit before returning to the hotel restaurant to enjoy a meal of Sydney rock oysters and John Dory, the tasty local fish, washed down with a couple of pints of Australian beer, of course. I fell asleep that night thinking that my vacation was off to a very good start.

I've always been an adventurous sort, tirelessly exploring the myriad attractions of whatever place I happen to be visiting, wanting to make the very most of my time there, and it was no different in Australia. The sheer vastness of the country proved a challenge, yet during my stay I managed to visit, among other sites, The Rocks, the oldest part of Sydney with its cobbled streets and colonial buildings, the world-famous Sydney Opera House, and Taronga Zoo, home to some of the country's unique animals. I even spent a day in the Australian Outback, where I got to see Uluru, or Ayers Rock, a site sacred to the local Aborigines. This great red rock towers into the sky and changes hue at dawn and sunset. Really impressive. But it's Bondi Beach that holds the best memories for me, for that's where I met Elaine.

It was my third time on the grand dame of Sydney's beaches and I was taking it all in, the glorious sunshine, the crystal-clear water, and perhaps most of all, the bevy of beautiful, bikini-clad women who seemed to be everywhere I looked. These Australian beach bunnies were, as my friend had said, absolutely stunning women, with their perfectly proportioned, well-tanned bodies—true eye candy for all red-blooded men, yours truly being one of them.

I was looking through a pamphlet on the Sydney Opera House when I was approached by a stunning woman of about my age, forty, in a one-piece blue bathing suit that neatly complemented her shoulder-length honey-blonde hair. She had only to open her mouth to ask me directions to the Opera House and I knew that here was a woman of style and keen intellect. Instantly attracted to her, I wasted no time engaging her in conversation, which eventually led to her gathering all of her things and bringing them over to my blanket. My pulse quickened at the possibility that she was as taken with me as I was with her.

We talked and talked and talked some more, neither one of us in any hurry to part company. And then suddenly it was dinnertime. "I was at a lovely place the other night," enthused Elaine, a never-married lawyer from New York whose mature sexiness I was beginning to find irresistible. "Would you like to . . ." Her voice trailed off as she gave me a small smile. "I'd love to," I said.

Elaine was staying at the Sheraton Wentworth, too, so we hurried back to the hotel and our respective rooms to change, then met in the lobby at the time we had agreed upon. Then it was off to Watson's Bay for a fabulous seafood dinner at Doyles on the Beach, after which I took Elaine to a pub in The Rocks that I had discovered my second night in Sydney. Here, amid some delightful characters, we downed a few beers before heading back to our hotel. The evening had been full of intelligent talk and laughter, making me feel good all over, and I didn't want it to end. Happily, neither did Elaine, which is why we ended up in my hotel room stripping off our clothes in a frenzy of lust and then toppling into the large bed in a feverish embrace, our lips mashing together passionately.

Emitting a little growl, Elaine dove immediately for my cock, which was already at full attention and throbbing in readiness. "Did I tell you that sucking cock is one of my favorite things?" she said, smiling up at me from between my legs. Before I could respond she was sucking me into her mouth, sexy slurping sounds accompanying this delightful exercise and making me all the hotter for her. Up and down her beautiful head bobbed, her lips gliding smoothly over my saliva-coated shaft, her tongue doing a merry dance on the sensitive underside.

At one point, she took her mouth off me and smiled broadly. "See how you like this?" she said with a wink. And the next thing I knew she had the entire length of my cock in her lovely throat, which almost made me lose it then and there. Damn, this woman was hot!

Several minutes later, realizing I needed to calm down

a bit and eager to taste my delightful new friend, I got her spread-eagled on the bed and commenced a serious tonguing of her fragrant pussy, lapping up her freely flowing juices like a thirsty adventurer who had gotten himself lost in the Outback and suddenly come upon an oasis. Elaine responded to my efforts with sighs and gasps and moans, her hips arching off the bed when I started in on her clit. Soon her hands were flying down to my head to hold it in place, my face mashed against her sizzling cunt, as she shuddered through an obviously very strong orgasm.

"God, you're good," she said when she could speak. "Where did you learn to eat pussy like that?" I told her I could ask her the same thing about sucking cock. We laughed then, realizing, I think, that past history was of no importance here, that it could even dampen desire, and neither one of us wanted that. This time was for us and us alone.

Staring down at my rigid member, Elaine said, "You'll fuck my pussy first and then my ass. Doggy-style. Okay."

Okay? Where had this marvelous woman been all my life? No sooner had she assumed a position with her head down, cradled between her arms, and her sweet bottom up than I was maneuvering into place behind her and sending my cock home in one strong, easy stroke. "Oh, yes, oh, yes," Elaine said excitedly. "Pound me, Chad. Make me feel it."

I did my best to comply, tossing finesse to the wind as I thrust hard and fast into my wonderful friend's warm, wet pussy and heard her answering gasps and cries of pleasure. As her climax drew near, she asked—no, she demanded—that I spank her, and I was quick to respond.

Several hard smacks to her uptilted bottom, on the left and right cheeks, had her shrieking into the bedsheet and then, very soon thereafter, crying out that she was coming. "My ass now," she said to me breathlessly. "Stick it in my ass."

Adjusting my position so I had the correct angle, I put the head of my excited cock at Elaine's pretty anus and pressed home. My cock slid into her rear passage with relative ease and then I was sawing in and out of her ass, again slapping her cheeks at her command. "Oh, yes, it feels so good in my ass," Elaine whimpered into the bedsheet. "Fuck me hard, lover."

I did as asked, drilling my cock into Elaine's bottom again and again as she alternately thanked me and urged me on to even greater effort. And then I simply could hold off no longer and blasted my seed into that curvaceous ass of hers, at which point Elaine informed me in a husky voice that she was coming, too. Thoroughly drained, I fell forward onto her back, my weight flattening her on the bed. We lay like that, breathing hard, with me desperately trying to remember the last time I'd had such a good time in bed.

Happily, Elaine and I had several more good times in bed before it was time for us to part company. We had one of those sweet, sad partings at the airport you see in the movies, kissing passionately and then waving good-bye as Elaine hurried off to catch her flight to New York and I took a cab back to my hotel. A day and a half later I was back at the airport, this time to board a plane back to California.

I spent the entire trip home wondering if I'd ever see Elaine again, mulling over the possible answers to all those questions a man asks himself when he's found someone special but isn't positive she feels the same. And I had all but convinced myself that I'd never see Elaine again when I got home and went to my computer to check my mail. And there she was.

Her e-mail was rather lengthy, but what I focused on, what I feasted on, was "I miss you already. We have to figure out this East Coast–West Coast thing. And fast." I felt like I'd just won the lottery.

—*C.Y., Los Angeles, California* O⟶■

CURRYING FAVOR WITH A SPICY BEAUTY
IN BOMBAY, INDIA

I suppose I love India because that's where I met my wife. I was taking a graduate course in engineering at the University of Bombay, and she was spending a year touring South Asia. With her handmade clothes, she was a free-spirited hippie type at a time when most women wore power suits with shoulder pads. Not that I saw a lot of that in India, but Anna's laid-back attitude and wacky sense of humor were still a breath of fresh air.

We met one night on Chowpatty Beach. I was strolling among the fortune-tellers, magicians, and locals when I saw her at a *bhelpuri* stand, buying some of the crunchy snack. I was startled to hear an American accent, and it wasn't until about a block later, when she stopped to accuse me of following her, that I realized I was even walking.

I apologized and explained that it was because I hadn't heard an American voice in so long. Upon hearing that I lived in Bombay, Anna asked for suggestions of things to do and see.

"I'm afraid I won't be of much help," I replied. "I haven't really gotten a chance to look around."

"Not even Elephanta Island or the Hanging Gardens?" she exclaimed. When I shook my head no, she made me promise that I would take a weekend off and join her for a few days of sightseeing. There was no way I could refuse, and I didn't want to. With her long strawberry-blonde hair, freckled face, and curvy body, she was as cute as a button, and even if my better judgment said that I should stay in and prepare for midterms, my cock dictated otherwise.

I met Anna at her hotel early Saturday morning, and we set out on our tour of Bombay. We first hit the Pherozeshah Mehta Gardens, and smiled at the couples hidden among the topiary. That started a discussion about how bold Americans were, which continued as we boarded a red double-decker bus. We rode through the traffic-jammed streets to Kalbadevi, the outdoor bazaar with its crowded streets devoted to different products. There, Anna enjoyed the Zaveri Bazaar, which sold jewelry, while I was more interested in Chor Bazaar, or the "thieves' market," which sold pretty much anything, most of it junk.

Then we took a boat to Elephanta Island. Its main attraction was the temples and shrines carved out of caves, dating back to 600 A.D. The main cave depicted the Trimurti, celebrating the trinity of Lord Brahma, Vishnu, and Shiva. Many of the caves had dark inner cells, and it was in one of these that I first kissed the woman who later became my wife. I just had to take the chance, so in a dark corner of one of the caves, when no one else was around, I grabbed her hands and pulled her to me. She didn't resist, but threw her arms around my neck, tilting her face upward.

Our lips met in a long, sensuous kiss, her tongue slipping between my teeth to feel around. She felt warm and soft in my arms and tasted of berries, which somehow didn't surprise me. My cock thickened and grew large, throbbing when Anna rubbed against it. I had one hand at the small of her back and the other on her breast, playing my fingertips over her hard nipple. Anna moaned into my mouth and ground against me as I pinched her nub.

We were both on fire, but not because of the hot Indian sun baking the cave. I wanted to fuck Anna, and when she moaned, "Oh, God, do me, do me now," I knew we'd never make it back to her hotel or my dorm. It was around lunchtime, so the caves were pretty empty, but just to be sure I took a quick look around. Seeing no one, I slipped a hand up her light sundress, smiling when I encountered nothing but smooth pussy lips that were already damp. Going pantyless in a modest place like Bombay was exactly something a girl like Anna would do.

She grabbed my wrist and moved my hand over her mound, so I quickly abandoned my thoughts. Then I rubbed my palm slowly over her pussy, but Anna was impatient, spreading her legs wider so that my hand brushed against her clitoris. When I made circles over her clit with my fingertips, I felt Anna's body shake. Then she let out a small cry when I slipped two fingers into her dripping hole.

I finger-fucked her pussy with increasing speed, my movements facilitated by her natural lube. Anna was breathing so hard that she couldn't hold our kiss, so instead she moaned into my neck as she sucked and bit my skin. I wondered how my professor would react when I showed up in class on Monday with a big red splotch on my neck, but I didn't really care because just then Anna was scrabbling at my belt buckle.

With my pants around my ankles and my cock in Anna's hand, I thrust my fingers in and out of her cunt.

She pumped my dick in her fist, squeezing my balls with her other hand. I could tell she was coming when her movements stopped and her grasp on my shaft tightened. To send her over the top, I placed my thumb on her clit and pressed hard. She cried out as her cunt pulsed around my fingers and her clitoris twitched beneath my thumb. Then she fell to her knees, drained.

I reached down to help Anna up, but she pushed my hands away and knelt in front of my bobbing erection. Sticking out her tongue, she swiped at the head, and I groaned. As I leaned against the cool stone wall of the cave, her tongue strokes covered my entire length. When she opened her mouth wide and swallowed me, I held on to the back of her head and guided my dick down her throat.

Anna moved back and forth over my cock, my balls practically resting on her chin at times. She steadied herself by gripping my asscheeks, her fingers pressed into my flesh. As she drew her mouth off the tip of my cock, she'd stop and suck just that. Then she'd run her mouth back over my length, covering me with warm saliva.

I was coming within minutes; there was no way I could hold back. Anna was a talented cocksucker, and after a few more passes of her lips and tongue I was shooting buckets of semen down her throat. She swallowed it, smiling, then licked my cock and balls clean of what little come she'd missed.

I pulled Anna up to me, my now-soft cock flat against her belly. When we heard voices, we quickly got ourselves together and made our way back out to the light of day. Squinting in the sun's glare and giggling, we got on the boat and headed back to the mainland. We were both famished, so we stopped for a late lunch/early dinner at a small restaurant serving South Indian delicacies, since Anna is vegetarian.

Afterward, we went to a Bollywood cinema, which Anna insisted was a necessity when visiting Bombay. However, the four-hour film was entirely in Hindi, a language that neither of us really understood, so we spent most of it necking in the back row. Then we strolled down the promenade along Marine Drive, watching the sunset, and I think we shocked some of the natives with our display of public affection. We couldn't keep our hands off each other, so Anna suggested we head back to her hotel in South Bombay.

Anna let us in and we immediately fell to the bed, tearing off each other's clothes. I landed on my back and pulled Anna down on top of me, her pussy resting on my stomach as her plump breasts flattened against my chest. She gave me a kiss, and even after a spicy Indian meal, she still tasted like berries. My cock bobbed impatiently against her ass, wanting a taste of its own.

Needing it as badly as I did, Anna moved down to impale herself on my member, letting out a long sigh as her wet heat swallowed me inch by inch. When she reached the bottom, she drew herself up, then shoved right back down. As her cunt slid over my cock, her breasts were bouncing against her chest and her hair flew wildly around her face. I reached up to pinch and twist her nipples between my fingers and her face contorted in total bliss. I'm sure I had a similar expression gracing my own face, as I had never before felt anything as heavenly as when her ass rested against my balls after a hard shove downward.

We were both racing toward orgasm, but I wanted to prolong the experience of making love with this incredible woman. Lifting her off my cock, I positioned her on her hands and knees and moved behind her. Then I lined up my cockhead between her puffy labia and shoved inside. Anna lurched forward with the impact, but quickly recovered and jerked back, filling her cunt with my dick. She wanted to bring us to orgasm, but it was my turn to take control. I grabbed on to her hips and held her still, sawing in and out. My balls slapped against her thighs as I fucked her, and soon her canal closed in on my shaft. It held me so tight I could barely move, and so I let go, my balls unloading deep into her womb.

Anna spent the rest of her vacation with me, and we kept in touch after she left. When my Indian program was complete, I returned to the States to finish grad school. Anna moved to the city to be with me, and it wasn't long before we were married. We couldn't afford a honeymoon in Bombay, but we plan to get back there as soon as we can. However, whenever I come home after a long day of work and catch the succulent scent of curry, I know that my wife is in a sensual mood and it's going to be a wonderful night.

—*C.H., Bridgeport, Connecticut* O╍■

OF SUSHI, SAKE, AND STRIKEOUTS

There are two things I love most in this world, travel and baseball. So I try to combine the two as much as possible, like road-tripping to minor-league games and visiting as many of the classic stadiums as possible before they all disappear. I've even seen a few Mexican League games. But I'd never been to a baseball game in Japan.

That changed recently, when I was sent to Tokyo on business at the height of baseball season. So I packed a mitt as well as my laptop, and then I set out for the Far East, filled with excited anticipation for sushi, sake, and strikeouts. Well, I got all that, plus a whole lot more!

After the long flight I went straight to my hotel. I'd had my assistant book me into a *ryokan,* which is a traditional inn complete with futons, Japanese meals, and rice-paper walls, rather than the Western hotel where my associates were lodged. When I arrived, I asked the innkeeper about getting tickets for a ball game. Unfortunately, he knew about as much English as I knew Japanese and wasn't any help. Then came a voice from behind me.

"I can help you," said a woman in heavily accented English. Miki worked for the *ryokan,* and it was my good fortune that she spoke fluent English and knew a thing or two about baseball. She offered to get me tickets and said she would even show me around the city if I was interested.

Of course I was interested! Not only did I appreciate

Miki's help, but she was a beautiful woman, with large, dark eyes framed by feathery eyelashes, high cheekbones, and pouty lips. Her hair caught the light from above and glinted black and navy. She was petite but feminine, with firm breasts that were slightly on the smaller side of average. My cock hardened as I accepted her invitation, and I briefly wondered if this was a service offered to all the guests or if Miki had just taken a liking to me.

I met her later that night for dinner. She took me to a restaurant that specialized in *nabemono,* a stew that you cook at your table by dipping a variety of meats, vegetables, and noodles in a large pot of boiling broth. It was delicious, and we washed it down with Guinness, which is one of the most popular beers in Japan.

After dinner, I gave Miki a kiss on the cheek to say thank you. As I did, she turned her head and kissed me back—full on the lips! I was really very surprised. Although I was attracted to her, I'd never expected anything sexual to occur. Responding to Miki's advances, I embraced her tightly as her tongue slipped into my mouth. Her breasts pressed against my chest and I could feel her stiffened nipples.

Then she pulled away and hailed a passing cab to bring us back to her tiny apartment. I slipped off my shoes at the door, and the rest of my clothes followed soon after as she practically tore them off me. She also got naked in a hurry and then pulled me down onto her futon.

Miki lay on her back and I kissed my way first up one leg and then down the other, at which point I stopped to suck on her toes. Then I kissed back up her legs again.

Her thighs parted each time I got close to her sex, and her arousal was evident by the scent of her feminine musk and the dampness streaking her thighs. Bringing my mouth to her pussy, I softly licked each flower-petal lip before delving into her hot, wet center. She sat up and gripped my head tightly in her hands as I furiously ate her. I sucked her tiny pearl of a clit until she was crying out with joy, and when I made my tongue into a point and fucked her with it she squealed words I couldn't understand, but I think she was telling me she was coming.

Satiated, Miki slid into my arms and gave me a long, passionate kiss. Licking her own juices off her lips, Miki moved to my nipples and sucked each one in turn. I am highly sensitive there for a man, and she had me groaning and shaking within minutes. My cock had become painfully hard, and she finally took it in her mouth, enveloping my dick in a wet heat that sent my senses into overdrive. My balls twitched as I came just a few seconds later and shot my come down her throat. I couldn't believe I'd come so soon, especially since I had really wanted to fuck her beautiful pussy. Miki said that we would find time to make up for it and gave me a kiss. Then she took me back to the *ryokan* so I would be well rested for my morning meeting.

I was still pretty tired the next morning, but the meeting was a success regardless. I bagged a new client for my company, even though my thoughts were mostly with Miki. When I was done I went back to the inn, where I washed up and changed. Miki was meeting me a little while later to take me to a baseball game. The Yomiuri Giants, who are the most popular team in Tokyo, weren't playing that night, so she'd gotten tickets for the Nippon

Ham Fighters, another one of the city's four teams and, I was to learn, her favorite. I didn't care who we saw—I was just excited to be going.

We took the subway to the stadium, which was packed. Right from the beginning the experience was a little strange, as everything seemed familiar yet different. The concession stand sold sushi and dried fish snacks, and I bought a cup of fresh draft beer from a girl dispensing it from a keg strapped to her back. But most surprising was the passion of the fans—they were even louder than those in America, if you can believe that. Everyone had a noisemaker, which they'd use at the slightest provocation. Miki cheered louder than anyone else there, especially since the Fighters were winning. I got caught up in her excitement, which she often exhibited by squeezing my thigh or grabbing my upper arm. By the end of the game I was really turned on, and I conveyed this to her by giving her a long, hard kiss while grinding my hard-on against her crotch.

Luckily, Miki was as aroused as I was and ready to fuck, but we didn't want to take the time to go back to her place or the *ryokan*. Instead we went to what the Japanese call a "love hotel," which is an accommodation that charges by the hour. They don't pretend they don't know what you're there for, but it's really private, as payment is made through a curtain so that the clerk never sees your face. Apparently, this is a fairly common practice in Japan and lots of people use them. I found it just a little bit nasty, which only fueled my lustful desire.

We stripped as soon as we got inside our room, since knowing that the meter was ticking brought our excitement up another notch. This time we decided to forgo the oral sex and barely bothered with foreplay—I was leaving for Kyoto the next day and wanted to fuck Miki before I did. She clearly wanted it as badly as I did and got on her hands and knees, wagging her cute ass in invitation.

I knelt behind her and reached around to pinch her nipples until they became stiff points. I had my own "stiff point" aimed straight at her cunt, so I grabbed her hips and wedged my cockhead in her hole. Miki leaned back to impale herself on my cock and her pussy sucked me in, swallowing my entire length as I let out a long, deep groan. She felt wonderful, warm and wet and inviting, and I stayed completely still for a moment just enjoying the intense sensation.

But Miki was unable to wait any longer, and her eyes flashed as she glanced back and demanded that I fuck her. "Yes, ma'am!" I laughed and began thrusting my hips back and forth, repeatedly filling her with my bloated cock. She shouted "More!" and so I gave it to her, pounding into her sweet pussy until we were bouncing on the bed and my balls were slapping against her upper thighs.

As I fucked her, Miki started cursing in Japanese again. At least I think she was cursing, and I was doing the same, yelling, "Oh, fuck, oh, yeah, damn, I'm gonna come," over and over. My cockhead scraped along her smooth passage as we frantically coupled, racing toward orgasm while at the same time trying to hold back as long as possible. Finally, we reached the breaking point, Miki a few seconds before me, and the pulsing of her pussy against my shaft triggered my explosion. As my dick squirted come I pumped into her more and more slowly, until my balls were empty. Then I pulled out and lay beside her.

We left the love hotel soon after. Miki escorted me back to the *ryokan* and kissed me lightly on the cheek as we parted. I still have a souvenir pennant from the Fighters' game to remember my Japanese travels, and hopefully my business will take me back to Tokyo someday so I can see Miki again. All in all, it was a very successful trip. Baseball and sex—what more could a red-blooded American guy ask for?

—*C.T., Via E-Mail* ⚬━■

VIVA PUERTO RICO! TRAVELING COMPANIONS
FIND NEW PLEASURES IN OLD SAN JUAN

My best friend, Sara, and I wanted to temporarily escape the rigors of our last year of graduate school, so we decided to head down to Puerto Rico for a relaxing and hopefully fun-filled respite that would offer us a little bit in the way of culture as well. We didn't pack much more than our bikinis, flip-flops, shorts, hiking shoes, and a couple of sundresses. In our late twenties, Sara and I are both active and athletic, but the demands of our doctorate program leave us little time for boyfriends, so we were looking forward to finding some hot guys to add a little spice to our vacation.

When we arrived in San Juan, it was still early in the day, so we stuffed our bags in a locker before heading out to explore Old San Juan. We approached the walled city and cobblestoned streets and breathed deeply, feeling as though we'd been taken back in time. Since both Sara and I are studying history, any time we are confronted with the remnants of an era long gone, it fills us with a sense of wonder and romantic nostalgia for the past. We share this intense passion for history, which is probably why we're such good friends and make such excellent travel companions.

As we walked through the narrow streets lined with buildings in an array of Caribbean pastels, we read passages from our guidebook that described the numerous attacks on Old San Juan. Striking images of tenacious fighting and struggles for survival filled our heads as we came face-to-face with the formidable fortress of El Morro, which dates back to the sixteenth century. We touched its walls—that we read were fifteen feet thick— and smiled at each other as we shared the pleasure of its rich history right before us.

Moving along, we bought a bag of *cenapas*—a local fruit that looks like a huge bunch of green grapes but has a tough skin that we later learned you had to bite through to get to the fleshy pink fruit inside—and then headed toward El Castillo de San Cristóbal, the twin structure of El Morro on the northeastern side of the city. We stopped to peer into the Casa Blanca and Iglesia de San José and every other courtyard and building along the way.

Feeling very touristy, Sara and I snapped pictures of each other in front of practically every building, futilely trying to eat *cenapas* and just being goofy and enjoying ourselves. As Sara posed in front of La Catedral de San Juan and I got ready to shoot, a man tapped me on the shoulder and offered to take a photo of both of us. Of course, he first showed us, in the most charming way possible, how to properly eat that elusive fruit, so we could pose properly with them in our mouths instead of fumbling with them in our hands. Then, letting my city-wise attitude fall away, I handed over my camera to this handsome stranger and joined my friend in a silly pose.

He said, "Smile," in a delightful accent and handed me back the camera as another man rushed quickly over to him. They introduced themselves to us, and it turned out that Rob was from New York and was in Puerto Rico visiting his cousin, Marco, our gentleman photographer.

Marco was showing him around Old San Juan before
they headed to Culebra, a group of islands off the eastern
coast, to snorkel and dive along its spectacular coral reef.
An invitation to join them followed soon after we all sat
down for a drink at a nearby café.

It quickly became clear that Sara and Rob were attracted to one another, she being a dark-haired beauty
with bright green eyes and he a tall, blue-eyed man with
sandy-brown hair. As for me, I couldn't stop staring into
Marco's coffee-brown eyes. I ached to touch the sun-
bleached hair on his darkly tanned, muscled arms.

It was decided that Sara and I would fetch our bags
and spend the night at Marco's apartment in San Juan
before catching a ferry to Culebra the next morning.
After dropping our bags off at Marco's, Sara and I
showered and changed into cute little sundresses, then
joined the men on the balcony before heading out for
dinner.

Marco came out carrying a tray of piña coladas for
us, with extra-spiced rum, and we all toasted the adventurous trip ahead of us. It was then that I really noticed
how sexy Marco was, with his freshly washed hair
slicked back off his chiseled face and his eyes dark and
penetrating. When he looked at me, admiring the curves
of my body in my tightly fitted pink dress, I felt as
though he were looking right through my clothes to my
naked skin!

After a gourmet dinner at a local restaurant, consisting
of *arroz con pollo, tostones,* meat empanadas, and the
local delicacy, *asopao,* Marco and I shared flan for
dessert, with him feeding me spoonfuls of the silky yellow custard. When I missed a spot on my mouth, he

leaned forward and kissed it off me, letting his lips just barely graze mine. My thong was so drenched by that point that I was almost afraid to stand up. But I did, without hesitation, when Marco asked me to dance with him.

Once on the dance floor, the band played a rapid Latin beat. Marco's strong arms held me tightly around my waist as my braless breasts bounced softly against his hard chest. In accented but perfect English, he told me I was beautiful and that he couldn't wait to show me more of his island. I thought to myself that I couldn't wait to see more of him, and when I felt the protrusion of his hard-on against my leg, I knew I wouldn't have to wait long. Slyly looking over and catching Sara's eye, I could tell that she and Rob were in much the same place.

Dinner over, the four of us strolled back to Marco's place, with Marco leading the way and pointing out sights along the scenic route he chose. Soon after arriving at Marco's apartment, Sara and Rob drifted into the back bedroom, leaving Marco and me seated on the living-room couch. He leaned over and kissed me deeply, with more passion than I'd felt in a long time.

Coaxing me back against the couch, he climbed on top of me. I nuzzled my face in his neck and tasted the skin there, slightly salty with sweat and deliciously macho. I undid the buttons of his shirt and saw the smooth expanse of his bronzed chest, with tiny hard brown nipples that I flicked with my tongue. He tossed his head back as I licked him and grunted his approval. Then he looked back down at me and slid my dress up over my head in one move, leaving me in just my soaking-wet thong.

He lowered his head to my breasts and slowly sucked

each nipple in turn into his mouth, his tongue making circles around the areolas and his teeth dragging along the crinkled nubs. He buried his face between my breasts and I pressed my flesh against his ears, playfully holding him captive there. He broke free and slid his tongue down my flat belly to my damp thong, resting his nose on my crotch and inhaling deeply.

"Delicioso," he said with a deep sigh and then pulled my thong down, revealing shiny wet pussy lips all plump and juicy for him to suck. Marco rubbed his face against my soft brown curls and kissed around my whole mound. Then, finally, his wet tongue slithered between my pussy lips and found my clit, which hardened under his tongue's hot ministrations. With every lick I felt my orgasm building in my belly. I bucked my hips up to meet his face, trying to push his tongue harder against my clit, but he held my hips down and forced me to endure this incredibly sweet, slow torture.

Marco pushed two fingers deep inside my vagina and fucked me with them while still sucking on my clit. I closed my eyes, imagining him licking me the way he sucked the pit of the *cenapa,* and I shuddered as my orgasm washed over me in a tidal wave of pleasure. I held his head firmly between my thighs as my orgasmic quivers eventually melted away.

He moved up my body and kissed me, coating my lips with the taste of my nectar. I reached down to unzip his pants and he helped me pull them off. His cock sprang hard and thick from his underwear, and it hovered above my face. I saw the drop of pearly pre-come on the cockhead and eagerly licked it off, savoring the tangy taste of it before taking as much of him into my mouth as I could.

He was straddling my chest by now and I reached between his legs to cup his balls, rolling them in my hand. He moaned as I managed to stuff nearly his whole cock down my throat. I grabbed his asscheeks, urging him into a thrusting motion, and soon he was fucking my face as I massaged his ball sac.

I ran my hand from his balls back between his asscheeks and dipped a fingertip into his hot asshole. He lurched forward in a final thrust and sent a torrent of hot sticky come down my throat. As he pulled out of my mouth, a few drops of his cream spilled over my lips and down my chin, and I licked them off my face as he leaned in to kiss me, helping me get every last drop of his passion.

The taste of his come just got me more excited to fuck him. We flipped over so that I was on top, and after sucking him back to full hardness, I eased my dripping pussy down over his cock until it was buried inside me to his balls. I rocked slowly back and forth until my clit was buzzing. Marco grabbed hold of my hips and moved me back and forth on his cock.

The pressure of my clit against his groin sent my orgasm spiraling through me, but I kept riding him, and when it faded away, I lifted off him and rubbed my pussy juice over my tight asshole. Then I slid my butt slowly down over his rigid cock. It took a few seconds to wedge him into my rear passage, but soon he was firmly implanted in my ass. He thrust upward, driving his cock deeper into my ass, and I cried out my pleasure when he shot a load of hot come inside me.

I rolled off Marco and we held each other there on the couch, listening to the ecstatic cries coming from the bedroom. We laughed happily knowing that our friends were having as much fun as we were. After a short rest, Marco took hold of my hand and led me out to the balcony. He held me close and I looked up at the opalescent moon, knowing that I was exactly where I wanted to be.

—*C.V., New York, New York*

TOUR GUIDE IN JAMAICA SHOWS
MARRIED COUPLE BEST PLEASURE SPOTS

When we looked out on the early morning horizon, the clear blue waters of the Caribbean sparkled. Judith, my wife, and I strolled along the beach in search of the perfect spot to take in the beauty of Jamaica. We settled on a spot that offered some seclusion from the other tourists and locals. After getting ourselves settled, we ran toward the water's edge. We jumped in and swam twenty feet from the beach. As we stood in chest-high water, Judith slipped her hands into my swim trunks. Wearing a smile, she stroked me to near orgasm, then submerged her body underwater and took my cock into her mouth. She sucked me until I was about to explode, then popped up out of the water.

Judith reached under the water and wiggled out of her bikini bottom and threw it at me. As I was about to throw it back at her, she leaped out of the water and I caught her in midair. She wrapped her arms around my neck and inserted her tongue deep inside my mouth. She wrapped her long legs around my waist and my cock brushed up against her vulva. As she kissed me, I palmed her ass and steered her pussy to where I could stick my cock inside it.

It was pure joy to feel the warmth of her pussy. I grabbed her by the waist and pulled her into me at a rapid pace. As the warm sun beamed down on my shoulders, I pounded her with great speed. She gave a loud scream as

I pulled out of her and my semen squirted in the water. She smiled and kissed my lips. "I love you so much," she whispered.

We made our way back to the beach and relaxed for an hour or so, taking the occasional swim. Judith wanted to see the marine life of the Caribbean, so she suggested we go out on a glass-bottomed boat. We approached the first boat that was advertised and asked the captain if he could take us out.

"No problem, mon," was his reply.

We hopped on board and then he steered the boat out to sea. He came to a coral reef and pointed down at the glass bottom. We saw all kinds of fish. Later, out on the horizon, I saw a deserted island and asked who owned it.

"I don't think anybody owns it," was his answer. After a brief pause he asked if we would like to go there.

"Not today," I told him, "but can we count on you to take us out there tomorrow?"

"No problem, mon."

Back on the beach, I paid the captain for the ride. We gathered up our belongings and headed back to the hotel. When we reached the room Judith strutted over to the bed and took off her swimsuit. Now fully nude, she sat on the bed, opened her legs, and smiled.

"Do you want some more, big boy?" she offered as she placed herself on her back and covered her pussy with her hand. She inserted her middle finger inside her pussy. Smiling, I moved toward the bed and began licking her sex. I teased her clit and ran my tongue up and down her dripping-wet slit. I sucked and kissed and poked at her pussy until she came. As I lapped up her love juices, I looked at the clock and realized that we were going to be late getting to Dunn's River Falls, one of Jamaica's main tourist attractions.

As we fumbled around the room putting on shorts and T-shirts, we gathered up a change of clothing and swimwear to take for the day trip. A receptionist with a Jamaican accent rang our phone to remind us that the shuttle bus was waiting outside the hotel. We threw the things in a bag and raced downstairs and onto the waiting bus. We found a seat behind a few other tourists and the driver took off, steering through the narrow streets of Montego Bay.

The one-and-a-half-hour drive to Ocho Rios didn't seem all that long because a beautiful young woman in a tight red dress with a nice smile talked about the different sites we passed along the road.

"I see you like that woman in the red dress," Judith said. "You may just get lucky after all."

I had no idea what my wife meant, and since I was at a loss for words I didn't respond. My eyes stayed glued to the woman in red as she spoke about the history of Jamaica. When we reached our destination, I got off the bus thinking that Judith was walking behind me. Suddenly I got a feeling that she wasn't, so I turned around and saw her engaged in a conversation with the woman in red. When my wife joined up with me I asked her what was up.

"You'll see," she said mysteriously.

The pristine water rushed down the rocks of Dunn's River Falls and emptied out into the pale blue waters of the sea. Judith and I and quite a few others followed the tour guide as he climbed up the small boulders of the falls. Water cascaded down the hill and soaked our swimsuits, giving us some relief from the tropical heat. Judith's nipples poked through her bikini top and her tits jiggled when she hoisted her hands to pull back her wet hair.

We looked at each other with hungry eyes, so we made our way to a bathroom. As we entered a stall in the men's restroom, Judith took off her bikini bottom and bent over. I entered her pussy from behind and worked her to climax. As she came, I held her quivering body in my arms. All eyes were on us as we strolled out of the bathroom arm in arm and slowly walked back to the bus.

"I enjoyed that," I said breathlessly.

"I always enjoy you," she replied happily. "You're also going to love your surprise."

"What surprise?" I asked.

"What's the one thing you've always wanted to do with me?" my wife asked with a smile.

"You don't mean . . ." I said with great astonishment. "You're kidding me." Judith had always promised me that she'd do a threesome, but she was very concerned about the third party—at least till that day.

On the drive back to Montego Bay, the woman in the tight red dress sat behind us, and on occasion I'd turn around and smile at her. When we got back to the hotel, Judith and I went up to our hotel room and took a shower together. After the shower, we snuggled together in bed and fell asleep.

At daybreak, Judith woke before me and hurried me along so we wouldn't miss the glass-bottomed boat trip to the small deserted island off the coast of Jamaica. We made our way to the dock and jumped aboard the ship. With a pleasant smile on his face, the captain said, "Good morning, sir. Ready for your ride?" He chuckled and winked at my wife.

He steered the boat out to the small island and docked. Judith and I told the captain when he should return to pick us up, then we laid our beach towels on the sand and quickly worked our way out of our clothing. I flipped her on her back and shoved my cock deep inside of her. As I got a rhythm going, I saw a shadow quickly approaching that startled me. I turned to see the smiling face of the woman who'd worn the red dress. She came out of the bushes in her birthday suit!

"Surprise!" Judith said.

The woman reached down, grabbed my ass, and introduced herself as Nina. She kissed my ass and touched Judith's tits. Nina lay next to Judith and opened her legs, exposing her hairy bush. I looked over at Nina's smiling face as I continued fucking my wife. I inserted my middle finger inside of Nina and massaged her clit.

As I was nearing orgasm, I pulled out of Judith and rolled over onto my back. Now the two women got on top of me. Judith lowered her tight ass to my face while facing Nina, who was guiding her tight pussy onto my stiff cock. The two wet pussies started throbbing as I licked one and fucked the other. As I licked my wife's clit, I heard the sounds of lips smacking. The women were kissing.

Judith ground her pussy down hard on my face as Nina bounced faster on my cock. As I was coming, both women gave out a shrill moan. They held each other as I exploded deep inside Nina. After a short break, the three of us started touching one another until we were ready to fuck again. I had the women get on all fours side by side and then I moved from pussy to pussy, doing each doggy-style.

After our escapade, we sat around and talked until the boat arrived. Nina hopped aboard for the ride back to land. (I later found out that our captain was in on the whole thing as he had dropped Nina off on the island before picking up my wife and me.) Nina went her way while Judith and I went back to the hotel. We did not make love that night, but we fell into peaceful slumber.

The next morning, the receptionist woke us to remind us that the shuttle van would soon be arriving to take us to the airport. On the flight back to the States, I looked over at my wife and smiled. "How did you manage to get Nina to agree to a ménage à trois?" I asked.

"Walter, you can get anything you want in Jamaica. Besides, a woman never reveals her secrets."

—*W.H., Bloomington, Indiana* ⊙┼☰

HORNY SERVICEMAN AND HIS HOT WIFE IN
JOYOUS CELEBRATION OF HIS RETURN HOME

My husband, James, recently spent four months away from home performing military duties. We are a very sexually oriented couple, so being apart for so long a time nearly drove us both crazy. We decided to make his homecoming a special one: a weekend of sexual adventures and exotic moments in one of the most romantic cities in the world, Paris.

Our trip started in Germany with a four-hour train ride to Paris. Fortunately, the modern train was equipped with four large bathroom stalls, which we discovered soon after finding our seats. As the train departed for France, James and I hurried to one of the restrooms, locked the door, and kissed passionately, groping at each other like the sex-hungry couple we were. Immediately, I could feel the big bulge in my husband's jeans, and I rubbed it firmly as I pulled up his T-shirt to lick at his tiny nipples. It felt so wonderful just to be touching him sexually again.

James, in turn, unzipped my pants and started rubbing my tingling cunt through my already-soaked panties. I couldn't remember ever wanting him so much! He continued stroking me as I wriggled free of my pants, kicking them out of the way. Grabbing my ass, he pulled me to him and rubbed his big bulge against my wet underpants. Then, stepping back, he jerked down his zipper and hauled out his cock, which I started stroking immediately. Perhaps it was sheer horniness clouding my thinking, but I couldn't remember him ever being so long and so hard!

Yanking down my panties, James pushed me up against a wall and quickly got my shirt off. He sucked on my pert nipples, mumbling something about how much he'd missed them. Then, lifting one of my legs up, he slid his beautiful cock up into my pulsating cunt. Gasping with pleasure, I threw my arms around his neck and wrapped my legs around his waist, holding on tight as he worked my pussy up and down his hot cock, his strong hands firmly gripping my asscheeks.

I moaned into his neck, relishing the feel of his cock inside me after four long months. I knew I wouldn't be able to hold off coming for long, and I was right. I pushed down hard on his cock, my pussy tightening around it as I was overwhelmed by one of the strongest orgasms I'd ever had in my life. It was all I could do to keep from screaming out my joy for everyone to hear.

My husband continued to lift me up and slam me down on his dick until he exploded inside me, holding me still as his come shot up into my cunt. His whole body was quivering as he came, and the feel of his hot cock throbbing inside me started me coming again. It was the most gratifying sex we'd had in a long time.

We put ourselves together and exited the restroom. We got a few knowing smiles as we made our way to our seats, but I didn't care. In fact, I liked the idea that some of the other passengers knew what my husband and I had been up to. Having just been soundly fucked after doing without my man's cock for so long, I felt deliciously decadent.

We continued on our way, arriving in Paris more or less on schedule. We found the bed-and-breakfast where we had reserved rooms and settled in. It was an old, quaint inn with a beautifully decorated lobby. Our room had a large feather bed with a comforter and pillows. Lying on a small table on the balcony, which offered a nice view of the most intoxicating city I'd ever seen, was a bouquet of fresh flowers.

After unpacking and freshening up a bit, we went downstairs to the café on the first floor where we enjoyed a light lunch of bread, meat, cheese, and fruit washed down with a glass of wine. Following an afternoon of shopping downtown, we returned to the inn to change for dinner. I felt like a queen as I dressed in a short cotton skirt and matching T-shirt and sandals. With the weather warm and breezy, I felt no need for anything else, not even underwear.

After a delicious meal, we decided to visit a pub across the street. Candles dimly lighted the interior and we were led to a table for two in a corner. The crowd was moderate with just the right amount of noise and commotion. After being served our drinks, I slipped off one of my sandals and caressed the insides of my husband's legs and his crotch with my foot. He responded by moving his chair next to mine.

I was getting excited as he snaked his hand up under my short skirt to my naked pussy, which he stroked teasingly. When I couldn't stand it anymore, I swung my legs up over his so as to give him better access to my aroused sex. It looked as if we were having a very intimate conversation. James unzipped his pants to reveal a wide-awake cock staring right up at me. I wet my fingers with some of my cunt juice and then started stroking my husband's erect cock, trying very hard not to be too obvious.

Right there, in the pub, we masturbated each other, James's fingers playing in and around my cunt while I continued to work my hand up and down his throbbing manhood. We kissed, sucking on each other's tongue. And then suddenly I was choking back a moan of delight as I came. My husband came seconds later, and I was able to grab a napkin from the table just in time to catch his come and keep it from splattering my T-shirt.

After another drink, we left the pub and returned to the inn. Our arrival there was a comforting one as the balcony windows were open and a warm breeze floated through the sunlit room. Our bed was freshly made and more cut flowers had been put on the balcony table, with dinner menus resting on each chair. Also on the table was a decanter of chilled wine and two glasses. It was the perfect atmosphere in which to end a delightful day.

I slipped into my new silk thong panties and stretched out on the bed while James poured us each a glass of wine. He brought the glass to my lips for me to drink, but some of the wine spilled down my chin, over my breasts to my stomach. Laughing, my husband said, "Here, let me clean that up for you." With that, he trailed his tongue down my chin and neck to my nipples, which he licked lovingly. He licked down my belly to the top of my panties, which he then carefully, almost reverently, removed.

My pussy was glistening with my juices as James brought my knees up and ran his tongue over my cunt to my asshole. I moaned softly as he began to gently rub my puckered rear hole with a finger while his talented tongue danced in my pussy. All I had to do was say, "Honey, stick your big cock in my mouth," and my husband was out of his clothes in a flash. He positioned himself over me with his head at my feet and his cock hovering over my face.

Eagerly, I took him into my mouth as he commenced a delightful licking and sucking of my pussy. Soon enough we were both coming, James pouring his creamy goodness down my throat as I glossed his handsome face with my juices. Then, truly exhausted, we fell asleep in each other's arms.

We awoke early the next day and set out to do some sightseeing. Paris is such a captivating city and we wanted to see as much of it as possible in the time available to us, so rather than wander around aimlessly we opted for a bus tour advertised in a brochure James had picked up in the lobby of the inn. That proved smart, for not only were we able to spend time at the obvious tourist attractions, like the Louvre Museum and the Eiffel Tower, we also got to sample the street life in Montmartre and note the difference between the Right and Left Bank of Paris. We even got to enjoy crepes and coffee at one of the charming outdoor cafés along the Seine.

Really hungry by the time we got back to the inn, we ordered up dinner and gobbled it down in our birthday suits, there being no reason to keep our clothes on as we weren't going out again. A full day of sightseeing hadn't dampened our desire for sex, so we fell into bed eager to fuck. As we fooled around, I happened to glance toward the balcony and realized that the curtains were open. I told James that there was a couple on the terrace across from us and they were looking our way. "So let's give the folks a show," he said with a grin.

Still naked, we stepped out onto the balcony and embraced. Not surprisingly, the couple across the way sat up and took notice, quickly arranging their chairs so that they were sitting side by side. By husband held me close to him with my ass pressed against his rapidly swelling cock. He fondled my tits, then brought one hand down to stroke my wet pussy. The realization that we were being watched excited us both very much.

Urging me to bend over one of the balcony chairs, James pushed his cock into my pussy and began fucking me with long, deep strokes. Reaching between my legs, I fondled his big balls as he did me from behind. I looked over at the couple across the way and saw that they were masturbating while watching us. And then a tingle of anticipation washed over me as James pulled out of my cunt and placed his cock at my asshole. Moments later, he was stretching my asshole, urging his cock ever deeper into my rectum, and when he finally had the whole thing inside me, we both moaned with pleasure.

Knowing that a man and a woman were watching me get fucked in the ass was mind-boggling. That, plus the wonderful feel of my husband's cock sawing in and out of my behind and my fingers rubbing my clit, was enough to send me over the edge. I came like crazy, crying out in ecstasy, and I was still coming when James gave out a yell of pleasure and shot his semen into my rear passage. Pulling his dripping cock out of my ass, he helped me straighten up and then drew me back against him. Together we watched the couple across the way get up from their chairs, laughing at how quickly they moved into their room, no doubt to fuck themselves silly.

What a fabulous weekend! Being without my man for four long months was certainly not fun, but we definitely made sure his homecoming would be truly memorable.

—*Y.C., Virginia Beach, Virginia* O┉▪

BAKERY OWNER SAMPLES A COUPLE
OF DANISH IN COPENHAGEN

For years my good friend Christian had been inviting me to spend time with him in the city of his birth, Copenhagen, Denmark. Finally, this past summer, I decided to take him up on his offer. I definitely needed a vacation and it seemed to be the perfect place to visit.

I was really looking forward to not only visiting Copenhagen, a city I'd heard and read good things about, but also seeing Christian again. We had met and become fast friends at school in Boston, where we were both studying hotel management. Following graduation, Christian returned to his homeland to help run his uncle's bed-and-breakfast while I looked for work here. I had finally snagged what seemed to be a nice position with a major hotel chain when fate stepped in to completely alter my plans.

My dad, citing poor health, suddenly decided to retire from the bakery business, to which he'd devoted so much of his life, and successfully, too. "Son," he said, "the business is yours. Your mother and I are moving to Arizona. Good luck."

All of a sudden, just like that, I was the owner of half a dozen small but profitable bakeries. For a while I considered selling them all and moving along with my original career choice, but then I got to thinking. A very successful business had been handed to me. True, I didn't know beans about bakeries, but I didn't have to because Dad had long ago installed a sound management team. Why work my buns off for someone else when all I had to do was sit back and collect a nice paycheck and perhaps pop into the bakeries once in a while and sample the goods? And so, I became the proud owner of six great bakeries.

I reflected on my situation as I flew to Denmark. How appropriate, I thought, that I, a bakery owner, visit a place known worldwide for its pastries!

As promised, Christian met me at Copenhagen International Airport, which is located just fifteen minutes from the city itself. In no time we were pulling up to his uncle's bed-and-breakfast, an inviting and most welcome sight after so many hours in the cramped quarters of the plane. Christian showed me to a cozy, tastefully furnished room, suggesting a nice late-afternoon nap before dinner. Sounded good to me.

Christian had made reservations at Grabrodre Torv 21, where we feasted on roast pork served with red cabbage and a rich gravy while engaging in a lively conversation befitting two old friends who hadn't seen each other in some time. Then, after enjoying steins of Danish beer at one of Copenhagen's many delightful cafés, it was back to the inn. "We have a full day planned for you tomorrow," Christian said, smiling. "You had best rest up."

I drifted off, puzzled by what my old friend had meant by the word "we." The mystery was solved the very next morning when, over a light breakfast at the inn, I was introduced to Karen and Margrethe. Statuesque, breathtakingly beautiful blue-eyed blondes with fair skin and friendly smiles, they exemplified all the best qualities I had read and heard about the fabulous women of Scandinavia.

So taken was I by their looks, I barely heard Christian say that the girls were friends and sometimes employees of his who had volunteered to show me around Copenhagen. "If that's okay with you?" he said. Needless to say, it was more than okay. And so, not much later, linking their arms with mine and promising me a great day of sightseeing, my two new friends steered me out of the inn and into a sports car the color of their hair.

We started with the statue of the Little Mermaid, from Hans Christian Andersen's famous story, located at Langeline, then visited Rosenborg Palace, next to which, in Kongens Hall, stands a statue of Hans himself. Breaking for lunch, we enjoyed a fabulous *smorrebrod*, Danish open-face sandwiches of unimaginable variety, at Ida Davidsen, all of which were washed down with the potent aquavit. Delicious!

After lunch, Margrethe and Karen took me to Tivoli Gardens, Denmark's enchanting amusement park, where we spent hours enjoying the rides and the music, pausing on two occasions for ice cream served in giant cones. In the late afternoon, before returning to the inn for the light fish meal Christian was going to prepare, we stopped at the Royal Copenhagen Patisserie for hot chocolate and freshly made Danishes. If only my people could make pastry this good, I thought.

No doubt Christian knew I'd be coming home stuffed to the gills, hence his light meal, which suited me just fine. Then, rather reluctantly, I excused myself and headed upstairs to my room, bidding my two gorgeous tour guides good night with the hope that I would see them again. Karen and Margrethe looked at each other and giggled, and Christian smiled. I thought this was a bit odd, but I was too pooped to examine it further and, without looking back, trudged up the stairs.

Around midnight, I was awakened by what I thought was a light tapping on my door. Couldn't be, I thought, and dozed off again. A few minutes later, though, opening my eyes, I nearly fell out of bed. There were the blonde goddesses, Karen and Margrethe, standing at bedside in all their naked splendor. I blinked several times, thinking I had to be having one wonderful dream, but no, the visions of loveliness before me were real. Oh, my!

"We enjoyed showing you some of Copenhagen today," Karen said. "And we'll be showing you more during your stay here."

"But tonight," Margrethe chimed in, "we thought you'd like to see some sights not on any Danish travel brochure." She looked at Karen and both girls giggled. "But perhaps you're tired from all our running around today and would like to rest."

Yeah, right, I thought, as my cock continued to swell under the blanket. I was still struggling to find my tongue when the girls, perhaps sensing my plight and eager to demonstrate just how friendly the Danes can be to visitors, simply climbed into bed, one on either side of me. "You t-two are just so beautiful," I breathed, realizing how inane that sounded even as the words left my mouth. Again the twin blonde goddesses giggled. And then they immediately got down to business.

With Karen on my right and Margrethe on my left, they began stroking me all over, their smooth, soft hands here, there, and everywhere. Karen leaned over my chest

and laved my nipples, lovingly nipping the crinkled nub-
bins of flesh. Margrethe, meanwhile, slithered snakelike
down the bed and took firm hold of my now fully erect
and throbbing cock. "Ooh, such a big one," she squealed.
"I love big cocks." She proceeded to prove it by licking
my swollen member all over, from bulbous head to hairy
base, cooing all the while. And then she plunked it right
into her warm, wet mouth and began sucking slowly,
teasingly, those big blue eyes of hers bright with mischief
as she looked up at me.

Karen, saying she wanted a taste, scooted down the
bed and tried wresting my cock away from Margrethe,
who finally relented and let it go. Now it was Karen's
mouth on me, her velvetlike lips gliding up and down the
shaft, her tongue dancing over the sensitive underside.
An impatient Margrethe took it away from her after a
minute or so, jamming it into her mouth with authority.
But then, after she'd sucked on it for a while, she passed
it off to Karen. And that's how it went, the two lovely
Danes passing my sturdy erection back and forth between
them, with both ladies oohing and aahing over its size
and rigidity.

Just as I started to wonder which of these beauties I'd
fuck first, Margrethe took control, pushing aside Karen as
she positioned herself over me and with a sigh sank all
the way down on my fleshy pole. Undaunted, Karen simply clambered up the bed and straddled my head, smiling
down at me as she lowered her sweet-smelling pussy to
my mouth. "Heaven on earth" was the phrase that came
to me as I began slurping up the juices flowing freely
from Karen's pussy, which, like Margrethe's, was surrounded by golden curls the texture of silk.

After a while the girls changed places, with Margrethe sitting on my face while Karen posted on my cock. To be honest, with my eyes closed, I couldn't tell them apart, but what did it matter when one gorgeous blonde was fucking herself on my cock while the other ground her flavorful cunt into my mouth with lusty enthusiasm. What I did know for sure was when both girls came, Karen's cunt contracting around my cock and Margrethe's glossing my face with its tangy juices, I sort of howled up into Margrethe's pussy, which made for a funny kind of noise, as I shot my load up into Karen's sweet sex.

And that was just the beginning.

With me totally revitalized, the weariness of a busy day on the go a distant memory, and my two gorgeous new friends seemingly insatiable, we sucked and fucked until the wee hours of the morning, stopping only, and with some reluctance, when Christian rapped on the door to say breakfast would be served shortly.

Karen and Margrethe stayed close by for the duration of my stay in Copenhagen. During the day we'd go sightseeing, either in Copenhagen itself or out in the countryside. Thanks to the girls, I saw more of Denmark in a week than most visitors see in a month. Marveling at the cleanliness of the streets and the friendliness of the people, I toured museums, visited castles, snacked at cafés, and dined in restaurants small and large, bohemian and elegant. At night, one or both of the girls would join me in my bed.

On my last night at the inn, Karen and Margrethe insisted I give them each a facial, which I did with relish, splattering both their lovely upturned faces with a copious amount of creamy come. Each wanted to be fucked in the ass, too, and of course, I obliged. Imagine, if you will, two outrageously beautiful blondes lying belly down on the bed side by side, each reaching back to pry apart her buttocks while urgently requesting my "big" cock in her ass. Yes, it was magic, all right.

On the flight back home I thought about my bakery business and then about the two tasty Danish I'd been fortunate enough to sample while I was in Copenhagen. A flight attendant, passing by with a tray of snacks, had to be wondering why I had this goofy smile on my face.

—*S.L., Via E-Mail*

COMING SPECTACULARLY ON THE SPECTACULAR GOING-TO-THE-SUN ROAD

Since my boyfriend, Alex, and I were still paying off our grad school loans, we didn't have much money for a summer vacation, though both of us desperately needed one. We'd recently moved to Montana, so we decided to just hop in the car and drive up the Going-to-the-Sun Road that takes us right through Glacier National Park and over the border into Canada. We'd heard it was a spectacular drive this time of year. It would only cost a few bucks, plus gas, and we planned to camp instead of spending money on hotels. Since there were so many beautiful hiking trails in the park and it was just the beginning of summer, we couldn't imagine a better or more romantic vacation.

Alex and I packed the car full of snacks, water, and camping gear and headed up toward Glacier. Every minute of the drive was wonderful, and finally being alone with Alex, with just the radio blasting and all the windows open, made me feel completely free and peaceful. It started to make me feel excited, too, knowing that we would be sleeping together under the stars in one of the most majestic places in the world. I couldn't wait until we were snuggled closely together in our sleeping bags, the heat of his body against mine, having glorious sex while breathing in the fresh mountain air. I was getting aroused just thinking about it—so much so that my pussy got really wet as we were paying the admission fee and starting our drive through the park. I had to squeeze my thighs together tightly out of fear that my copious juices would drip onto the seat.

Alex looked over at me as we passed the toll at West Glacier and got our booklet guide to the park. He said that he recognized the look on my face. When I asked him what he meant by that, he said, "You're thinking about fucking, aren't you?"

It still amazes me that he knows me so well, and I had to laugh at his accuracy. I leaned into him and kissed the side of his neck as he started us on the Going-to-the-Sun Road. I could taste the faint vestige of sweat on him and licked my lips, nuzzling my head into the crook of his neck. He kept one hand on the wheel and placed the other on my knee, gently squeezing it and then lightly trailing his fingers over my thigh and under my very short shorts. He tickled the sensitive skin mere inches from my cunt, making even more honey ooze from my pussy as my mind raced with oh-so-naughty thoughts about fucking my boyfriend.

It got to the point where despite how beautiful the view was from the car window as we passed Lake Mc-Donald on the way to Logan Pass, I couldn't keep my mind focused on anything except sex. I clenched my thighs tightly, trying to stave off my need to come and pay attention to the scenery, the lush green trees, the amazing rocks and rows of wildflowers, and the crystal-blue streams that we passed along the road.

But it was all in vain, since having my sexy man beside me—all six feet of him, his lean and muscled chest, his head of thick black hair, and those penetrating green eyes—was such a distraction that I couldn't help but focus on his natural beauty instead of the nature that was completely surrounding me.

Alex noticed me squirming in my seat and asked what was going on. I told him to pull over at the next lookout point, and luckily, there was only one other car there and it was pulling away as we drove in. Alex opened his door and started to get out, but I yanked him by the sleeve of his T-shirt and jerked him back. Pulling him close to me, I gave him a frantic and intense kiss that told him exactly how I was feeling. He kissed me back and ran his hands underneath my shirt, squeezing my breasts and pinching the tips of my nipples with the urgency I craved. I leaned over to the driver's seat and pushed the lever that released the seat fully back. Then I slid on top of Alex, covering his body with mine.

"I guess you don't want to get out and read the plaque," he said with a grin. I answered with a little laugh and fell back on top of him, lifting up his shirt and peppering his stomach with little wet kisses that soon became longer and more languid licks with my tongue. His skin tasted so good, and smelling him was enhancing my arousal. He ran his fingers through my hair as I deftly unbuttoned his shorts. With some maneuvering in the small space, I managed to release his cock and slide it all the way into my mouth.

I could hear the sounds of the wilderness around me and the whizzing of cars as they drove past us, but I was concentrating on sucking my boyfriend's cock, wedging his long hard shaft into my mouth and down my throat. I cupped his heavy balls in my hand as he moaned deeply in pleasure. I rolled them in my palm as he urged me on, gently scratching his fingertips through my hair, sending a wonderful tingle through my body.

I slid his penis in and out of my mouth in slow deep glides, holding the base of his cock as I rested my ass on the steering wheel for better balance. I pulled his dick out of my mouth and rubbed it over my pursed lips, spreading the wetness across my face, meeting his eyes with mine, showing him how I loved sucking his big juicy cock. I kissed the tip again and laved the head, getting it good and wet. Then I shimmied out of my shorts and panties and ground right down on him, forcing his hard cock all the way up into my ready pussy.

I sat there atop him for a few moments, enjoying the sensation of being all filled up. But soon, Alex started moving his hips, driving his cock deeper inside me. I matched his rhythm and quickly we got a good thrusting motion going as he reached up and grabbed my breasts, squeezing my nipples as I rode him slowly and then faster and faster. My juices spread all over his groin as I slid my squishy cunt against his skin, both of us getting close to coming in minutes.

Before I let him come, though, I managed to turn myself around so that he could grab hold of my asscheeks and grip them hard as I held on to the steering wheel and bounced up and down on his cock. My clit ground against him each time I brought my ass back down on him, sending sharp shocks of ecstasy through my sensitive nub. I needed to be filled even more, so I lifted off his cock and slowly eased his stiff member into my asshole, easily pushing past my relaxed sphincter muscles and sliding his thick shaft into my back passage.

That was it. It felt so good being stuffed full of his

cock, and I heard Alex gasp as my rear tunnel clutched his dick tightly with each up-and-down motion. I looked out through the windshield as the vast beauty of the park overwhelmed me and each push of his cock brought me closer and closer to my amazing orgasm.

Just as I was reaching my peak, my clit hard and throbbing, my pussy walls tightening and my ass grabbing at Alex's cock, making him groan that he was about to come, I saw a deer hop across the road. For a moment I couldn't believe what was happening. Then I was flooded with the richest and most mind-blowing orgasm of my life as Alex's come spurted deep inside me in hot thick torrents that I could feel painting my insides. There we were, out in the wilderness, and I had just had the most incredible sex of my life!

I carefully climbed off my boyfriend, feeling his warm come dripping out of my asshole as his softening cock slid out. I turned around to face him, kissing him tenderly on the lips with a big satisfied smile on my face. We took our time regaining our composure and getting dressed. Eventually we started the car again and got back on the road, stopping at the visitors' center at St. Mary and taking in the view of the snowcapped mountains and waterfalls along the way. Then we worked our way back into the park to Many Glacier near Swiftcurrent Lake where we set up camp for the night.

As we got into our tent that night, sliding our clothes off once we were in our zippered-together sleeping bags, Alex pulled me on top of him and gave me another amazing ride on his cock, and then he licked my pussy till it was clean of his cream and my juices. He made me come with nearly every swipe of his tongue as I begged him to fuck me again more in my eager ass.

We spent the next few days meandering around the park, driving from trail to trail, getting out to make love in the wild outdoors whenever we could and taking full advantage of the spaciousness of our car. Taking this vacation made us realize how passionate sex outdoors can be, and we've decided to make the drive through the glacier an annual event. Next time, though, we hope to see a black bear or a grizzly, although I'll never forget the hop of that deer!   —*M.S., Helena, Montana* ⚬┼▄

TWO VISITORS TO GREECE GIVE NEW MEANING TO THE TERM "TOURIST ATTRACTIONS"

I've enjoyed reading *Penthouse* Variations for many years and I thought you might like to hear about an experience of mine that happened when I was on vacation in Greece. I met many girls in Athens, but there was one who was extra special. She wasn't what you might call beautiful, but she had a sex drive that wouldn't quit. After all, not all girls are *Penthouse* models, but it doesn't mean that they don't want to have sex!

I had visited the Acropolis, which was of course heavily populated with tourist groups. A short, rather plump American girl caught my attention in one of the tourist parties. All the people in her group were wearing name tags, so I could see that her name was Jodie. Having nothing to lose, as I was there on my own, I approached her and said, "Good morning, Jodie." It's surprising sometimes how such a direct approach can get results—she smiled prettily and said, "Good morning to you."

Jodie was only about five feet tall, with small breasts and a very wide bottom, and I could feel my attraction to her growing, especially since I've always favored fully proportioned women. Once introductions were made, I walked with her around the Acropolis for some time and told her what I knew about the ruin's history. Eventually she had to meet back up with her group, but we arranged to have dinner together at my hotel that evening.

We had a very pleasant meal of fresh seafood, and during the course of the evening, it became increasingly obvious that Jodie knew what was on my mind—and didn't mind one little bit. After we'd finished our baklava and coffee, she happily accepted my offer of a nightcap in my room, and so we retired there after I'd paid the bill. We shared a glass of brandy, and then we started to kiss. Given no discouragement whatsoever, I unbuttoned her blouse to reveal her perky little breasts.

I stroked and licked her rosy nipples, and they stiffened like tent pegs under my touch. Running my hand up her thigh, I discovered, to my surprise, that she wasn't wearing panty hose as I had expected, but a rather luscious garter belt and stocking set. I reached the crotch of her panties and discovered that they were wet, her juices soaking through the fine material. She was hot and willing, so I thought I'd try for one more thing.

"Jodie," I began, "I've got my video camera over there. Would you mind if . . ."

"No," she was quick to respond. "If you want a souvenir of your trip, it's fine by me." She was so enthusiastic that I could hardly believe my good luck, and I quickly set up the camera and returned to the bedside. In the meantime, Jodie had stripped off her blouse, skirt, bra, and panties and was lying back on the bed dressed only in her garter belt and stockings.

I was enthralled by this Rubenesque beauty with her rounded stomach and full ass, hips, and thighs. Seeing her displayed for me like that and knowing it would all be captured on video gave me an enormous erection. I started stroking my way up her thighs and soon came to her pussy. Rubbing her clitoris in small circles, I guided her head toward my hard cock. She needed no urging and readily took my length in her mouth, gulping down as much as she could. My cock responded, and before I could even try to hold it back, the floodgates opened and I came in Jodie's mouth, without being able to warn her.

She looked surprised that I had come so soon, but didn't seem to mind. In fact, she never stopped sucking and seemed more than happy to swallow my entire load. I felt that she should be rewarded for that, and so I got up, pushed her back on the bed, and positioned myself between her legs. Going down on her, I plunged my tongue deep into her wet cunt and licked at her clit. I didn't neglect her tight little asshole, either, licking my way around it and tickling it with my fingertip. Jodie loved it all, squirming and jerking under my grip, and I'm proud to say that I brought her to a powerful orgasm during which she screamed her pleasure.

Eating her pussy, though, had stiffened my cock again, and I wanted to take full advantage of her sexual willingness. I asked her to turn over on her stomach and raise her ass in the air so we could fuck doggy-style. The video camera recorded every second as I positioned myself behind Jodie and slowly pushed my erect cock into her cunt. She responded to my thrusts with excitement, thrusting back at me, and soon I could feel my orgasm building again. Not wanting to come so quickly this time, I pulled back suddenly, so much so that my cock slipped out of Jodie's pussy.

I had to put my cock back somewhere, and her asshole was so inviting that I pressed the tip to that tight crimp and pushed it easily inside—obviously she wasn't new to anal penetration. Jodie squealed in surprise, but her noises turned to delight as I slipped my full length into her anus. I began fucking her, but not for long, because she was crying out with sheer joy as I pumped my dick into her ass. When she tightened around my shaft, my second orgasm was triggered and I pumped shot after shot of hot cream deep into her rear canal.

Spent, I pulled out and we both collapsed onto the bed, sweaty and entangled. We kissed and caressed each other for a while, and then we took a shower together, after which Jodie spent the night.

In the morning, Jodie decided not to go back to her tour group and spent the day with me instead. We stopped at her hotel so she could put on some comfortable sight-seeing clothes, and then we went to the Plaka, which is the neighborhood right below the Acropolis. The streets there are lined with cafés and tourist shops, as well as tons of tourists. We walked around for a couple of hours, buying souvenirs for ourselves and for friends at home. I even bought Jodie a gold bracelet at a small jewelry shop.

We stopped at the Folk Art Museum and listened to the street musicians. Then we had lunch at a *taverna* whose tables spilled out onto the street. It was a perfect place to sit and watch interesting people walk by, and we commented on almost everyone who crossed our path as we sipped ouzo and ate moussaka and souvlaki. Before leaving, we stopped at the oldest distillery in Athens, walking upstairs so I could purchase bottles of their wonderful ouzo to bring home with me.

Although we hadn't done much that day, we were both tired from our lack of sleep the evening before, so instead of heading out to see more ruins as we had planned, we went back to my hotel for a little rest. Of course, we didn't end up resting that much. Seeing Jodie lying on my bed in just a tank top and shorts was too much for me, and my dick strained toward her like a dowsing rod. I didn't want to push my luck, though, so I just sat next to her and massaged her shoulders.

Jodie pressed against me, so I brought my hands around to her front and began massaging her breasts through her top, feeling each nipple harden. When she pushed me away I was disappointed, but it was just long enough for her to pull off her shirt and shimmy out of her shorts and panties. I just sat there for a moment, amazed at my luck at meeting such a lusty lady on my vacation to Greece, but Jodie grew impatient and started pulling at the front of my pants. Soon she had them undone and was fishing out my cock, which throbbed in her firm grip.

This time Jodie took control, rolling us over so that I was on my back and she was straddling my waist. I held the base of my cock so that she could position herself on top of it, and then she slowly lowered herself down, swallowing my shaft inch by glorious inch. When she had reached the bottom she began to grind her hips and move up and down, riding me like a pro.

I grasped her fleshy ass and squeezed it tight around my prick and helped her with her ride. The way her cunt swallowed me again and again felt amazing, and when she started to come the feeling got even better. Her pussy clasped my cock in a tight grip, and as she cried out her pleasure, my balls exploded. I filled her with blasts of my hot come, and then she slumped over on my body, satiated.

We lay there like that for a moment, until my spent cock slipped out of her cunt. Then we got up and showered again and spent the rest of the afternoon sightseeing around Athens. In fact, we spent the rest of the day and the evening together. In the morning I called for a taxi to take her back to her hotel, and I said good-bye to my sweet-natured, sexy American girl. Good thing I'll always have this lusty video to remember her by!

—*G.W., Via E-Mail* ⊙┝━

IN THE FLORIDA KEYS, WOMAN UNLOCKS A LUST FOR TWO MEN AT ONCE

My girlfriend of one year, Janet, is truly gorgeous. She's tall, with long blonde hair and a beautiful smile. Her breasts are perky and firm, and she has no need of a bra. We enjoy a wonderful sex life and are totally uninhibited when we're together. We experiment with toys. We've tried light bondage. We've had sex in unusual places, including the conference table in my office.

Still, there was one thing I could not get Janet to do. In the past, I had enjoyed an ongoing threesome with my ex and my best friend, the two of us giving her all the sex she could handle. I had offered this option to Janet a few times, but surprisingly, she didn't want it, saying that she was mine and mine alone.

Recently we vacationed in the Florida Keys at a posh resort. It was our first real trip together, and we were having a wonderful time—the weather was absolutely perfect, and the white sand and blue-green water were beautiful. We ate fresh seafood with tall, frosty drinks every night and had hours of amazing sex afterward. Plus, we got to sleep in late every day before we hit the beach. It was like being in heaven. Little did I know that our first trip together was about to get even better.

One afternoon, after several hours of tanning, we headed to a bar on the beach. We sat and sipped mai tais as we enjoyed a cool ocean breeze, Janet wearing only her French-cut bikini. That told me I would be in for some great sex later, because sitting around like that in public and showing off her body really turns her on.

After a little while, a guy sat down on Janet's other side and they struck up a conversation. Brent was a commercial airline pilot taking an extended layover in the Keys. His wife was to join him there a few days later. He was nice-looking and in his forties like us. After a while, Janet asked if his constant travel was hard on his wife. He explained that if she got too horny, there was always Ray.

"Ray?" Janet asked. "Who's Ray?" Brent explained that he was their best friend and next-door neighbor.

"You're okay with that?" Janet asked, dumbfounded. He said he was, and that sometimes they even did her together. Janet looked at me and said that Brent was as bad as I was. Then she just shook her head in disbelief and excused herself to go to the ladies' room.

When she got back she had regained her composure somewhat and the conversation turned to more mundane matters. After our next drink, Janet announced, "Okay, I want to try this." I asked her what she meant and she replied, "To have sex with the two of you, right now." Surprised but extremely pleased, I looked at Brent and told him that if Janet wanted to do it, then it was okay by me, too. He immediately accepted our offer. We paid our tab and went up to our room.

When we got there, I made drinks for us from the tiny bottles in the wet bar and Brent went into the bathroom. While he was gone, Janet looked at me and said, "I'm going to suck him until he comes in my mouth, and I hope it's a huge load. Then I'm going to fuck him. Are you sure this is okay with you?" I assured her it was, as long as she enjoyed herself.

"That," she said, taking a long swig of her drink, "you can count on!"

Brent returned and sat down with us on the couch and we engaged in idle chatter for a while. Then Janet stood up and turned her back to me. She leaned over and kissed Brent passionately, their tongues working feverishly. Then she broke away from him for a moment. "Undress me, darling," she said to me. I unhooked the clasp of her bikini top and slid the straps down off her shoulders. Janet held it up by cupping it to her breasts while Brent looked at her in anticipation. Then she let it fall to the floor. I hooked my thumbs in her skimpy bottom and she lifted up her ass so that I could slide it down and over her long legs.

What a turn-on it was to have her standing naked between us! She then told us to lose our bathing suits, and we quickly complied. Brent sat back down on the couch while she checked him out. His cock was a nice size, and hard as a rock, complete with a drop of pre-come perched on the dark red tip. Janet glanced back at me and said, "Ready, darling? I'm going to suck Brent now." I just nodded dumbly, still somewhat amazed that this was happening. If this was what Janet was like while on vacation, I remember thinking to myself, then we'd have to go away more often!

Janet slowly sank to her knees and took his cock in her hand. Then she began to lick up and down his length and rubbed his wet member against her cheeks until her skin was glistening with moisture. Deep-throating him easily, she began a steady bobbing motion with her head. Brent just leaned back and savored the wonderful sensations he was being treated to. After a few moments, he groaned loudly, and soon I saw his hips begin to jerk. Then he cried out in bliss as he flooded her mouth with his come.

I could hardly believe what I was seeing: Janet stayed with it and swallowed as much as she could, the rest drenching her hand and chin. She then turned to me and announced that it was my turn. Diving on my cock, she treated me to the same pleasures Brent had just enjoyed. When he had recovered, he knelt next to her as she sucked my dick, fondling her breasts and then slipping his finger in her pussy. "Boy, she's wet," he observed. I said that she seemed to be enjoying herself.

Soon I felt that familiar boiling in my loins, and seconds later I was filling Janet's mouth with its second load of the afternoon. When she finished with me, she wiped her chin and hands and returned to her drink.

After we had all calmed down a bit, Janet moved over and lay down on the bed. Spreading her legs, she said to Brent, "Come here and fuck me, please." He was there in a flash, climbing between her legs and preparing to enter her. Impatient, she reached down, grabbed his cock, and rubbed it against her clit. Then she placed him at her entrance and pulled him in. "Now, Brent, let's do it nice and slow like I like it, okay?"

Brent began fucking Janet with a nice tempo, and she moaned and bucked her hips with his every thrust. Soon she began to tremble like she does when she's about to come. "Come in me, Brent," she begged. "I want it so bad." He picked up the pace and grunted loudly as he deposited his load in her at the same time she cried out her release. They kissed and collapsed in each other's arms.

After a while, Brent rolled off Janet and she summoned me. I wasted no time climbing on and filling her cunt with my cock. Boy, was she wet! Their combined juices let me slide right in. I was so incredibly turned on that it didn't take me long to add my load to Brent's. After I came, we kissed passionately, and then all three of us relaxed a bit, watching a porn flick we ordered on TV.

Soon the now insatiable Janet wanted more. She sucked my cock until I was good and hard again, then pulled me back on top of her. I happily slid back into her pussy and began to fuck my delightfully horny girlfriend. "I think you've created a monster, lover," she said to me between gasps. "I love this!" Then she told Brent to join us so that we could come in her together.

Brent arranged himself so that she could get his dick in her mouth. She swallowed him with glee and sucked him in earnest. It was amazing: The cock in her mouth was just inches from my face. She sucked him with that voracious appetite of hers and soon he groaned that he was about to come, which set me off, too. Janet got her wish as we both filled her with our hot cream at the same time.

Brent and I spent the rest of the night pleasing Janet. The next morning, he got up and left to call his wife to tell her all about the fun he'd been having. I wanted a cup of coffee, but Janet wanted a couple more hours of sleep. I splashed some water on my face and headed downstairs for my java. I was sitting at the table when the waitress brought me a cordless house phone. It was Janet, telling me that Brent had come back for his watch and they were ready to fuck again after some heated foreplay.

I told her I'd be right there, but she insisted, "No, darling, stay there and just listen to us. Then come back up and fuck me." I agreed (how could I not?) and listened to her sexy narrative. "He's putting it in me now. He has such a nice dick," she said. Then she moaned and told Brent to fuck her hard. Soon I was treated to the chorus of moans that punctuated every thrust. When I heard him announce that he was coming, I almost came myself. My dick was really hard by then, and I couldn't wait to get upstairs and fuck my horny girlfriend. Then Janet gasped that she was going to come, too, and I heard their cries reach a crescendo as they reached their orgasms together.

As soon as she said good-bye, I signed the check and went upstairs. Brent had left, but Janet was still spread-eagled on the bed. I quickly stripped and mounted her, kissing her as I slipped into her pussy. She asked if I could taste Brent's come on her tongue, and actually, her mouth did have a different taste.

We spent the rest of our week in the Keys enjoying the afterglow. Although we never got together with both Brent and his wife, we did agree to meet sometime back up north, and perhaps plan a vacation together. Today, Janet is a different woman, and I have Brent and the Florida Keys to thank for that.

—*J.D., Hartford, Connecticut* ⚬┼■